RECKONING

Gathering of the Storms
Volume 2

TJ MICHAELS

USA TODAY & NY TIMES BESTSELLING AUTHOR

Reckoning (Gathering of the Storms) ©
Copyright 2003 – 2016 by T.J. Michaels
ALL RIGHTS RESERVED.
First edition published 2016 Bent West Books
Edited by LM Editing
Cover Art by Syneca of Original Syn
ISBN: 978-0-9975063-5-8

DEDICATION

This book is, as always, dedicated to my kids. They have been super supportive from day one. This work is of special importance because it's the one I wrote when they were little. I set it aside to raise them and establish my career, and it sat on the shelf for a long, loooong time. Now, I share with you what was truly the beginning of my journey as a writer.

The world created for Gathering of the Storms is rich, full of family and love, power and deceit. Magick and mayhem. So without further ado...

Welcome to Draema!

INTRODUCTION

There is one truth: Once passion is awakened, it is as potent and lethal as any storm.

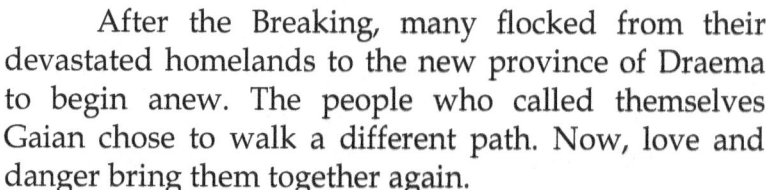

After the Breaking, many flocked from their devastated homelands to the new province of Draema to begin anew. The people who called themselves Gaian chose to walk a different path. Now, love and danger bring them together again.

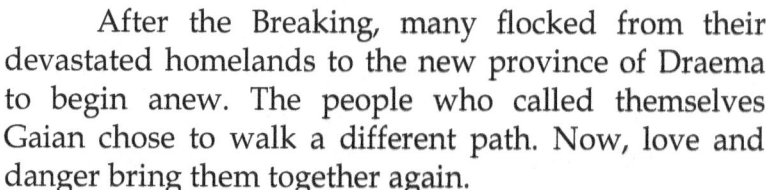

The threat to Rhia Greysomne, First Heir of Draema, has struck time and again. Each plot, darker and more devious than the last, closer to family and loved ones.

How did a creature only known in fairy tales come to possess the magick of the Gaian clans? And how does he keep eluding the Realmwalkers, only to strike where they least expect it?

The Wind Storm and the Fire Storm have run out of time. Since their enemy can't seem to get to Rhia, her husband, RuArk Miwatani, Protector of the Realm, is now firmly in the cross-hairs of their unseen foe.

So Rhia will do what she does best — kick ass and take names, Draeman style. A reckoning is at hand...and Rhia will be the victor. Period.

WARNING: Cunning, but gorgeous bad guys with extra-long teeth abound. Laser pistols, katanas and bows all meet in the ring, complete with hunky swagger.

CHAPTER ONE

RuArk lay motionless, barely breathing. Linc managed to help roll him over as Rhia pressed strong, but trembling fingers to the large vein in his neck. His heartbeat was much too faint and fever flashed out of nowhere. He was suddenly so warm, the still-falling rain should have evaporated the second it touched his body. The blood was everywhere. She reigned in panic as RuArk stirred, and a tired groan slipped from his lips. She might not be a perfect Gaian woman, but crisis? Crisis she could do.

"Rhia..." He tried to lift his injured arm to touch her, but the weight of it seemed too much. It flopped into the mud in a puddle of red-tinged water. The ripped sleeve of his tunic fell away and she saw it—a huge gash across his left shoulder. The skin and muscle lay wide open and she could see clear down to the bone.

Her temper flared. "How long did he fight with his shoulder hacked open? Why didn't any of you take care of him?" she snapped at the group at large. Right now she didn't care who answered.

"RuArk, lay still," Rhia barked as he tried to get up. By the third time he'd almost tossed her onto her butt, she straddled him to keep him from moving. The man might be only half conscious, but he was wholly pissed off and determined to get up off the cold wet ground.

RuArk stumbled to his feet as she continued to cling to him. "I can take care of myself," he hissed, throwing her own words back at her. He fell heavily against her chest, clutching the front of her soaked tunic. His lips tipped up into a half smile and Rhia wondered what the hell he found so funny while he was dying before her eyes.

When his breathing became short and raspy, Rhia had had enough. She stood up on her tip toes, grabbed him by what was left of his tunic and whispered for his ears alone.

"Listen up, RuArk, because this is your only warning. You're. Going. Home. Don't make me take advantage of the situation by having you dragged there." She softened her demands with a gentle, "Please, don't be boneheaded about this."

He looked down at her but said nothing. They both knew she'd won this little battle and this time when he hit the ground like a fallen tree, he remained unconscious.

Warriors gathered around the Protector of the Realm and tried to push past Rhia to gather up RuArk's prone body. They obviously didn't realize who they were dealing with. The first warrior who inadvertently put his hands on her landed on his head next to RuArk. The next found himself standing on the toes of his boots. While he tried to get away from the agonizing pain shooting up his arm Rhia had twisted behind his back, her thumb worked a sensitive nerve at the base of his spine that kept him immobilized.

"All of you step back," she yelled, then turned to

Linc, Dalmore and Osgar.

"Linc and Dalmore, take him home as fast as you can. Osgar, send someone across the river to the Grandfather, then tell Drefan to double check the security on the gates. All of them."

The two men caught RuArk underneath his arms. Their muscles strained with the weight. In the end, it took four warriors to get RuArk up the hill to the villa.

Lunis met them on the front porch with a wicked black fireplace poker in his hand. One look at RuArk and the poker was forgotten, left to clatter loudly on the stone at his feet as he ran ahead to prepare their bed and get extra linens. Rhia still shouted orders.

"Lunis, after you help us get him upstairs, send a runner to the Society of Physicians and the Gaian Healers. Have them set up a triage area. Use the security force's barracks for the more serious cases. Then find Brita and have her bring her medicines. Sharyn, too. Tell those women to get their asses up here immediately."

RuArk lapsed in and out of consciousness as his body continued to burn at an alarming rate. Rhia grew more and more nervous as he approached delirium. There was no reason he should have a fever this fast.

But then, this whole business was strange. No Draeman colony, nor any of the colony's townships had been attacked since the wars and reconstruction after the Breaking. Who were those men who'd dared attack her home? And how had they gotten into the township? There hadn't been anyone in front of or behind her when Drefan waved her through the inner wall's gates. What the hell was going on?

Lunis put down a plastic-like material on one side of the bed and placed clean sheets over it. The warriors settled RuArk on top of it, removed his boots and leggings, and then filed out of the bedroom solemnly. Linc stayed behind.

Rhia threw a towel over RuArk's groin while Linc removed his underclothes. An already serious expression hardened as he helped remove RuArk's ruined leather tunic.

The wound was horrendous. The only thing holding RuArk's shoulder to his body was the bone itself. The slash was deep, but thankfully the cut was clean. So why did it look like this? The bleeding had slowed, but a strange yellow fluid mixed with the blood seeped out of the gaping flesh, bubbling as it came up out of the wound.

The skin around the cut was a sickly gray that faded to a putrid-looking raw pink. She'd been in endless blade fights and countless skirmishes, but she'd never seen anything like this. Rhia stopped breathing.

His skin was scalding to the touch. She sponged the wound as best she could and then covered him with light linens. Then for the first time in her life, she prayed.

"His fever is raging, Linc. Please go see what's keeping Brita and Sharyn." He didn't move right away, only stood watching her with a stoic expression. Hell, she didn't have time for this. "What, Linc?" she barked as she brushed a stray lock of hair back from RuArk's forehead.

"I respect your strength and courage, fighting alongside us as you did, but if he leaves this realm, I will never forgive you."

Her fingers stilled at the coldness in the First Commander's voice.

"What does this have to do with me?"

"The Wind Storm refused to have his wound seen to because he was more concerned for your whereabouts and safety than his own life. He continued to fight until he saw you were safe. If you had been where you were supposed to have been, he would have been under the care of the healers long ago, and much more assured of life than he is at this moment."

Linc left the room without another word, and quietly snapped the door closed behind him. What else was there to say? After all, he was right. The battle may not have been her fault, but RuArk's current state of health certainly was. There was no arguing that he would be in much better shape if he'd been treated earlier. Now there was absolutely nothing she could do except comfort him with cool towels and wait for Brita and Sharyn to arrive.

The two women had taken two steps through the main door into RuArk and Rhia's apartment and were no further than the living room when Rhia appeared at the threshold of the bedroom, blade at the ready. The bastards who'd attacked had gotten past the gates once and she wasn't taking any chances. Relieved to see her friends, Rhia dropped her blade with a muffled thud on the thick carpet and blurted out her concerns.

"Brita, what do I do? What do you want me to do? Linc and I removed his wet clothing and covered him lightly, but his fever is so high. The wound looks horrible. How can I help?"

"You can help by leaving us to our tasks," replied Sharyn, already marching into the bedroom toward RuArk's too-still body.

"Are you crazy! I'm not going anywhere," Rhia growled.

"Rhia, nobody said you have to leave, but we can't tend him if you're damn-near on top of him," Brita said as she joined Sharyn at the side of the bed. She nudged Rhia aside to get a good look at RuArk's large flushed body. She pulled a digital steth out of her bag and placed it on his chest.

"His fever is high, but his heartbeat is strong, though a bit erratic. His lungs don't sound clear. Strange, since the wound is on his shoulder. I'll give him some meds to stave off infection. When he awakes tomorrow, his fever should have come down significantly." Brita dropped the steth back in her bag, then snatched two small packets of crushed brown something-or-other from an inner compartment.

Thank god Brita knew about medicines. It was times like this Rhia wished she'd paid more attention to the woman's instruction when she was growing up, rather than chasing young boys with wooden swords.

Sharyn changed places with Brita, closed her eyes and let her hands move about RuArk's temples. Rhia pulled in a swift breath as goose bumps jumped across her skin. A familiar tingling sensation tickled the base of her skull. She knew Sharyn was using her Gift on RuArk.

"What are you doing to him, Sharyn?"

"I am listening to his body. We must determine where to begin the healing before Brita gives him the fever medicine. The wound in his shoulder is... wrong. The yellow substance oozing from it is almost alive with a vile taint. I can sense it. I am afraid it will take both of us to heal him."

"Both of us?" Rhia shrieked. "What the hell am I

supposed to do? You know I can't control my Gift yet. In fact, we don't even know what my Gift is."

"Come here, Rhia."

She hesitated, unsure and afraid for the first time in ages. "Sharyn, if I screw up, I'll be responsible for RuArk's death."

"Come here. Now."

Even in her concern, Rhia couldn't keep her brows from flying upward. Sharyn hadn't raised her voice, but her tone dropped into a deep octave that took the option of refusal off the table. Rhia moved next to her friend and prepared for who-knew-what.

"You do not have to know how to use your Gift to help him, Rhia. Just open yourself to me. My skill and knowledge of my Gift of Healing will join with your innate power, and magnify it."

"Then what?"

"Then we wait. The rest will depend on his strength and will. If he were a weaker man, there would be no hope for him, regardless of our Gifts."

"Please, just tell me what to do. He's starting to wheeze. Hurry up!" She was beside herself with worry and didn't realize she was practically strangling the other woman until Sharyn looked calmly down at the hands clutching the collar of her tunic. Blushing, Rhia quickly removed her fingers and let her arms fall to her sides.

"Just relax, Rhia and follow my lead. Reach for your Source and allow the Gift to come to the surface on its own. If you open to it, it will come. Once you feel it, let me take control from there."

The two women knelt on the top step of the huge platform bed next to RuArk's body, and placed their hands on his chest and belly with their fingers touching.

Rhia closed her eyes and opened herself to her Source. She sensed rather than saw a faint light flare to life, then grow brighter as she made contact with her Source. She felt Sharyn gently take control of it, taking Rhia along for the ride. She felt everything Sharyn felt, saw what Sharyn saw.

They could see the wound now from *inside* RuArk's body. Sharyn probed down through the layers of skin, the fibrous bands of muscle, the veins and blood vessels, everything. Then she zoomed in on the source of RuArk's distress.

Poison. Blood poison. Rhia had no idea how she knew, but the knowledge was there none the less. She also instinctively knew it would take an amazing amount of strength to neutralize and remove the taint and heal RuArk's torn and shredded muscles, nerves and tissue.

Sharyn spoke into Rhia's mind. *"Rhia, we will remove the poison first, then heal the severed nerves. That is all we can do."*

"But where will the blood poison go?"

"We can expose it to the light, to pure Source energy. Think of it as a laser of sorts. It will dissolve it... unmake it, in a manner of speaking."

"Okay, I think I get it. Can we heal him and seal him up completely?"

"No. It's going to take all our strength just to remove the poison, and we're going to be close to completely drained by the time we are done. If our strength fades while we are still linked to RuArk, we can become infected, lose him and kill ourselves as well. We will do what we can, then Brita can mend the torn tissue. Are you ready?"

"Yes. Do it."

The next instant, Rhia felt a tremendous surge of energy rush toward and then through her. It reached into RuArk, who jerked and bucked as they worked. Thankfully, Linc had returned in the middle of the healing session and between the three of them, they managed to keep contact with RuArk's body and each other.

When they were done, they released their Source with an inaudible whoosh. Rhia promptly collapsed into the nearest cocoon-like comfy chair and willed the bright spots and sparkles behind her eyelids to go away. Linc helped Sharyn up from the spot on the floor she'd crumpled onto.

Lunis entered with a tray of tea and broth. "Ladies, you should eat something to regain your strength." He set the food down on the small table between them, but Rhia wasn't sure she could move enough to eat anything just now.

"Linc, help me," Brita called from across the room. "I need to get this down his throat."

"What is it?" Linc asked quietly.

"Clear broth with paracetinil for the pyrexia..."

"Py-what?" Linc asked.

"Pyrexia. The clinical name for fever. And meds for the pain and swelling." Brita mixed a pungent-smelling concoction from several vials on the table, then moved swiftly toward RuArk.

Linc held up the head of a semi-conscious RuArk as Brita slowly spooned the liquid into his mouth and massaged his throat to make sure it went down. After she'd done this several times, Rhia watched her prepare a packet of flexible, clear surgi-thread.

Though the blood vessels and nerves had been healed by Sharyn, the layers and layers of muscle and skin, Brita mended by hand with the smallest of stitches. Rhia was thankful that her lifemate felt no pain and that the surgi-thread would dissolve on its own. When Brita was done, RuArk had nine-inches of red, angry skin that oozed just the slightest bit of blood.

After carefully moving him to the other side of the bed, Linus and Linc changed the linens. Then they all settled in on couches, chairs and even on the floor, unwilling to leave RuArk for a second.

CHAPTER TWO

It was well past midnight when Rhia snapped awake. Something had stirred her. Laying perfectly still while her eyes adjusted to the darkness, her senses were on full alert. Slowly, she sat up, tested each stiff, achy limb, and looked around the huge bedroom full of slumbering bodies for the source of her unease.

Finally, she spotted something moving. She stumbled toward the glass wall of windows and peered out onto the terrace. Finally, she spotted something moving. After what seemed like endless moments of stretching her neck trying to see off into the distance, Rhia froze. Commanding her fatigued legs to steady underneath her, she leaned as far over the railing as she dared.

"Oh my god!" she gasped, and then turned and ran headlong into a haggard-looking Sharyn.

"Rhia, what is it? What is wrong?"

Sharyn staggered, but Linc was suddenly there. His arm shot out and grabbed Rhia as she tried to fly by. Shaking off his grip, Rhia ran out of the bedroom, through the living area, and out of the apartments. Sharyn and Linc were on her heels, hissing for her to stop.

Stop? Not an option.

Linc caught up to her just as she threw open the towering front door and jumped into Joan's arms, which caused Joan to fall backward against a man who looked just like Linc—his twin.

"Joan!" Rhia shrieked. "It's really you! Oh my god, it's you!"

Thank the Ancestors. Which she certainly believed in now, given the earthly magick she'd witnessed tonight. Rhia hugged Joan so tight, the shorter woman let out a muffled cry for mercy. Linc embraced his brother. Sharyn, seeing that all was well, turned and signaled the okay to Lunis, who again wielded the fireplace poker. The fireteam of warriors who'd quietly been guarding the place silently dispersed.

Once Marth learned RuArk had been wounded in battle, he refused to leave. Joan wouldn't leave without Marth. Brita was determined to stay in case RuArk awoke and needed more medicine. Sharyn dug in simply because leaving RuArk when he was hurt was out of the question, though she was too wrung out to actually help if anything arose.

Drefan came up to see his cousin, and camped out in the living room. After Dalmore and Osgar returned from their rounds, having promised to let the others know how RuArk was doing, they'd come up to the villa to see for themselves, then decided to hang out with Drefan.

Rhia looked around in disbelief. Dawn was still a couple of hours away and her place was packed with big warrior bodies, Housemen running in and out, messengers coming and going with reports from the First Commanders and responses to numerous requests for updates on RuArk's condition from, well, everyone. Lunis had the foresight to have breakfast sent up for all of them as the sun rose.

Thankfully, RuArk slept through it all.

Forcing herself to remain on her feet, Rhia checked on her husband one more time. A horde of guests was out on the terrace, which stretched the length of the apartment, from the bedroom to the living room. Linc urged Joan and Marth to quickly recount their tale while Rhia and Sharyn ate — or rather, tried to eat.

They still had no idea who had been behind the abduction, but Marth had left spies in Draema Proper to get to the bottom of it. And when Marth got to the part about joining with Joan, it was near impossible to chew or swallow given all the good-natured ribbing aimed at the happy couple.

Rhia grabbed Joan's hand and rose from the table. "I'd like to talk to Joan for a moment. Alone. You all head back to your own places. I promise to call for you if RuArk awakes."

"Rhia, do not overtax yourself," Sharyn said tiredly. "It will take a couple of days for us to regain the energy we gave tending to the Protector."

With a nod, she twined her fingers with her friend's and led her to the far end of the terrace to the bedroom doors. Just before they stepped inside, Marth's long legs quickly carried him to Joan's side. "I will come for you in half of an hour, and then we will bathe and get some rest."

Joan nodded amicably and gifted him with a blinding smile when he kissed her hand. He lifted a single finger and played with her dimples before he turned and walked back to his comrades. Joan's gaze was glued to Marth's tight butt as he followed his twin and everyone else off the terrace. A few moments later, they heard the apartment door open and close and knew they were alone, finally.

Once to the base of her bed's platform stairs, Rhia let go of Joan's hand and slowly climbed the six steps to RuArk's side where she pressed the back of her hand to the hollow of RuArk's neck.

"Well?" Joan asked.

"Fever seems to be coming down, thank the Ancestors," Rhia said quietly.

"Ancestors? Wow, I never thought I'd hear a Draeman say that," Joan teased. "Oh come on Rhia, don't scowl at me. I'm just kidding. Besides, you know we've always believed in science and architecture. If we can feel it, touch it, then it's real. But the bond I'm developing with Marth is certainly not something that can be explained by any of our scientists. It's beyond quantum or anything else I've ever heard of."

"Tell me about it," Rhia responded, plodded down the steps and plopped into a chair. She threw her legs over the side and let the soft cushions cradle her body. She turned stern eyes on Joan, and said, "Ok, Joan, out with it."

"We already told you what hap—"

"No, girlfriend, you told us *some* of what happened. I know you left out the, uh, intimate details you wouldn't share with everyone listening at the table. And I want those deets, woman, right this minute. So spill it."

"Rhia, you look like you're about to nod out."

"I'm running on pure adrenaline right now from you being here, so hurry up before I crash. I know there was sexin' involved!"

"Alright, alright," Joan laughed, and then snuck a peek over at RuArk to make sure her guffaw hadn't disturbed him. "Well, it started like this..."

Joan told about the would-be kidnappers who'd mistaken her for Rhia, followed by her and Marth's adventure trying to get to Province Springs via airship, train, horse and, finally, a very long walk.

And this time, she left nothing out. She reminded Rhia of the first time she'd met Marth that night at the stables when she thought he was Linc, and how Marth rescued her on the Wind Storm's orders.

"I'm going to kill that man," she said with a yawn. It didn't have quite the effect she was going for. "He only told me there was an attempted abduction, but wouldn't give me any details. He just let me wonder and feel guilty."

"Well, you deserved to feel guilty, Rhia," Joan told her matter-of-factly. "You're my girl and all, but I told you not to run off, and I certainly told you I didn't want to go on that blasted errand in your place wearing your clothes, on your horse, blah blah blah."

"I know, and I've felt terrible about it. I'm sorry for putting you in danger. What kind of friend am I, anyway?"

"You're a good friend. You were just out of sorts and unsure of what course your life was taking, is all. But now you know, right?"

"Well, maybe."

"What do you mean, *maybe*? Think about it, girl. This man is everything you've ever dreamed of. I know for a fact he's been more than generous and beyond patient with you."

"What? How?"

"Marth and Linc is how," Joan grinned. "They can always communicate. It's called mind linking. It's their Gift. Linc kept Marth and me up to date on everything going on from the moment you left the High City. Oh, and did you know that the Wind Storm knew you were planning to run all along?"

No. No, she hadn't. Well, surprise, surprise.

"Instead of interfering," Joan continued, "he let you run to your heart's content. In the meantime, he planned everything for the joining ceremonies along with all the stuff in this house, with my help of course."

At Rhia's shocked expression, she chuckled. "Yes, woman, that's right. With my help. In fact, at the same time you were talking me into running that dumb errand for you, RuArk had already started sending instructions to the township on what he wanted done. He also asked me what kind of things you like, so this house would be all done up before you got here."

"I had no idea. I-I didn't know."

"Did it ever occur to you that you don't have to know everything, Ree?"

"Well..."

"Oh, hush, I'm not done."

Rhia rocked back in shock. Her best friend had given her a piece of her mind before — was the only one, besides Brita, who dared. But this? This bordered on nanny-vs-kinderchild fussing.

"Furthermore, he's given you something you've missed since your mother died — a family, Rhia. Marth told me all about how Gaian society is built on extended family. You have a new mother, a father who is King of one of the most powerful lands in the world, and a slew of aunts, uncles and cousins. To them, you may as well have been born into their clans because they don't see you as any different than their own children. Now try to find *that* in Draema, woman."

Rhia lowered her gaze to the carpet. Hot tears gathered and threatened to spill. With a deep breath, she pushed them back.

"Listen, I gave my heart to Marth because I'm willing to trust him. And I'll continue to trust him unless he gives me a reason not to. Period. So, why can't you do the same? What if RuArk had been killed tonight?"

The lump in Rhia's throat was the size of a small melon. She'd never been so scared in her life than when RuArk had passed out in the mud, barely breathing. As she listened to her friend, Rhia couldn't help but ponder her words. Joan was right. She had a new, huge family, even if she wasn't quite sure where she fit just now.

If she'd lost him she had no idea what she would have done. Did it take almost losing someone to admit she didn't want to lose him at all?

At the subtle knock on the bedroom door, Joan rose, hugged Rhia close and said, "You know I love you, Ree. Otherwise, I wouldn't have bothered tearing you a new one just now. But Rhia, this is it. He's the one. No matter what you think of his rules or requests, you're responsible for how you treat him. Just love him, and let him do his job. What have you got to lose, other than the man of your dreams?"

"Myself," she whispered.

"That's ridiculous. Other than change your clothes, has the man asked you to change anything else about yourself?"

"I can't go out unescorted or practice my fighting skills on anyone other than him. How fair is that?"

"You can't go out alone, but you can still go as you please. You can't practice your skills with his men, not yet anyway, but you can still practice them. If we were at home in Draema Proper, I'd be the one running around with you and practicing with you. So what's the difference between doing it with me, and doing it with him?"

It was true that RuArk hadn't asked her to stop being a soldier. He'd only asked her to be a lifemate in addition to a fighter, and let him ensure her safety.

"Well, I don't appreciate the domestic crap," Rhia huffed.

"Oh please." Joan rolled her eyes. "You've run your father's house and the entire Citadel since you were twelve years old."

Well, Joan had her there.

The knock sounded again. When Marth opened the door, Joan was there to meet him. He bent down and kissed her sweetly on the lips. Joan winked and Marth smiled back. It was such a tender moment, the tears Rhia had held a tight grip on slipped down her cheeks. It was the most beautiful thing she'd ever seen—two people in love who didn't care about the differences in their cultures, or who had the upper hand between them.

Short, feisty, beautiful Joan, with her cropped platinum curls and creamy cacao skin, left with her six and a half foot, green eyed Gaian warrior, whose black-as-sin hair hung freely down his back.

The sun slipped higher into the sky and Rhia's last thought as she drifted off was that her best friend would make some beautiful babies with her warrior mate one day.

RuArk drifted in and out of consciousness. Groggy, his head felt stuffed full of cotton, but he was aware enough to realize Marth and Joan were safely in Province Springs. Not only had Joan arrived, but she'd laid into Rhia pretty good and hadn't spared her feelings one bit. He'd also learned that his little warrior had been by his side every waking moment.

He cared quite deeply for her, but hadn't known whether she really returned the feelings. Until now. A faint smile drifted across his lips as he slipped back into slumber. He wished he could stay awake longer. It was amazing what people said in front of you when they thought you were asleep.

CHAPTER THREE

By midday, the puckered, gray, angry look of the surrounding flesh had diminished significantly to a much healthier dark pink. The swelling had gone down quite a bit, and even his fever was lower. And both Rhia and Sharyn were completely wiped out.

While Sharyn rested and RuArk slept, Marth and Linc stepped in and covered for them. Lunis and his team of Draeman and Gaian Houseman, kept the household running smoothly. Sharyn had warned her that using their Gifts in such an intense manner would tax their bodies tremendously. But Rhia had to admit that she hadn't really believed Sharyn.

Joan came to hang out, as she'd done since they were kids. Bored senseless, and beginning to feel beyond useless, Rhia welcomed the company.

"Right now, I feel like I've been run down by a hover and backed over at least twice," she groaned, sprawled out on the floor in front of the fireplace. "But once I'm at one hundred percent, what am I going to do?" Rhia let out a frustrated sigh. "Being bored is not something I'm used to."

"I am definitely going to order a medical pod from the High City. Being this far out from the center of the technology capital of the world sucks."

She sat up to sip her third cup of a disgusting muddy-brown restorative tea Brita had sent up. She wished it would hurry up and start restoring.

"Blazes, this stuff tastes like boiled ass."

"I don't even want to know where you thought up that analogy, Rhia," Joan laughed. "Hey, I have an idea. Why don't you talk to RuArk about setting up a training class for the women?" Joan reached for a warm loaf of honey bread. "Even the Draeman men who aren't soldiers might be interested."

"What kind of class are you talking about? Blades? Art of war? Lost Arts? What?"

"Just your typical run-of-the-mill self-defense. From what you've told me, they certainly could have used it the night you all were attacked. If not for the Gaian warriors, who've handled blades since before they could walk, and the few Draeman soldiers assigned here, Province Springs could have easily been lost."

"Agreed. But what I'd like to know is who were those bastards that attacked us. They couldn't have possibly been men from this province."

Rhia turned toward the door and frowned at Linc who'd barged into her bedroom unannounced. Good thing she'd risen and dressed already. The man leaned against the wall just inside the threshold and mumbled an apology that seemed less than heartfelt. Obviously he had news, so she let it go. Marth, Osgar and Dalmore hung back, not stepping into her space until she waved them in.

None of them looked happy.

She turned to Joan. "Uncanny how much that one and Marth look alike. Can you tell them apart now?"

Joan nodded and gave her friend a "well duh" look and said, "Of course. There are little tells, plus Marth's energy is different."

Different energy, eh? Rhia guessed it had more to do with her friend spending time between the sheets with the man who now made a beeline for her. Joan automatically held up her cup for him to take a sip of steaming coffee. He declined and kissed her on the cheek. Moss-green eyes twinkled above a sincere and beautiful smile as strong-looking fingers caressed the curls at the base of Joan's skull. Freshly showered and in traditional Gaian tunic and leathers, Marth's long black hair was now pulled back into a silky braid that brushed across the middle of his broad back.

An incredulous Rhia turned wide eyes on Joan. The woman looked as if she hadn't a care in the world. There was no hint of concern, no grumbling about not getting enough sleep. No short fuse. It was downright disconcerting. Then understanding dawned, and Rhia's scowl faded.

"Are you really Joan Rouillard? You're much too calm to be my lifelong girlfriend. Wouldn't have anything to do with mating would it?"

Without bothering to look up from her cup of coffee, Joan replied with a bit of her usual sauciness. "Good loving can do wonders for your disposition, Ree." And she wasn't the least bit embarrassed to say so. She looked up over her shoulder and flashed Marth a scorching wicked smile that he obviously understood well, if his answering growl was any indication.

Dalmore and Osgar cleared their throats as a broody Linc pushed away from the wall and said, "The attackers. They were not men. They were Noman."

"What?" Rhia rose from her spot on the floor so

quickly she bumped into the coffee table and her nasty tea toppled onto the plush cream carpet. "Why the hells would Noman come here? Stalking me on the road here is one thing, but to attack the township?"

"I will tell you more when the Wind Storm is awake. It is not proper for me to do so until he gives me leave," Linc said, his tone flat.

Rhia weaved ever so slightly on her feet, yet still managed to fume. "Excuse me?"

"Rhia, sit down before you fall down." A large dollop of whipped cream disappeared into another steaming cup of dark coffee as Joan said, "You still haven't quite recovered from all the energy expended while healing RuArk. Linc will tell us what he knows when he can. It wouldn't be proper to tell you before he tells his commanding officer. Brita says he'll be awake soon anyway."

Joan was right about the warrior pecking order. Draeman soldiers wouldn't have hesitated to give her the details, considering she outranked them all. But these weren't Draeman. Linc and company reported to RuArk, regardless of her giving orders right after the man had been wounded. However, the knowledge did nothing to remove her irritation at not getting any answers.

She wanted to know what the hell was going on, but that blasted Linc wasn't budging an inch. In fact, he stared her down with a glare, as if he wanted to say something more. She was really getting sick of his funky attitude and her neck moved slightly to the side as her hand found its way to her hip. Just as she was about to ask him if he had a problem, he excused himself.

The day, along with the next one, passed in a blur

of nasty tea, bites of food and fading into and out of the oblivion of restorative sleep. She awoke to a quiet room and realized that for the first time in almost two days she didn't feel as if she were going to keel over. She rose and made her way to the bathing room by the light of the moon that filled the space with its glow.

When she was done, instead of bunking down on the couch again, she climbed the steps and eased beneath the covers next to RuArk. He didn't stir one bit. Rhia sat there for a moment just watching the rise and fall of his chest, the flutter of his eyelids that said he was dreaming.

RuArk was a good man. She could almost see the gray twinkle of his gaze when he was being mischievous with her. Almost smell the scent they created together when they made love. Feel his arms around her.

As she sat, a peace that she hadn't experienced in many years came over her until it overflowed her heart center.

I'm just relieved that my lifemate will live. *That's my story and I'm sticking to it.*

Smiling at her own silliness, she lay down and once again let sleep claim her.

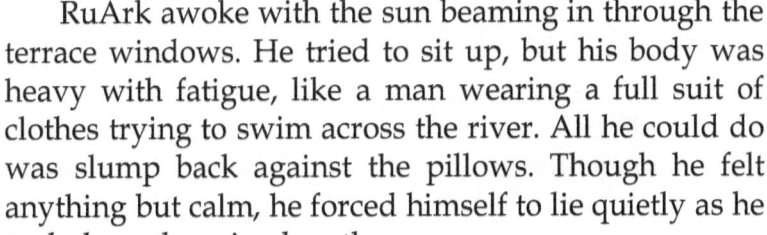

RuArk awoke with the sun beaming in through the terrace windows. He tried to sit up, but his body was heavy with fatigue, like a man wearing a full suit of clothes trying to swim across the river. All he could do was slump back against the pillows. Though he felt anything but calm, he forced himself to lie quietly as he took deep cleansing breaths.

A quick glance around told him he was at home, in his own bed. But why? What in blazes had happened? He tried to remember the exact events of that night, but his thoughts remained fuzzy around the edges. He shook his head briskly to clear it, but the action did nothing except start a wicked pounding at his temples.

In his mind's eye, he recalled Rhia drenched in rain and covered in blood. There'd been darkness and agony. Cold cobblestones, thick slippery mud, pain. A wide-eyed Rhia had screamed at him, but he couldn't hear her words, only the thick pounding of his own heart. Then there'd been peace.

He reached for his Source and the memories came—his shoulder had stung, then burned like fire, even in the raging storm. As he looked down at his body, his energy waned, and his hold on his Source along with it.

The injured limb was wrapped snugly in clean strips of gauzy white material and bound securely against his chest. His free hand rubbed against his still-pounding temple.

Focusing on the sounds around him, he heard someone open the door to his apartments and walk toward the bedroom. He hoped whoever it was would come in and give him some news on what had been going on while he'd been out of it. But the footfalls paused in the outer room, turned around and went back out the way they'd come.

Not long after, he heard footsteps again, but these were much heavier and moved a bit slower than before. They could only belong to a man. His door opened just wide enough for an old man with long gray hair to stick his head through the opening.

"Good, you are awake. How do you feel?"

"Grandfather? When did you arrive? How long have I been asleep?"

"Rhia sent word that you were injured in battle. We were not worried with Sharyn here, so I waited until this morning to make the journey across the river to see you and promised to send word to your parents about how you are doing. You have slept for several days. What do you remember?"

"Other than getting injured, not much at all." RuArk grunted and rubbed his slightly feverish chest. The muscles felt as if they were stretched too tightly across his ribs, sending a dull, but potent pain through his upper body. Perfect, a pain in his chest to match the one in his head and shoulder. He was sore all over. Had someone spent the last few days beating him? Moving his uninjured arm to stretch the muscles, he winced with each movement.

"Your wound was life threatening. The healing required great amounts of energy, which caused your muscles to seize. You will be tender for some days to come."

"What happened to me? The last thing I remember was seeing Rhia fighting off two men dressed in black. It was raining and the courtyard was full of mud and puddles of blood. Where is my lifemate?" RuArk was trained to be free of fear in every situation, but the thought that something happened to Rhia while he'd been laid out brought him to the edge of his control. He had to get up.

"You are not to rise, grandson," the Grandfather said sternly. "I am too old to fight with you, but I will thrash you if I must. Make this too difficult and I will simply send for your mother."

Warlord or not, Queen Mila was the last person he

wanted to see. If left up to her, he would be ordered to bed for the next two cycles.

Nodding his agreement to behave, he watched the Grandfather rise from his spot on the top step of the platform bed, his hand on the pommel of his blade.

"You came to me armed?" RuArk was incredulous.

"As I said, I will thrash you if necessary." The old man smiled and RuArk shook his head at his elder's antics. "Besides, if you are concerned for Rhia, there is an easier way. Simply invoke the life bond and you will know she is well. You may not have enough energy to hold strong to your Source, but the life bond should be effortless."

And he was right—it flared and RuArk immediately felt her. She was close and perfectly well. Her voice popped into his head and he went still. It wasn't coming through the bond. It felt more like a vague memory, just out of reach. She'd been having a conversation with Joan about him. About loving him? But had it been just a dream?

The Grandfather sat down again at his bedside and told him everything he'd learned since his arrival this morning. He left out nothing, including how Rhia and Sharyn linked their Gifts together to dissolve a rather nasty blood poison.

"Blood poison?" RuArk wrinkled his brow, but let the Grandfather continue.

"Yes, most likely smeared on the blade that sliced through your shoulder. Both Rhia and Sharyn exerted a great amount of energy to save you, grandson. It took Rhia two days to even get out of bed after that. Perhaps the healing would not have wiped them out had you been a skinnier warrior, eh?" With a chuckle and a wry grin, he parted the light woven tunic and bared

RuArk's upper body so he could lay his hands on his bare chest. The elder's Source burst forward like pure light, and then flowed outward to wrap RuArk in comforting warmth. The Grandfather listened to RuArk's lungs and heart without bothering to use the steth sitting nearby. Amazing considering the tech that Draeman relied so heavily on still couldn't pull off such a feat.

"The fever has just about broken, and your lungs are clear. But you still have some healing to do. You must listen to me in this and heed the instructions given to you if you wish to regain your full strength. I have already given Lunis instructions on what you are to eat and drink. You must also rest seven more days."

RuArk started to protest, but the pain beating against the back of his eyes caused him to clamp his mouth shut. *What a headache.* And he still hadn't seen Rhia.

The Grandfather helped him sit up and then rose and made his way down to the floor.

The old man waved goodbye and walked out into the living room without another word. But where was Rhia? RuArk wanted some answers and he wanted them now. Just when he felt his temper slip, the bedroom door opened again and his scowl faded into a smile. A warm glow began low in his body and it wasn't from the remaining fever.

CHAPTER FOUR

A moment after the Grandfather left, Rhia rushed into the room.

"I'm here, RuArk."

Much to RuArk's liking, she wore a very short peach-colored silk robe. The poufy bun on top of her head accentuated her high cheekbones and luscious lips. The scant bathrobe barely covered her strong thighs. A belt was tied neatly around her middle and the smallness of her waist enhanced voluptuous breasts—breasts that threatened to spill out. He could hardly stand it.

Oh, if only she knew what she was doing to him, and in his condition, too. Her jaw was set in full Blademaster challenge mode. She was obviously determined to carry out some task, but her warm smile and gleaming amber eyes gave her away. She was glad to see him.

His gaze was glued to her thighs and the sleek play of muscle as she circled to his side of the bed and climbed the steps. All his senses tuned in to this woman. She bent to set down a breakfast tray, he couldn't take his eyes off of her. His blood heated when her breast brushed against his arm as she leaned close and tucked a large linen napkin under his chin.

When she fluffed the pillows behind him, the warmth of her soft skin seeped through her wispy silk robe. He breathed deeply to wash his mind of its wayward thoughts only to be overtaken by the clean scent of her hair. He felt like a dirty old warrior alone with a beautiful young woman, with devilish thoughts coursing through his brain.

As she lifted the spoon to feed him what looked like porridge, he clamped his lips shut and glared at her.

"Seriously?" she asked. Clearly, she thought he was just being difficult about being fed. On the contrary, he couldn't bear the sight of the crevice at the top of her robe. It led down to a pair of the most inviting breasts he'd ever laid eyes on. His mouth watered as he recalled the taste of those sweet taut mounds.

"You need to eat to recover quickly, RuArk. We can do this the easy way, or I can get Linc to hold your mouth open while I feed you. Your call, truce or torture?"

"Tell me again how long I must stay in bed." He eyed her guardedly, and waited for the answer. Gods, he would go crazy if he had to see her barely dressed for a week and not be able to sink into her sweet core.

"The Grandfather said about seven days."

"Will I get to see you in that robe every morning?"

Not bothering to hide what he knew was a predatory grin, satisfaction filled him when she shivered. One side of her mouth lifted as she stated flatly, "No."

"Fine. Truce."

After he'd had enough of the warm porridge, Rhia placed a cup of creamy coffee into his free hand. He hated that his grip was unsteady in his current weakened state and he appreciated that she left him alone about it. When he was done, she took his empty cup, put it on the tray and removed all the dishes to the coffee table across the room.

RuArk had hated every second of being fed, but he certainly appreciated that she cared enough to help him. And he sure as hells appreciated the view. She returned to the bed and settled next to him on her knees. RuArk's gaze burned into hers before he let it travel to the spot where her robe rode seductively high up her thighs. He simply couldn't resist reaching out with his good arm to slide his hand along her bare leg and up underneath her silken material.

Rhia jumped when he made contact with her skin. It felt like it had been forever since he'd touched her, and her skin felt so good against his fingers. When he gently pressed his hand between her knees, he almost sighed with relief when she opened without hesitation.

When she leaned back on her heels and spread her legs wide, a deep groan seeped up out of his chest even as her need became a sensual spark in her beautiful eyes.

"RuArk, we shouldn't be doing this yet. You need to get better first."

He touched the short cropped curls between her legs and gently slid a finger between her dewy flesh. Up and down. Up and down. The sweetest friction imaginable.

"RuArk, you'll hurt your arm if you continue to… oooh."

"I like it when you say that."

"W-when I say what? Mmm…"

"That." The tip of his tongue glided over his lower

lip. He wished his tongue was somewhere else. He knew she did too when her hips began to roll ever so slightly. He was enjoying their sensual dance.

Wanted to dance the most primal of steps with her.

"RuArk. You shouldn't."

"Let me pleasure you, Fire Storm. If I cannot sink my cock into your sweetness, let me at least touch you."

"But you're supposed to be rest—"

"Relax, Rhia," he whispered.

"Resting your... arm."

"Let me, sweetheart." He picked up the pace, moving the pads of his fingers over, in and through her sensitive folds until they were slick with her honey. Her unique scent wafted up from between her spread legs. Such a sweet aphrodisiac.

Her inner thighs quivered when he gave his attention to the blooming bud stiffening against his fingers as he spread her dewy sweetness all over it in slow, agonizing circles.

"Come for me, sweet." He was weak from his wound and tiring fast, but he was determined to push her over the edge. He wanted, *needed* to feel her melt for him. Blood pounded in his ears and flowed down to his cock until it filled to near bursting. He'd almost died a few days ago and all he could think about was burying himself to the hilt in his lifemate's hot center. Right now, her sweet sex was his whole world.

RuArk wanted to tease his wife with words of what he'd like to do to her, but putting more than two words together was impossible. Her hips tilted forward to give him better access, and the walls of her channel gripped the seeking finger he plunged inside her. The belt of her robe had come undone, and the silky covering fell open just as her head fell back onto her shoulders.

RuArk's tongue stuck to the roof of his mouth when Rhia palmed her breasts, kneaded and caressed them until the nipples were hard as polished stones. She was wound up and the spring only pulled tighter. Yes, this was what he wanted—for her to welcome it, reach for it, knowing he would give her sweet release. Bucking against his hand, she was almost there.

"Wind Storm, the Grandfather said you were awake and—"

"Fucking hell," Rhia hissed, quickly drawing her knees and robe together. RuArk hoped the garment hid what he'd been doing to her underneath it.

Slamming to a halt, a red-faced Linc turned away from the erotic scene. RuArk grinned wickedly at a frazzled Rhia, and lifted his fingers to inhale her fragrant scent.

He opened his mouth, swirled his tongue around the finger that had just been inside her and licked it clean.

RuArk grinned. "Mmm, you taste so sweet."

Rhia looked as if she might swallow her tongue and barely managed to paint on a scowl at his torment. RuArk lowered his hand to his side just as Linc reappeared in the doorway with a cup.

And RuArk was still grinning in spite of the interruption.

"You are such a blasted tease," she whispered, then scooted sideways a bit so he could see past her to view Linc better.

RuArk turned his eyes to his First Commander and pinned him with a glare. "Linc, I believed your rooms were in the barracks?"

"Sir?"

"Perhaps I am mistaken since you entered these rooms without knocking."

"I just received news you were awake and did not think to call out for entry."

"It is a poor excuse for disrespecting my lifemate. This is her space, our space. Don't let it happen again. I don't want Rhia to find herself in an embarrassing situation not of her own making."

Rhia blushed to the roots of her dark, flame streaked hair and elbowed RuArk in the thigh. "Will you shush, already?"

"I apologize, sir. And my apologies to you, Fire Storm."

Rhia nodded, but said nothing, and RuArk wondered at the coldness between the two.

Linc walked up the steps and offered RuArk the fresh cup of brew, this one fragrant with a blend of chocolate and spices. It tasted almost as good as Rhia. Certainly much better than the bland porridge she'd forced him to eat earlier, or the medicine he could still taste on the back of his tongue from whatever he'd been given while he'd been unconscious.

"Your report, Linc?"

"Yes, sir." Linc glanced distractedly at Rhia, then finally spoke in his usual matter-of-fact tone. "We were attacked by a band of Noman."

RuArk's hand froze halfway to his mouth. Passing the cup to Rhia, he forced himself not to interrupt knowing there was more to the story.

"They did not breach the main gates, but entered the township by way of an overgrown, and obviously long forgotten set of small wooden gates behind the stables."

RuArk's brows rose. "The villa's stables?"

"No, sir, the public stables of the Society of Breeders on the westernmost side of town. They're built into the inner wall that surrounds the entire township. How they knew of these gates, we are not sure."

Both RuArk and Rhia frowned as Linc relayed the rest of the events of that fateful evening.

They'd lost several warriors and had many more wounded because of the stealth of the attack. But in the end, the Noman had been slaughtered almost to a man with only a few escaping into the darkness of the night. And they had no idea who was behind it all.

At the knock on the door, RuArk looked to Linc with a raised brow.

"Drefan guards the apartment doors. No one enters without his knowledge."

RuArk called out permission to come into the bedroom. A granite mask hid his surprise when Ricard Shae walked in with Brita on his heels.

Rhia must have caught the look that passed between RuArk and Linc because she leaned sideways and whispered into her husband's ear.

"I know you don't like the man, but I've known him my whole life. You don't think he had anything to do with this, do you?"

"We will talk later." RuArk then turned his attention to Ricard and Brita, who seemed strangely out of sorts.

"Brita, are you well?" RuArk asked.

"Huh? What?" She appeared completely shaken, her mind obviously elsewhere.

"Are you well?" RuArk asked again. Gray eyes narrowed at her discomfiture.

She fidgeted, but finally responded, though her gaze remained focused on the floor. "Yes, yes, I'm fine. Just a bit tired is all. We've been working well into the night tending other wounded. I think I'm just a bit weary."

Ricard's face was hard and unfeeling as he watched Brita speak to RuArk. He looked at her without a single emotion. No care. No concern. Like a shell. His presence, his energy seemed... foreign. When the man caught Rhia's gaze on him, the strange expression evaporated as if it had never been.

Rhia appeared to have dismissed it. RuArk, however, did not.

Ricard broke the stifling silence. "I'm glad to see that you're well, RuArk."

"Truly?" RuArk asked stonily.

"RuArk," Rhia hissed and poked him in the ribs. "You don't have to be rude." He ignored her as Linc stepped a bit closer to Ricard.

"Have you been of help to your sister since the battle, Ricard?" Linc inquired quietly.

"Actually, I was wounded. One of the nurses from the Society of Physicians bandaged me up." He held up his arm, showing the neat wrappings of clean white linen. "I took a good slice to the ribs as well. I can finally move my arm without too much pain," he said with a wince as he gingerly attempted to stretch the place where he'd been cut.

"How bad is the cut? Do you mind if I see it?"

"No, my lord," Ricard grimaced as he stiffly raised his loose tunic to reveal a sparkling white linen bandage wrapped deftly around his midsection.

"Take care not to overtax yourself. You would not want to take a fever," RuArk drawled. Something niggled at the back of his thoughts. Something dark and sinister. The longer he looked at the little Draeman man, the stronger the sensation grew. He knew Ricard was involved somehow, but proving it was another matter. Perhaps he would simply throw him into one of the cells in the lower levels of the villa until he could be sure.

Brita offered RuArk a dose of pain medicine. He refused, choosing instead to face his scowling lifemate. The last thing he wanted was for Rhia to worry, but he needed to be clear-headed and completely aware of what was going on around him if he was to get to the bottom of this. Rhia made no bones about expressing her thoughts—she thought he was nuts for choosing the bone-rending pain rather than a mild sedative.

Ricard and Brita left just as Marth and Joan entered. RuArk noticed that Ricard moved awfully well for someone with a wound to the ribs.

"Linc, did you learn anything while you were watching Ricard since he arrived some days ago?"

"RuArk you couldn't possibly think Ricard was involved in this?" Rhia protested, again.

"Why not?"

"He would never hurt me. He's been in love with me forever."

Linc, being the voice of reason asked, "But what if the goal was not to harm you? What if the goal was to harm the Protector, leaving you unprotected?"

Rhia tilted her head and seemed to think on what was being said. After a moment, her unwavering gaze found RuArk's. "Considering the lengths that my father went to just to get me mated to you, I can't dismiss the seriousness of the situation. As much as I don't want to believe it, I can't rule Ricard out. The

Noman you introduced me to on the way here was bad enough, but to learn that they somehow knew how to get inside this township is another deal entirely."

Linc, Marth and Joan all nodded at her sound reasoning.

"You will be careful Rhia. No arguments. No excuses." RuArk gave her a moment to protest, and was relieved when she didn't. "Given the number of dead and wounded, your life is not the only one in danger here. Marth, you know what to do. Between you and Dalmore, continue to watch our unexpected guest. Where is Sharyn?"

"She is securing the gates where the Noman entered." Linc replied on his way to the door. He eased it open, and then stopped. "Do you believe Ricard is truly injured, Rhia?"

"Why do you ask?"

"Because he has not been seen since right before the battle. We did not know until now whether he was among the living or the dead, as we are still accounting for our people, both Draeman and Gaian."

RuArk sat stone still as his anger flared and Rhia's calm reassurance reached for him through their bond. The throb in his shoulder became a wash of pain as his energy began to flag. He might need to rest, but his mind was already thinking of all kinds of imaginative punishments for Ricard Shae if he learned the man had been involved.

Easing down beneath the covers, he spoke around a huge yawn. "Bring me word as soon as you know where he has been, Linc. Have Dalmore look after Ricard while you join Sharyn at the gate. The two of you decide if this gate should be sealed, or if it should simply be patrolled from now on. We may come to need it someday."

Linc nodded, then spoke boldly, but sincerely, to Rhia. "I ask your forgiveness, Fire Storm. I was wrong to blame you for the Wind Storm's actions the night of the battle. He is his own man and makes his own decisions. You have my respect for your strength through this ordeal. Forgive me for my disrespect. I will never disregard you again." He turned on his heel and was gone before she could respond.

Meanwhile, RuArk whispered instructions to Marth, whose report later that evening was of no comfort. Ricard had disappeared again. Sadly, no one missed him. Not even his sister, whose current hobby was walking around in a daze.

CHAPTER FIVE

"You have failed again, Behn. You are totally incompetent. The Gaian is still alive and Rhia is safe and sound in Province Springs. Where's the good news you promised me when you sent your filthy Noman kin to carry out this latest farce you call a plan? What good are you if you can't bring me one little woman?"

"Your whining is beginning to bore me, Father. If you cannot have patience, then why don't you ride into Province Springs and retrieve her yourself?"

"Impudent, useless freak. Of my two sons, you're supposed to be the one who has rediscovered magick that makes you indispensable. Perhaps not, eh?"

"Watch it, old man," Behn said on a bored sigh. His sharp eyes caught the slight flicker of fear in Collaidh's eyes. "You need me to do what you cannot. So do not push me further."

"How dare you, you white eyed, black hearted Noman piece of shit. You're no better than your filthy Noman mother."

Behn growled menacingly and let his already elongated fangs lengthen further.

"Don't you dare threaten me," Collaidh ranted. His face turned an alarming shade of purple as he returned

Behn's growl and bared his own perfectly white, straight, small teeth.

It didn't have quite the same effect.

"Do not worry," Behn said quietly. "I would not stoop so low as to take your cowardly, mewling blood into my body even if I lay dying." He stepped close, so close he knew his father caught the scent of aging blood on his cool breath. "My mother was more of a woman than you will ever be a man. Her only mistake was trusting you. You disgust me."

Behn's mother had been completely infatuated with Rama Collaidh and believed him brave, seeing he'd been the only man to ever purposely go into her hunting grounds. He'd told her he was on a diplomatic mission to bring their cultures together. In truth, he'd been nothing more than a young and foolish Draeman noble who'd taken a stupid dare while drinking with friends. He had to sleep with a Noman woman... and live. In his arrogance and drunkenness, he'd accepted.

Effortlessly, Behn peeked inside his father's mind, saw what he saw, heard what he heard as the man relived the very story that Behn had grown up with.

She'd been alone in the High Desert, just outside of Draema Salone along the outer wall. Beautiful, ethereal, her pale skin was almost translucent with a pearly sheen. Her long white hair curled to her waist and reflected the bright glow of the full moon. One look at her and Rama had been so overtaken with lust he'd have done anything to have her spread underneath him.

He'd lied, declared that he'd been watching her and finally come to claim her. He'd had such a cunning tongue, she'd sensed no deception, and believed he'd been as primal in his choice of mate as any Noman would have been. Rama had touched, kissed and fondled her boldly. She'd pulled his hair and nipped him with her sharp teeth, leaving little love bites all over his chest and neck. It had been the most fulfilling, wild and primitive loving he'd ever experienced.

He certainly hadn't thought beyond the sex, but he'd won the dare and his friends paid up with round after round of good Draeman ale and the promise to keep his secret.

While visiting the western counties he'd stopped to see a wench who lived near that same outer wall he'd snuck through a year earlier. A pack of strong, feral Noman found him and taken him to *her*. Taken him to see his sons—twin boys barely a season old, Behn and BBehn. One was Noman, the spitting image of his beautiful mother with white eyes and wavy little tufts of snow-white hair. The other was a brown eyed human with black hair just like his father's.

While the pack had slept sheltered from the sun, Collaidh had taken the human child, who he renamed Bryan. The other, he'd left behind.

That was twenty-five years ago. He'd never laid eyes on Behn again. Until now.

Behn had grown into a creature to be reckoned with. Though he was Noman, he was, in fact, brilliant—a scholar who had rediscovered how to touch and use his Source and walk the Dream as none but the Gaian had done for centuries. While Behn Collaidh had become a leader with his own personal Noman army, his brother, Bryan, had turned out to be an abject failure. A failure who still didn't know he had a twin. And if their father had his way, he would never know.

Collecting his thoughts, Collaidh took a deep breath. Behn felt the old man push the disgust and rage he felt for a creature of his own flesh and blood, down to the bottom of his emotions.

"I apologize, Behn. I was wrong to speak of your mother in such a manner. She was innocent in the whole affair."

Slipping out of his father's thoughts, Behn regarded the man who had fathered and left him behind all those years ago. With his resentment masked carefully, he accepted the apology and turned to leave. Collaidh hindered him with a question Behn had no intention of answering. He could care less about his father's apology. All that mattered was revenge and Rhia.

Patience would give him both.

Soon he would become a natural in the Dream, and eventually learn to *Seek*. The Ancestors had no favorites and would guide him as they did anyone who sought their council, whether for good or ill. He would teach his children to master their Source and perhaps develop a true Gift. He would harness that power and use it to rule the weak-minded. Use it to bring the Noman out of the northern lands to take their rightful place as masters in a land of plenty. He would start in Draema. And the end? There was none in sight.

"What do you plan to do now? Whatever it is, I'll accept it," Collaidh said

"I have another that I am sending to Province Springs, someone from Rhia's own Society of War."

"One of the soldiers she's trained or served with, perhaps?" Collaidh asked.

"Yes." But that was all the information he was giving up. Everyone seemed to want Rhia, but Behn was determined he would be the one to have her. No one, absolutely no one, would put their plans ahead of his. Including his no good father or the overstuffed Council of Seven that he thought he controlled.

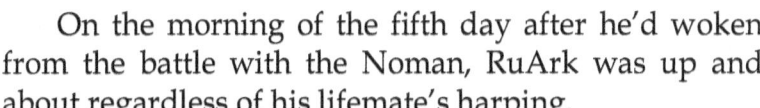

On the morning of the fifth day after he'd woken from the battle with the Noman, RuArk was up and about regardless of his lifemate's harping.

Rhia grumbled all the way to Sharyn's apartments on the other side of the villa. She was still muttering to herself when she walked right through Sharyn's partially open door.

"He's out there working his shoulder," she gestured wildly toward the direction of the lower courtyard. "And after we took all that care to heal the blasted man. He actually had Marth unbind his shoulder while I was downstairs ordering his breakfast. That sneaky, rotten... Hell, what if he re-injures it? What then, huh? If he expects me to wait on him hand and foot, he can forget it."

Rhia stopped raving long enough to finally notice Linc sitting at the small luncheon table next to the far windows. Rhia's eyebrows climbed practically to the top of her forehead as her mouth snapped shut. Sharyn completely ignored the look.

Curiosity overrode her irritation at her husband, and she flopped down on one of the overstuffed couches and waited.

Linc rose, took a final gulp of coffee and left the warm mug on the table. It smelled of peppers and spice. In spite of the odd combination, the scent made her mouth water.

Spices and peppers? In coffee? And it actually smells wonderful? Ack! I must be ill or something.

The handsome warrior paused meaningfully in front of Sharyn, his expression tender, his tone serious. "We shall finish our talk later."

Rhia's head tilted a hard left at the request-that-wasn't-a-request. Damn these Gaian giants and their arrogant attitudes. What if Sharyn didn't want to finish the talk later? What if she had something more important to do? What would the big warrior do then? To her surprise, Sharyn dipped her head demurely and agreed.

As soon as the door closed behind Linc, Rhia was ready to get into her friend's business.

"Well, it's obvious you two weren't talking about First Commander duties and schedules for the night patrols. What's up?"

Sharyn ignored her question and launched right into the day's lesson.

Fine. Rhia would let it go for now, but later on, all bets were off.

"How would you oversee the cleaning of the estate, both the villa and the surrounding grounds?" Sharyn asked.

"I would find Lunis and have him see to it."

"No, Rhia. You alone are mistress here. Master these skills, show you have no problem running this estate as your lifemate asks, and he will give you anything you wish."

"Oh, please," she scoffed. "He'll never give me everything I wish. The man wouldn't even stay in bed like he knows he should. He's too much... *warrior*. I've never had to do this kind of stuff before. Why can't I just do what I do best-fight?"

"Remember, you are denied the thing you want most because you fight *too much*. Eventually, this will sink into your brain. You understand duty, but you do not understand the nature of a man. Your lifemate wants nothing more than to see you happy."

"Could have fooled me. He's out of bed and won't listen to a word I say, but I'm supposed to jump and do whatever he wants?" Rhia glared. She couldn't help it.

"It is not difficult to bend a man if you know how to do it."

"Well, what's the difference between running the Citadel at home, and running this blasted place?"

Sharyn lifted her brow, and flashed Rhia a secret smile. "Exactly, Fire Storm. Exactly."

Finally, the light bulb flared on in Rhia's mind and she had the answer. There was *no* difference. How could she have missed it? RuArk had told her plenty of times that there was no need for her to become the perfect Gaian woman. All she had to do was run the place.

Sneaky bastard had let her think there was some super-secret Gaian code to what he wanted from her, when in truth, he'd said exactly what he meant. It wasn't his fault she'd read way more into it than he'd said, but she wasn't going to admit that right now.

Instead, she thought about how her father managed to take care of their homeland without running himself ragged. It was too much for one person to do alone, so he delegated many of the tasks. When she'd lived at home, she'd been one of those delegates. Well, didn't she have a whole township full of warriors, soldiers, and Society members to delegate to?

"Now answer the question again," Sharyn urged, obviously realizing that Rhia had put two and two together in her head.

"To have the estate cleaned, I'd find the head of the Houseman, which is Lunis. I'd ask him to make a list of all of the rooms in the villa and all of the buildings on the grounds that need care, along with a list of who does what. Then, I'd ask him to get all the staff together so I could personally tell them what I wanted done, first making it clear that Lunis is in charge, and second, instruct them to see to the items on Lunis' list. Then I would leave it to them and go practice my hand-to-hand knife fighting with you."

"Perfect! You are a fast learner after all," Sharyn said proudly, nodding at the stylish cut of Rhia's sarand. She'd stopped griping about wearing it, and was happy as long as her blade, hanging low on her hips, and her mother's dagger strapped around her thigh, accompanied the outfit.

"Let us move from these couches down to the floor. Sit cross legged and we will practice reaching the Source."

"Finally." But it didn't take long for thoughts of RuArk to lead her down the path of distraction. She wondered what he was doing, felt the bond kick in and knew he was still in the courtyard with some of his men. She felt a faint twinge, a dull ache in her mind.

His shoulder is tender.

"Rhia, concentrate."

"What? Oh, sorry Sharyn. I just can't believe him. He's being totally foolish."

"He is a warrior. It is not his nature to stay in bed."

"But the Grandfather told him to rest. He shouldn't be working that shoulder for a couple more days yet." She jumped to her feet and paced back and forth in front of Sharyn who watched her from her seat on the finely woven rug.

"He is his own man, Rhia. There is nothing you can do about that. Besides, would you really want him if he gave in to you all the time?"

Rhia glared at the other woman, and settled back down on the rug.

"I did not think so. You would not want a man you could walk over, and you know this for truth."

"Yeah, whatever. Let's just get back to it," she grumbled and closed her eyes again.

This time she successfully reached her Source. The sensation was exquisite. She'd only been able to reach this place within herself a few times, and only with Sharyn's help. This time she was on her own and the sweet, addictive surge of energy was almost overwhelming. Off in the distance, she heard Sharyn giving her instruction on how to better control it now that it coursed through her.

Rhia gently clamped down on the raw energy. She allowed it to continue to flow, but controlled the power and strength of that flow. Swirling images danced in her mind, came close until she could almost make them out, then they retreated again. The images seemed wispy and transparent. She opened the flow of her Source just a little bit more, then focused harder. Then, she saw it.

"Fire Storm? Fire Storm, wake up."

"What happened?" Rhia asked, sitting up groggily. "What am I doing on the couch?"

"Something happened with your Gift while you were connected to the Source. You were controlling it expertly when you began to tremble. You opened your eyes, but did not respond to me. Then you fainted."

"Fainted? I've never fainted in my life."

"Well, that is no longer true. Tell me what happened."

Now that she was awake, the memory flooded her thoughts with a clarity that was frightening. "I saw something, Sharyn. It seemed so real. And there was so much blood…"

She trembled as the scenes played themselves out before her eyes and brought with them all the feelings of dread and death, as if she were experiencing them right here, right now.

Rhia took a deep breath and pushed the words out of her mouth. "Our men were on their way to the High City. I could tell because I could see the walls from where I sat my horse. It was like I was there, watching. Like I was outside of myself or something."

"What happened after?"

"RuArk, Linc and Marth, they all rode into a trap. The warriors with them were taken prisoner and put underneath the High City somewhere. RuArk was taken into the Council chambers and accused of being a traitor and… and an assassin. Sharyn, he was sentenced to death."

"Who said he was a traitor?"

"I don't know. I couldn't see any of their faces. I could only see RuArk. He was badly wounded and bleeding everywhere, yet he stood before the Council of Seven with that blasted granite face he wears. Then…"

"Then what?!"

It was the first time Rhia had ever heard Sharyn raise her voice.

"They killed him, Sharyn, right there in the Council

chambers. His blood was all over the floor. Why would my father do such a thing?"

"Your father? You saw him? But you said you could see no faces?"

"Who else would it be? No one else in all of Draema has authority to conduct a Council meeting, and no one else has the authority to order someone to death." Dread settled into the pit of her stomach as she thought of what this could mean. Sharyn put her thoughts into words.

"Rhia, this Gift may be Foreknowledge. If it truly is, it is possible someone else had the power to order RuArk killed."

"But that would mean my father is not High Counsel in the vision I saw."

"Not Vision. Foreknowledge."

"Vision or Foreknowledge, so what. Who cares?"

"Even in something this troubling you must know what you are dealing with. The Gift of Vision shows us what may come, but it is shown in parables and symbols. If you see a songbird, it could represent spring or freedom, as birds sing in springtime and have freedom to fly where they wish. Interpretation is subjective. With Foreknowledge, you get exactly what you see. Death is death. Pain is pain."

And fucked was fucked.

"Sharyn, link with me. Please. I can't control my Gift enough to do this again by myself, but I have to try to see the vision again."

"Rhia it is very dangerous. We linked our Gifts when RuArk was injured because neither of us could have healed him on our own. But it was a dangerous undertaking. You know this."

"If RuArk's life is on the line, I've got to know

what's supposed to happen. And so do you."

Sharyn shook her head, yet resigned herself to the wisdom in Rhia's words. They joined hands and reached for their Source.

The scenes came more quickly this time. Rhia could feel Sharyn reaching into her to help her control the images. This time they saw enough to determine the timing of the horrors. Late summer. The summer season had just begun, so they at least had a little bit of time to figure out how to stop this treachery. But it didn't make either of them feel any better.

That afternoon Rhia sent a letter to her father telling him what she suspected. She admonished him not to trust anyone and that he should consider her warning as part of the original reason he'd called RuArk to the High City in the first place. They were still in danger. All of them.

CHAPTER SIX

RuArk healed quickly and jumped right back into his duties as Protector of the Realm. A quick trip across the river to Gaia to get the patrols along the borders and the land bridge redeployed, had been quickly followed by the organizing of a large hunting party. The plan? Track down and annihilate the Noman who'd attacked Province Springs—an attack that had nearly cost RuArk his life.

With summer fully upon them, both Rhia and Sharyn had expressed concern about the coming hunt. She'd even told him about her Foreknowledge, which hadn't gone at all as planned.

Rhia tucked her head against her lifemate's chest and blurted out her fears.

"RuArk, you can't go. It's not safe."

The covers fell down around his waist as he swiftly sat up and looked at her as if she'd lost her mind. She quickly launched into her tale in hopes of heading off their imminent clash of wills.

"RuArk, Sharyn thinks I have the Gift of Foreknowledge. Aaaand there's the imperious raising of the brow," she chuckled. He rolled his eyes at her dry humor, and she continued. "While we were practicing touching my

Source, right after you got out of bed that first day, I saw something. Something terrible. RuArk you died, horribly. And it was in summer... which is right now."

"You know that the Gifts are not always exact."

"But..."

"Rhia, you've worried more about me since the attack. Don't roll your eyes, you know it's true. I appreciate it, but we can't lay down our responsibilities, lay down who we are, what we are, and go live in a cave."

"But, RuArk..."

"Your life was in danger the day I walked back into your life. Your life is in danger now. I will not sit aside to save my own skin. Not now. Not ever."

"You know," she snapped, "it's a good thing Sharyn insisted that I learn how to reach out to the Ancestors for help because thanks to you and your bone headedness, I've been doing quite a lot of that lately."

"Thank you," he said, nuzzling her ear.

"I'm not sure if you're welcome or not, damn it. You should just give it up and let me go with you," she insisted, trying to squirm out of the arms that had come around her to hold her close. "You're trying to distract me."

"Is it working?" he asked. She smacked him on the arm, but only succeeded in hurting her hand.

"Ow! Must I remind you that I'm First Heir of Draema and a Blademaster in the Society of War? Since we're still officially in Draema province, I have every right to go with you if I bloody well want to."

"And must I remind you that you're my lifemate before anything else and your first duty is to be safe." He kissed her soundly. "And listen to me, of course."

Rhia snorted and almost burst out laughing until he reminded her that his recovery time hadn't counted towards her "Yes RuArk" days.

"Are you seriously bringing that up now, RuArk Miwatani? Really?"

"I am. And don't forget the time added for that fight in town. With warriors. While you were dressed inappropriately with not a sarand in sight."

Damn it, she'd completely forgotten about that little dust up, which hadn't been her fault at all. Not to mention, Linc had been the consummate tattletale.

"Officially," he said sarcastically, "You have two more days of total obedience. Of course, you have the option of challenging me again to have them dismissed."

Being no fool, she quickly declined.

RuArk then proceeded to make her forget about wanting to go Noman hunting or anywhere else outside of their bed. God, how he made her scream. Not to mention, he did some screaming of his own.

Blazes, the man had been gone for all of two days and already she missed him terribly. She rolled over, grabbed his pillow to his chest and inhaled his scent. Rolling out of bed, Rhia headed to the bathing room to dress while forcing herself not to reach for him through their bond. It wouldn't do to interrupt him if he were in the middle of a fight

Though it was early yet, it was clearly going to be another scorcher of a day. Ice cold juice in hand, Rhia sat on the terrace under a cloudless blue sky and observed a self-defense class down the hill in the courtyard. She smiled, pleased to see a Gaian captain teaching hand-to-hand basics in her own Draeman style to a mix of Tanners, Horse Breeders and other Society members.

The battle with the Noman had been a wake-up call to the people here. People who finally appreciated that their Gaian neighbors had dealt successfully with the menace across the land bridge for ages.

As she watched the students learn the fundamentals of fighting stances, she got up and went to the kitchen, her mind drifting to the language exercises she was supposed to go over with Sharyn later this morning. Rhia usually looked forward to her Gaian lessons, but frankly she was so tired even her favorite tasks lacked appeal. Exhausted and ravenously hungry, not one thing came to mind that could possibly explain this ridiculous fatigue.

Determined to stuff herself with something savory, the second she entered the kitchens her stomach lurched and roiled. Spicy sausage, herb-laced hard cheese, fresh bread—smells that usually made her salivate—had her running the opposite direction. Maybe she was coming down with something? A message to Brita for some vitamins to ward off the illness and regain her energy was most certainly in order.

But later, after a nap.

Sharyn flagged Rhia down just as she started to climb the stairs back to her apartment.

The other woman hadn't gone hunting with RuArk and the other First Commanders. Even if the other woman's sole purpose was to keep her sister of the blade from earning any new punishment upon RuArk's return, Rhia was glad for Sharyn's company, and doubly glad for Joan and Brita's.

"Rhia, where are you going?"

"Back upstairs for a nap."

"A nap?" Sharyn said doubtfully as her eyes conveyed her thoughts. Rhia could practically hear the woman's amazement. Usually up with the sun, driving herself relentlessly until the dinner hour, a nap this early in the morning sounded ridiculous, even to her own ears.

Sharyn grabbed Rhia by her chin, placed a hand under her neck and ran her fingers over Rhia's skin. "The sun is not even at midday. Do you have a fever? Are you ill?"

"I don't know what's wrong. I don't feel sick, but I've been wiped out lately. I barely have the energy to do anything but observe what's going on around here."

Brita came out of the kitchens and strode down the hallway, heading right for them. Her step was sure, but her expression was strangely vacant. Just as she passed by, Rhia called out. The woman jumped a foot into the air and gasped in surprise as her hand flew to her throat.

Rhia frowned.

Wild-eyed and afraid, it took a moment for the woman to calm enough to speak.

"Dammit, Rhia, you scared me!" Brita snapped frantically, trying to catch her runaway breath.

"How? You were walking right past us," Rhia stated matter-of-factly.

"I was? I... Well, I guess I've just been so preoccupied with getting the new medicine stores sorted and put away that I'm kind of loopy."

Sharyn looked at her out of the corner of her eye, not quite convinced. "Hmm. Are you sure you are not ill? I was just asking Rhia the same question. Perhaps you should go see the Physician in the township, or one of our Healers?"

"Me? Sick? No, no," Brita stammered, her fair skin blushed to a bright red. "I'm fine, really. I'm just tired. I haven't been sleeping well, but I'm sure it's nothing." Then she hurried away.

"That was weird," Rhia murmured.

"I will not disagree with you on that. It was almost as if she was someplace else as she walked past us. Strange." Sharyn turned back toward the kitchen, then called over her shoulder. "I will send Lunis with a meal for you."

"Thanks, Sharyn. See you later."

Rhia dragged herself up to her apartments, stripped in the bathing room and then headed to her huge bed. Thinking about her husband's "come hither" eyes and lazy smile, she recalled every minute detail of his face, his body. Even his voice as he whispered naughty words into her ear.

Without her meaning to invoke it, the bond she shared with her husband kicked in the second she touched her Source and flared up in her chest stronger than she'd ever felt it. Then RuArk was there, alive and vibrant in the back of her consciousness.

She pulled a pillow over her head and groaned as her body responded to his scent on the blankets and sheets. Hopefully, the hunt would end quickly and he'd be home soon. She didn't want to go any longer than necessary without his touch or his company. Her skin and breasts tingled, eager for her husband's touch. In fact, she was a big tired, tingly mess.

Too sleepy to hold onto the bond any longer, she released it. Her last thought as she drifted off was how wonderful sleeping a year sounded, and for the first time in her life she didn't feel the least bit guilty about it at all.

"Rhia? Rhia, wake up will you?"

Groggy, her eyes heavy with fatigue, Rhia finally managed to crack them open enough to focus on Joan's worry-lined face.

So much for sleeping a year.

"Wake up, get dressed and hurry up." Joan's agitation seemed to vibrate from her curly platinum head to the bottom of her sandal-clad feet.

"What the blasted hell is going on?" God, her body weighed a thousand pounds and her head felt full of wet linen.

"The warriors on the outer wall wouldn't let him in at first because Wind Storm left strict orders that both the Borderland and Province Springs walls and gates were to be closed and guarded around the clock. The low walls that surround the estate are patrolled, too. Nobody from outside the township is allowed anywhere near you except for the Grandfather and the warriors coming across the river from Gaia while he's away."

"So why did they open the gates against his orders? And who did they decide to let in?"

"I'm getting to that," Joan snapped. Clearly, whatever news had come from the High City was pressing enough to shake her. And a shaken Joan was something to be concerned about.

"One of the warriors came up from the gate. There's an urgent message from your father."

That was enough to get her moving. Fatigue forgotten, she was out of bed. Joan filled her in as she ducked into the bathing room to retrieve the light gray sarand she'd shed earlier.

"As I was saying, he showed them a letter with the seal of the High Counsel on it. Whatever was in it was enough to get the gates open and an escort through the township directly to you."

The second her clothes were arranged, Rhia was out the door, practically running down to the great hall with Joan on her heels. Once inside the main hall, she pounded to a halt. Sitting at a long polished table on one side of the huge main hall was a man looking up at several amazingly tall, weapon clad, and obviously distrustful, Gaian warriors. That clammy looking, pale skinned, black haired man, dressed in black and more black was none other than Bryan Collaidh. What the hell was he doing here?

Ewan, one of several scowling warriors, looked over to see Rhia standing at the entrance to the hall. He walked silently to her and quietly gave her a full account of everything that had occurred since Bryan's arrival in Province Springs.

"Where are his men?" Rhia asked, not taking her eyes off the man of her nightmares across the room.

"They were taken under guard to the outer barracks, sir."

"The outer barrack?" she asked, eyes raised up to Ewan with true surprise. That building was an old stone building, windowless and scarcely furnished. Barely comfortable and used only for the occasional storage of supplies, its sole purpose was to eliminate the need for warriors patrolling the outer walls to ride the several miles into town to replenish whatever they used while on duty. It was also the only building that locked from the outside. If there was ever a need for a quick holding cell, the outer barrack would be it.

"He came with six men, all unarmed. We would not allow his men into the township. For this reason, they were taken to the outer barrack, their horses with them. I do not trust him, sir."

"They came all this distance with such a small force and no weapons?"

Ewan didn't bother to answer the question. The hard glint in his dark eyes made his stance clear — one wrong move and Bryan was history.

"I don't trust him either," Rhia told the warrior. "Thank you, Ewan, for such clear headed thinking." She chuckled, shaking her head at the typical warrior 'Well-what-did-you-expect' expression that crossed the tall man's face. With that, she plastered on her diplomatic mask with a less than diplomatic smile and walked into the hall. She made a beeline to where Bryan sat watching the circle of warriors with a look that bordered on wonder.

"Bryan, what are you doing here?"

"I have an urgent message from your father." He reached slowly, deliberately into his cloak to retrieve the letter, just as every warrior slowly, deliberately, reached for a long knife or blade strapped to their midsections, sheathed in interesting looking shoulder harnesses.

Rhia watched him closely. He wasn't afraid, but rather seemed to be contemplating. But contemplating what? She took the letter from his steady hands and examined the seal. She was actually disappointed that it looked authentic.

So much for a reason to kick Bryan out of my home... again.

Her brow furrowed as she quickly read the letter from top to bottom, then went wide as she read it over again. Pinning Bryan with an angry glare, she practically snarled her words at him.

"Who else has read this?"

"I have, my lady," Ewan said quietly from over her

shoulder. "The seal was intact when he arrived at the gate. It was I who opened it that I might judge whether he should be allowed to pass through."

She turned to Ewan, her eyes still on the letter as she murmured, "I understand." Looking back to Bryan she asked, "Do you have any idea what's in this letter?"

"No. My father only said it was urgent. I was to give it to your husband, but was told at the gate that he's not here."

Rhia didn't bother hiding her skepticism, but before she could question him further, he brought her up short. "Though not always in his good graces, I am still a Collaidh. Why wouldn't my father trust his son to deliver something important?"

Well, he had her there. A deep frown creased the skin between her brows as she looked away from Bryan and tried to keep her emotions together. The room was completely silent except for the soft patter of Rhia's short boots on the marble floor. Finally, she turned back to her 'guest'.

"Leave us, all of you. Ewan, you can stay, but stand over there," she said, motioning toward the entrance doors to the hall. "I need some privacy with Bryan, here."

Without a sound, the room quickly emptied. Ewan stopped at the great hall entrance and leaned casually against the wall. Rhia knew his casual stance meant nothing. The man was ready to spring at the slightest hint of distress. Rhia motioned Bryan over to the man-sized marble fireplace at the rear of the room.

"Bryan, my father is gravely ill? How could you be in the High City and not know that?"

"Before I answer your questions, I owe you an apology." That caused a wary, raised eyebrow from her. With a much too serene expression on his face, he blew off her surprise and continued. "I was lost without you all those years I was banished to the borders. When I returned to the High City I wanted you so badly I acted improperly."

"Improperly? Are you on medication?"

"No. I mean it, Rhia. Please accept my apology."

She didn't buy it for a minute, but said, "Fine. Now, about my father?"

"I haven't been to the Citadel since the night your husband threw me down your stairs." Rhia couldn't believe it when the man actually chuckled. She'd never known him to be this mellow. Except when he was trying to manipulate her, of course.

"Thankfully, my father never heard about that little incident," he said, rubbing a spot on the back of his head. "I owe you for that. I've also been training and working hard. I really want to earn back the trust of the Society of War. And your trust, as well."

This was uncomfortable. He was being too nice. She quickly changed the subject. "The letter says my father is so sick he may not last more than another week or so. Obviously, I've got to get to him."

"I didn't realize." He sat down heavily in the nearest chair and looked down at the floor for a moment. He raised his face on a sigh and said, "Look, we can leave as soon as you like."

"Keep quiet. These warriors won't let me out of here with RuArk away."

"Perhaps I can ask them, let them know how urgent..."

"Don't be stupid," she hissed when he started to raise his voice and motion toward a deceptively laid-back Ewan at the door. "These are Gaian warriors.

They're loyal to RuArk and his orders overrule everything and anything. And they certainly overrule anything you suggest."

"Well, with your husband away, maybe you should just send a note back to your father. I don't want to be the cause of any problems, Rhia." Was that a hint of sarcasm in his voice? Perhaps she was so upset about her father's letter she was being a bit sensitive. Then again, she'd have to be crazy to trust Bryan Collaidh. But what choice did she have? This was her father who was dying. Her only comfort right now was that she'd taken Bryan down once. There was no doubt in her mind that if she needed to, she could thrash him again.

She paced back and forth in front of the fireplace. Her mind worked furiously, recalling when the warriors changed shifts, where security was lightest and when. What to do? What to do? She glanced toward the door and saw Ewan no longer leaned against the wall. As soon as she'd started pacing, he'd stood at the ready with one hand on the steel blade at his hip. She looked away quickly, schooled her features, and forced her stance into a more relaxed one, hoping he couldn't see the determination in her eyes.

"I'll have to find a way to sneak out," she said quietly to Bryan. "Return to the gates and tell the men on patrol that you've delivered your message and you'll leave at dawn. I'll meet you five miles southeast of here just off the main trade road. Be prepared to cut out of here fast if we're going to get to my father in time. Never mind if any of RuArk's men, Draeman or Gaian, get wind of me leaving here with you."

"No problem. I have an extra horse tethered outside the main gate for any one of your guards, if you want to bring a chaperone."

"No, they wouldn't be able to keep up the pace I plan to set. My father doesn't have time for that."

"I understand. I'll see you at dawn then. And don't worry, Rhia, we'll get there in time. Draema Neine has a train stop two townships over, and there's room for the horses. It's how we got here so fast. We can get there in no time."

Unfortunately, she'd never been to that depot and had no idea where it was. Committing to blindly following Bryan's plan wasn't an option. At least not right now. "We'll see," she said.

He bowed and turned to leave, paused briefly, then looked back at her. When their eyes met, the hair on the nape of her neck stood at full attention. And this was no reaction to someone using the Gifts. It was as if he watched her through someone else's eyes, his expression vacant, yet assessing, and strangely possessive.

It was absolutely creepy. Now that she thought about it, it was eerily similar to the look Brita wore earlier when Rhia had scared her in a very busy hallway. As quickly as her keen mind began to analyze, it was gone. Her hackles lowered and she stood wondering what the hell she'd just witnessed.

There were no answers forthcoming as Bryan left the hall, escorted by a glowering Ewan and a dozen other warriors who melted out of the woodwork.

CHAPTER SEVEN

Bryan and his men waited exactly five miles southeast of the gates of Province Springs. Rhia waved as she rode swiftly toward them. There were always scouts riding this terrain, and since she had no idea who else was around, she kept her mouth shut until she'd caught up to them.

Bryan was off his horse in a flash and waited for her. Rhia immediately noticed something different about his party. There weren't six men with Bryan. There were more like twenty, all well armed. The conciliatory Bryan had obviously been just visiting, and the asshole had returned. How could she tell? Perhaps it was the way he yanked her off of the back of her horse.

"Bryan, what the..." was as far as she got when the first blow landed on her right cheek, knocking her to the ground. She rolled, came to her feet ready to battle hand to hand when she was brought up short by the point of a very sharp blade at the base of her skull.

She ducked and spun, drawing her own blade. Her leg extended and caught whoever had come up behind her, and her blade followed quickly, slicing him across the chest. He went down in a heap. She took out four of them in a blink, but there were simply too many ready and willing to take their place. She cursed as Ricard was yanked from behind a tree, his hands bound behind his back and a knife at his throat. Bryan grinned in triumph. Dammit, the bastard knew he'd produced the leverage to make her behave.

"Make one more move, Rhia, and I'll order his neck sliced so clean you could put it in a frame and hang it over your mantle."

She forced herself out of her fighting stance, and raised a blood tipped sword up in the air, in a sort of half-surrender gesture. She wanted to fight until she couldn't stand up, and let Ricard handle himself. But training, reasoning and common sense, kicked in. It would be better to find out what was going on here.

"I'll drop my weapon if you let him go, Bryan."

He laughed! Actually laughed at her. "It's amazing that you think you're in control here, Rhia. But I have the whip hand and I won't hesitate to use it." And he certainly did have a literal long, slender, well-oiled whip at the ready.

"So why did you lure me here. And yes, I expect to have my question answered." She bristled when he said, "I'm taking you back to Draema. Your presence is required."

"If my father needed me, why didn't he send for me? Why is a kidnapping necessary?" Gesturing as she spoke, she took in the men surrounding her, both those lying on the ground bleeding and those still standing and bristling with weapons.

"I don't recall saying your father needed you. Actually, I didn't say much at all. I only delivered a piece of paper. But don't worry, Rhia. You'll be well taken care of. All you have to do is come back to the

High City and marry me."

"Marry you? Are you nuts? I already have a husband, dumb ass."

"So what? My father has already made arrangements to have your marriage set aside. You see, we Collaidh's are ambitious men who intend to rule Draema. So, you've become quite necessary."

"How the hell do you expect to rule Draema when my father is the High Counsel, you—"

His fist shot out with a blow that had her reeling before she'd even finished the question.

Ow, that was stupid. She moved her jaw side to side after another good wallop across her right cheek. She lifted her face—didn't have to lift it far considering he was barely taller than her—spit a wad of blood at his feet, and glared murderously. "To hell with this," she snarled and raised her fists to give him a taste of his own medicine.

But she wasn't fast enough. As soon as her hands went up, two Draeman soldiers caught and secured them in some pretty effective bonds. With the cords knotted tightly around her wrists and yanked behind her back, she was pushed roughly down to her knees.

"Well," Bryan went on smoothly, circling her slowly, deliberately. "I believe I rather like you on your knees. After we're married, I'll make sure you're in that position often."

"Oh, please," she snorted. "Put your cock in my face and you'll draw back a nub."

He raised his fist, but she refused to flinch no matter what he did to her. If she could just get free for a few minutes, she'd give him what she hadn't had a chance to finish that night in her apartments. The idiot obviously didn't realize RuArk had actually saved his life by throwing him down the tower stairs. She'd hurt him pretty bad that night, and she knew he would make her pay. And pay. And then pay some more.

Or at least he'd try.

"Well, Rhia, if you don't wish to marry me, you can always marry my father. One Collaidh is as good as another. Either way, we get what we want. You were promised —"

"Promised? How could I possibly be promised to you or anyone else when my father arranged my marriage to RuArk? You're blasted deranged."

"Call me whatever you want, but there are powers at work here you know nothing about. They've set the stage for this little drama, and they do have the means to promise me anything. Including you."

The last thing she remembered just before her head exploded with blinding pain was the smile of a wild-eyed Ricard Shae as Bryan cut the man's bonds and freed his hands.

Bastards.

When she came to, it was twilight. Her head throbbed. She reached back to press against the pounding, but couldn't reach it. As the fog cleared from her brain, she remembered her hands were tied. It took another second or two for her to realize she was also moving, thrown over the back of her horse like a sack of Gaian coffee. Her ribs ached from riding face down over the stiff saddle. Bile rose up in her throat and she grimaced, trying to keep from throwing up.

Ugh. Wish I'd stayed knocked out.

Then a slow smile tipped up one side of her swollen mouth. So, they'd had to knock her out to get her on her horse, eh? Cowards. She would have laughed if she hadn't felt so miserable.

"Bryan," she called out weakly. She raised her head as much as she could and gulped in the cooling air in hopes of keeping her stomach from turning inside out. "I have to hurl. Please, stop."

Her horse came to a halt and she felt herself hauled off his back. Her knees buckled the second her feet touched solid ground. Harsh retching hammered her belly until there was nothing but dry heaves.

She looked up to see a concerned Ricard with a flask of iced water. She allowed him to place it to her lips and took a long swallow. She swished and spit into the thick carpet of leaves and twigs and asked for a little more. This one she swallowed, thankful the cool liquid immediately calmed her stomach.

She mumbled a grateful, but irritated, "Thank you," as he helped her awkwardly to her feet and to the base of a nearby tree to sit. Ricard made no effort to rescue her, so he obviously wasn't here to help her. So, why the hell was he here?

"Rhia, I know you have questions," Ricard said cautiously as he glanced over his shoulder at Bryan, clearly not wanting to be overheard.

"What are you doing here, Ricard? Does Brita know where you are?" she whispered.

"I'm taking you to Draema."

"Oh, for goodness sake, not you too?" she growled quietly.

"Can you keep a secret?"

Motioning with her head to the traitors surrounding them a distance, she asked, "Who in this lot would I tell, Ricard? And what happened to you? A couple of days after the Noman attacked us, you disappeared."

"I let the Noman in."

Rhia's mouth fell open.

"After that day, someone was always following me around, watching me. At your husband's order, I'm sure. He's a very smart man, the Wind Storm. Obviously, I couldn't afford to be found out, so, I couldn't hang around once we knew your husband would live."

"But why would you let the Noman into my home? I could have been killed, dammit. Me, your sister, Joan, any of us that you've known all your life could have died," she hissed angrily.

"I had his promise that you would be kept safe."

"His promise? Whose promise?" The man was obviously a lunatic.

"The Dreadlord, of course. He came to me in my dreams. Promised if I let the Noman into Province Springs, they would get rid of that brawny warrior husband of yours."

"But to what end, you idiot?"

"So I could bring you back to Draema to marry me."

"Oh, this is ridiculous. I can't be married to RuArk, promised to you, and promised to Bryan and his father, too." She'd never heard such outrageous notions in her life. They were all crazy.

"Bryan only thinks you're promised to him, but it's only to get his cooperation. I saw it all in a dream. It's a ruse."

Rhia caught the mad glint in his eye, the gleeful set of his shoulders. She wasn't even surprised when he quietly crowed with delight. In all the years she'd know this man, Rhia had never imagined he was mad. She kept her mouth shut and let him prattle on about their life together once they got to Draema Proper. How could she have been so stupid to walk into this mess?

And that left another question—how did Bryan get hold of her father's official seal to make a letter appear so authentic? Maybe this was the Foreknowledge coming true? Maybe her father was already dead? Her gut cramped at the thought as she sucked in gulps of air in an attempt not to throw up again.

As Ricard rambled, she half listened, trying to figure a way out of this.

Wait a minute.

A soldier off to her right caught her attention. She recognized him, had in fact, personally trained him a few years back. At least he had the decency to blush and lower his head as he brought her something to eat along with a single skimpy blanket.

Bryan bellowed for Ricard and he scurried away just as the soldier motioned to her bound hands. Rhia nodded her agreement not to cause any trouble. After carefully releasing her, she accepted the food and took a small bite of grainbread slathered with calmonut butter. She'd forgotten what synthetic Draeman food tasted like.

Ewww!

If she was going to get away, she had to keep up her strength so she forced down another mouthful as the soldier stood and watched. She whispered to the man. "Why are you doing this? Why are you helping them?"

His answer left her speechless.

"I don't know, Blademaster. I hate Bryan Collaidh. Sometimes it's like I'm watching someone else do these things, but all the while it's me. When I lay down at night I have terrible nightmares of what will happen if I don't cooperate. Horrors worse than you can imagine..." His voice trailed off as he simply walked away, clearly tormented and shaking his head in confusion.

Rhia settled uncomfortably in her blanket and tried to think while appearing to doze. It seemed impossible with Bryan on the right, Ricard to her left, and a circle of Draeman soldiers all around. They'd taken her sword, her long knives, everything. Even her mother's prized jeweled dagger that she always wore strapped to her thigh.

When Bryan's hand slid possessively up and around the cheeks of her butt, she instinctively reached for her Source wishing there was a Gift of Broiling or a Gift of Singe or something she could use to ash the bastard. She looked up through the trees to the dark sky above and concentrated on RuArk with all her mind and strength.

The bond blazed with power, amplified by the energy of her Source as she silently called out to him as loud and strong as she could. Though her crazy captors had her on the road a full day, RuArk would find her. She just knew he would.

CHAPTER EIGHT

They'd been tracking the Noman for three days when RuArk was yanked out of his sleep. His hands silently gripped the hilt of a dagger as he squinted into the darkness. He held his head and body completely still while his eyes roamed left and right across the small clearing where they camped. He saw nothing but trees silhouetted against the night sky. Heard only the breathing of his men as they relaxed in sleep.

He feigned a snore and a grunt while the hackles on the back of his neck danced. Body poised for battle while pretending to quiet down in deep slumber, RuArk allowed his senses to reach out into the darkness. They told him what his eyes could not. Blood. Putrid, foul, old blood. On breath. On clothing.

Noman.

The air, mild and humid, held the stench like spoiled fruit on a rotten tree. He waited. The scent faded. No one and nothing appeared. But the danger was out there somewhere. He could feel it as keenly as he felt the misty dew floating across the grass against his skin.

Then the life bond flared within, pulled at his insides and lit up his consciousness like a blaring distress beacon.

Rhia.

The real threat centered on her and she called out to him urgently.

The thought of Rhia in danger pushed his temper up. On the brink of tossing away his legendary self-control, he forced himself to be still, reached for his Source, then called on his Gift of Vision. And unfortunately, the Gift did not disappoint him. Suddenly, everything was clear. They were being baited. Noman allowed them to get just close enough to follow their tracks before disappearing again. He shot out of his blankets and called to his men.

"Get up! We break camp and ride east in five minutes."

"Wind Storm, what is the matter? What has happened?" asked a groggy Dalmore as he rolled from his blankets with a double-edged long knife at the ready.

Gaian were a dangerous lot, sleepy or not.

"Rhia is in danger. This entire hunt has been nothing but a distraction." Five minutes were up. He vaulted into the saddle and headed to the road at breakneck speed, a pack of angry warriors at his back.

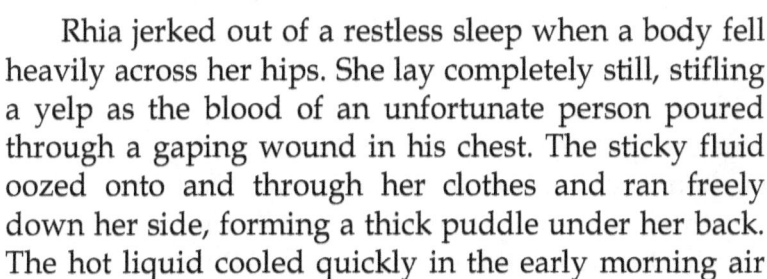

Rhia jerked out of a restless sleep when a body fell heavily across her hips. She lay completely still, stifling a yelp as the blood of an unfortunate person poured through a gaping wound in his chest. The sticky fluid oozed onto and through her clothes and ran freely down her side, forming a thick puddle under her back. The hot liquid cooled quickly in the early morning air and made her skin crawl.

She frantically reached for the bond as she had several times during the night. *'RuArk!'* she called over and over. A familiar awareness brushed against her mind, and the next instant he was there, larger than life. And from her position on the ground, underneath a stiffening body, he seemed *really* large!

The corpse tossed aside, he cut the bonds from her wrists.

"RuArk!" she yelled. He moved slightly to the left as she rolled to the right, and a heavy curved ax hit the ground between them with a sick thud.

Without bothering to look back, RuArk brought his blade around in a sharp arc, catching the ax wielder in the midsection with one hand, while he had a long knife at the ready to deflect another blade aimed at his neck.

Rhia wasted no time. Relieving the corpse next to her of his weapon, she joined the battle. She turned to see Linc with his back to Marth, the two warriors fighting off three of the Draeman. The lush leaves and foliage hid another soldier sneaking along the wide limbs of a huge tree overhead. She ran as fast as she could, trying not to slip on the blood soaked leaves covering the ground. The sneaking soldier swung down by his knees intent on planting a long knife firmly in the skull of one of the O'dann brothers.

Snatching a bow from a fallen foe as she ran, she let fly. Her aim was true, thanks to all of Sharyn's tutoring with the weapon. The O'dann's were a bit startled when they'd dispatched what they thought was the last of their enemies just to watch another fall from a tree not three feet away from them with a lovely piece of jewelry firmly imbedded in his neck — Rhia's arrow.

By the time the sun was fully up, the fighting was almost done. There was only one more piece of business to be handled.

Bryan and RuArk faced each other, blades drawn. Rhia knew it would be no contest. The look in Bryan's eyes said that he knew it, too. But if he was going to die he would do so bravely. Or at least appear to be brave.

"Do your worst, you filthy barbaric Gaian!" he taunted.

RuArk gave him no response. Instead, he turned and took in the bruises and blood, her tattered clothing, and dirty boots. Rhia knew in that moment that he was remembering a similar time—her face, bloodied and bruised the night he'd thrown this same piece of trash out of her apartments in Draema Proper.

"Rhia, come to me."

She made her way through the wall of warriors that had encircled RuArk and stepped to his side, relieved that none had fallen in the fighting. "Yes, RuArk?"

"I have the right to kill this man for laying hands on you. However, seeing how he has wronged you most gravely, I will give that right over to you, if you wish."

Her eyes traveled up to RuArk's unreadable face. She could tell, could *feel* there was something more to his question. Was he asking if she wanted to fight Bryan because he felt she should, or because he hoped she'd let him do the honors as her Protector? Or... Hell. she had no idea. And just how was she supposed to think at a time like this? Emotions soared as adrenaline and bloodlust pulsed through her body, making truly rational thought almost impossible.

RuArk repeated the question, his voice hard, cold as he looked Bryan up and down, "Rhia, do you wish to challenge him?"

Her amber cat eyes peered into Bryan's cold gray ones. "He's mine, RuArk."

One of the warriors found and tossed her her blade. Snatching it deftly out of the air, shoulders squared, Rhia stepped into the circle and laid out the terms of the challenge.

"Bryan, I challenge you for kidnapping me and for your previous attempts to rape me." Every Gaian warrior growled at those words. "For beating me, and basically for being an all-around bastard. The rules — no Draeman weapons, no laser cannons. Blades only." He didn't answer her right away, and looked almost puzzled.

"Are you trying to say I've done something wrong?" he asked. Sarcasm? Not a good thing right before you died. She knew the idiot was goading her and it took all her will power not to skewer him on the spot and be done with it.

She ignored him and said, "If I win, you will..." The words died in her throat as he engaged without warning.

A slender blade flashed out at her midsection. She recovered quickly and countered with a smooth strike of her own. Their blades met with a loud clang in the still morning air. He poured all of his strength into each thrust, each stroke. Rhia welcomed it, letting him dish out all he wished while she measured, observed, and calculated the moves that would take him out.

When she didn't die immediately, he grew wild

and reckless, yelling obscenities while she continued in her smooth, unhurried style. To this point, Rhia had only blocked Bryan's blade, now she would give *him* something to block.

Moving forward to meet his thrusts as before, but this time she continued her advance with precision at twice the speed of her opponent. Bryan was quickly flustered and bleeding, able to block only one of every three strokes.

A loud yelp resounded through the trees when cold steel cut him across the chest. His heavy battle tunic now hung in two large pieces. He continued to curse her, but she heard nothing, felt nothing, except the need to finish this.

Her next stroke sent him reeling. Before he could regain his footing, Rhia's fist shot out and punched him square in the eye.

"Now we're even, you creep." She spat on the ground at his feet as the pale flesh below his eye began to immediately redden and swell. "When they find your cold dead body, at least it will have a little color to it."

He ran at her with a wild, blood curdling yell.

Spinning deftly to the side with her sword trailing behind her, she caught him across the back of his thighs as he went flying by. He turned back toward her screaming, his hand reaching for his hamstrings, where skin and muscle were sliced clean through.

She'd taunted him with death during their little fight, but she didn't really want to be the one to take his life. With her blade pressed to his throat, she ground out, "Do you yield?" She hoped he wouldn't push her into actually killing him.

"Never!" he screamed, as the blood flowed freely

from his body. Hobbling pitifully, he yelled back, "Do *you* yield, you bitch!"

Sword lowered, she waited.

He raised his blade, but the stroke never completed. The next moment, Bryan Collaidh was face down in the dirt, his throat cleanly sliced through. Rhia wiped her blade on his ripped and torn clothing and walked away, leaving his body where it fell.

Seeking solitude, she found a quiet place away from everyone and sat down on the ground, her weapon at her feet and thoughts scattered to the four winds.

She looked up when RuArk squatted next to her just as Bryan's stiff body was being dragged away. The man's cocky swagger was now a thing of the past, and his pristine black-on-black clothing now covered with dust, grime and blood.

RuArk reached for her, enfolded her in his arms and whispered against her filthy hair. "You fought well, Rhia. I understand how you are feeling. In time it will pass."

"God, RuArk, I don't know what to feel. Why did he make me do it? Why did he make it necessary to kill him?"

"I am relieved he is being dragged away instead of you. That his family will receive news of his death rather than your father, and your friends, and…me." She felt a slight shiver course through him as he held her.

"I feel so stupid. I actually fell for his ruse and walked into this nightmare. Oh, RuArk, I'm so sorry," she wailed. "This is all my fault. I've been in too many fights to count, but never have I been the cause of one. I mean, all those Draeman soldiers that died today, it could have been the other way around, you know? Then what would I have done? It's just... Hell, I don't know." She sighed against his chest and stifled a loud sob. She might refuse to allow a warrior to see her cry, but right now this was her husband, and she would allow him to see her truly, emotionally naked.

After a few minutes of blessed silence, her muffled words sounded against his chest. "Are you mad at me, RuArk?"

"Yes, I am very angry with you," he replied softly.

"But RuArk..." she pleaded.

"It is a conversation for another time, Rhia."

"I know I shouldn't have left the security of the township by myself, but I thought that my father..."

"Rhia. Leave it." He paused, hard gray eyes conveying he was much closer to losing it than she'd thought. "I have never seen you in a true fight before, other than the time you tried to kill me in your father's training pavilion. Right now, let us thank the Ancestors that you are indeed as deft with a blade as you are with those feet of yours."

Eye closed, she felt his jaw move and knew he was smiling.

So why didn't she feel any better?

CHAPTER NINE

With the dead Draeman left to rot in their chosen place of treachery, Rhia rode close to her husband. She knew she sounded tired and defeated as she told him everything, even how she'd snuck away from the safety of their home, duped by her father's supposed letter and Bryan's feigned kindness.

"Give me this letter," RuArk demanded quietly.

She took it from the pocket inside her tunic and handed it to him. When he noted the official seal, his eyes blazed with anger. "I understand why you would believe this, Rhia, but I do not see why you would have so little faith in our warriors that you would not bring any of them into your confidence. Do you trust *any* of our people sworn to protect you?"

Boy, he really knew how to make her feel low.

"I wasn't thinking along those lines, RuArk," she said with a sigh. She sat up straighter in her saddle, looking directly ahead, trying to keep the stiffness in her spine when all she really wanted was to slide off the back of her horse, roll on the ground and sob.

Instead, she snapped, "I was told you left strict orders that I was not allowed outside the township walls. Who's going to disobey you, RuArk? Tell me, who? I had to get out any way I could. My father's life was in danger, may *still* be in danger for all we know."

Then came a pitiful wail from behind.

"Help! He's going to kill me, Rhia, please help me!" Ricard, the damn lunatic, looked as pitiful as he sounded as his eyes darted back and forth between the two warriors he rode sandwiched between.

His face was calm, but RuArk's eyes glittered so dangerously, she almost flinched when he turned to her and asked none too nicely, "What is his part in this, Rhia?"

Face a granite mask of calm, his eyes continued to smolder and flare anew as Rhia told of Bryan and Ricard's treachery. When her story was finished, RuArk called a halt.

Rhia's blood froze in her veins when her husband lifted his face to the sky and released a blood curdling war cry, spooking several horses, including her own. Sidestepping wildly, Moonlight threw his head back and whinnied. By the time she got him in hand, RuArk had dismounted faster than Rhia had ever seen a man get off a horse and moved with lethal determination toward Ricard.

"Untie him!" RuArk bellowed as he approached. She ran after him, calling his name, begging him to stop. RuArk didn't slow as the stoic expressions of the warriors melted in astonishment at the Wind Storm's unusual display of temper.

"RuArk! RuArk, please don't kill him. You can't..."

He rounded on her. "You will cease to tell me what I can and cannot do, woman. Back on your horse. Now."

Visibly startled and eyes wide with terror, Ricard tumbled from his mount, landed flat on his face and wheezed as the breath was knocked out of his chest. No one, not even Rhia, moved to help him as RuArk's boots came scarily close to the man's face.

"Tell me your plans for my woman, worm," RuArk gritted through his teeth, towering over the man. Linc and Marth moved to flank him, giving him nowhere to run. RuArk's hands were clasped deliberately behind his back. But Rhia knew better. Her huge warrior husband was as quick as the wind and would be on Ricard faster than he could draw his next breath.

"I had a vision from the Dreadlord. He came to me in a dream."

Rhia had heard this story before. It made her skin crawl then, and this time was no different. However, the echo of concern from RuArk rang through their bond, and with it came a combination of shock and rage. He cast her a glance that conveyed a wealth of meaning, yet betrayed nothing to their enemies.

Ricard and this so-called Dreadlord, were indeed their enemies.

"Continue," RuArk demanded.

"He told me I could have my heart's desire if I served him." Looking toward Rhia as he spoke, the fear in his eyes was replaced with something that bordered on zealous idiocy.

The O'dann's stepped to RuArk's side. "Does this lord have a common name?" Marth growled.

"I don't know his name, but he promised if I brought Rhia back to the High City he would..." Ricard paused.

"Yes?" Marth and Linc barked in unison.

Ricard looked at them as if they were slow of mind. "He would give me Rhia."

"Why? What in all the hells does he want with

Rhia?" RuArk asked through clenched teeth. When he stared mutinously at RuArk, her warrior grabbed Ricard by the collar, snatched him up from the ground and shook him until his neck snapped back and forth. "Why. Does. He. Want. My. Woman?"

"The Dreadlord doesn't have to reveal all his plans to those who serve him." Sneering down at RuArk, he added, "Does that Great Spirit of your Ancestors tell *you* everything, you barbaric savage?"

RuArk didn't respond, choosing instead to dig for answers. "Does this lord ever come to you in the flesh?"

"No, you idiot, I said he comes in my sleep! But I can feel him when I awake, as if he's been in the room with me, watching over me. Protecting me."

"Did he tell you what would happen if you should fail in your mission?"

"He didn't tell me, he showed me. The horrors were unspeakable." Ricard blanched and his gaze was suddenly far away... and horrified. "Far worse than anything you could do to me, so do your worst, Gaian."

"And what of the Noman we were hunting?" This from Linc.

"I told Rhia that I let them into Province Springs." Ricard began to laugh maniacally. Spittle flew from the corners of his mouth and his eyes flashed of something familiar, but Rhia couldn't quite place it. It was almost as if someone else looked back at them in Ricard's stead as the man continued to laugh as if he had a secret. "You stupid, muscle-bound back births. He'll have what he wants and there's nothing you can do about it."

"Ricard?" Rhia called softly, puzzled at the strange look that crossed his face. It was the same expression she'd glimpsed in Bryan's eyes after he'd talked her into leaving home. The same look Brita wore as she'd wandered around the villa looking lost. It gave her the creeps. She silently pushed her feelings to RuArk through their bond.

At his subtle nod of understanding, she tried to reach her former friend again. "Ricard?" she called, looking for any sign of her old childhood friend. "By letting those creatures into our home you put not only my life in danger, but your sister, Joan, all those innocent townsmen who happened to be in my courtyard at the time of the attack. Any of us could have fallen in that fighting."

He waved her words away and said, "The Noman were under strict orders and you were not to be harmed, Rhia. They were after this huge walking tree of yours, not you."

Aaaaand, that was something he hadn't shared in their little talk earlier.

"Who in all the world can command Noman? It is fucking unheard of," Rhia snapped. Well, unheard of until now.

"Put him back on his horse," RuArk ordered. Rhia turned away, headed back to where she'd left her own mount. At a loud yell she turned around in time to watch Ricard leap at one of the mounted warriors, snatch a dagger out of a sheath on the warrior's boot. With a cackle in his throat, he plunged that dagger into his own heart.

He was dead before he hit the ground. At least in death he looked somewhat like himself again, minus the wintery smile plastered across his bluing lips.

———◆———◆———

Sheltered for the night in a heavily wooded grove, they were a good distance from any commonly traveled road with the closest wide open space several miles away. If what Ricard and Bryan said was true, they were being hunted. While it would be difficult for them to spot anyone traveling through this wooded area, it would be equally hard for anyone to track them, whether human or Noman.

The scouts that Marth had sent out just before they'd left the scene of the skirmish now rode into camp. Sharyn, Joan, Ewan and a fully armed contingent of Gaian warriors were due to arrive right before the evening meal.

Hiding, uh, *cuddling* in their tent, both RuArk and Rhia heard the horses thundering through the trees long before they entered camp, but she refused to join RuArk in greeting the riders. She had no desire to see any of the warriors she'd duped by sneaking away. She might not be an all-around coward, but she was in no hurry to face their disappointment.

Peeking through the smallest hole imaginable, Rhia watched as Joan spotted Marth the second they rode in. The first one off her mount, she hopped over fallen limbs and dry timber with her sarand floating around her knees. Marth, squatting down to stack large rocks into a makeshift fire ring, looked up just in time to see his wife launch herself at him. He wrapped his arms around her as her momentum carried them backward. Even with the breath knocked out of her body, she could still manage to talk and kiss him at the same time.

"Marth, oh thank goodness! I knew you'd be safe, and now I'm going to kill you!" And on it went, with Marth grinning like a fool. Rhia bit the inside of her cheek to keep from laughing. However, the rest of the crew had no problem letting their humor show.

RuArk chided, "Well, O'dann, I see you've been swept off your feet."

"We know what you'll be having for dinner tonight, eh O'dann? Even better than Osgar's cooking, eh?" called another.

Untangling their arms and limbs, Marth helped Joan up and picked twigs and leaves out of her short platinum curls. "I am pleased that my mate is so glad to see me. Perhaps I will skip dinner and enjoy her sweetness, as was suggested." And they disappeared into Marth's tent even as Joan threatened to skewer him for putting himself in danger in the first place.

Rhia ducked away from the little hole in the tent flap as Sharyn's gaze moved her way. She might not be able to see the woman, but she heard her just fine when she asked, "Where is she, RuArk?"

Well, damn.

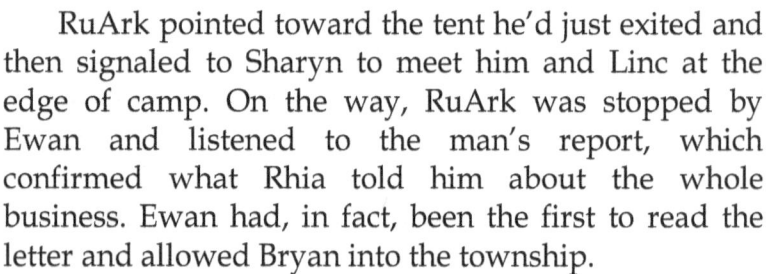

RuArk pointed toward the tent he'd just exited and then signaled to Sharyn to meet him and Linc at the edge of camp. On the way, RuArk was stopped by Ewan and listened to the man's report, which confirmed what Rhia told him about the whole business. Ewan had, in fact, been the first to read the letter and allowed Bryan into the township.

"I have failed in my duties, Protector. I let that filthy worm into the city, into our home. I was the one that saw that he was taken to the First Heir. I was charged with her safety and I did not fulfill my task."

"It is no fault of yours, Ewan. I have seen the letter

and the seal. I do believe I would have been fooled as well."

"It is not my place, sir, but I am angry that the lady put herself in such danger. And I am angry with myself for not seeing through the plot."

"I am angry enough for the both of us, Ewan. Let it go. She is safe and I have no fault with you, and neither does the lady. She realizes what she has done."

With a nod, Ewan dismissed himself and went to see to his horse and gear.

Sharyn listened as RuArk and Linc told of the so-called Dreadlord.

"We should speak with the Grandfather about this," Sharyn suggested. "It sounds like someone with the ability to walk the *Dream*. Someone skilled enough to manipulate others in that realm, which is not an easy thing to do."

Linc cut in, concern evident in his voice, "You believe one of the Realmwalkers is behind this?"

"I am not sure," Sharyn replied.

"I do not believe it is a Realmwalker," RuArk said thoughtfully. "The High Counsel was taught to walk the *Dream* by Rhia's mother long ago, and he is not a Realmwalker. In fact, he has no Gifts that we know of, yet he can walk into the *Dream* with ease. Perhaps another has been taught how to do the same?"

They looked at one another as the enormity of RuArk's words sank in. "The Grandfather will know. In the meantime, we must guard this closely. Tell no one, trust no one. We have no way of knowing who has been touched in their *Dreams* by this so called 'Dreadlord'."

That night, without being asked or prompted in any way, Rhia stood before the whole camp and gave her deepest apologies. She asked forgiveness for her recklessness and lack of consideration for how her actions would affect those she'd left behind. RuArk felt immense pride as she held her head high under the granite stares of his warriors and accepted the cool reception her apology received.

CHAPTER TEN

After returning home, Rhia was quiet and withdrawn. Keeping to their rooms, the woman was so solitary RuArk wasn't sure what she needed or wanted. Where was her passionate nature, her spark, her fire? He had no idea, but by the fourteenth day, he'd had enough.

She hadn't allowed him to touch her since her rescue, and her self-imposed abstinence was wearing on his nerves. Watching her come awake each morning as she stretched sinuously against the sheets was torture. Each movement brought to mind a memory of how her skin felt rubbing against his, slick with the sweat of their passion and their scents intermingled as his arms encircled her body.

Every breath overwhelmed him as her natural, enticing scent wafted up from under the covers. His mouth watered with thoughts of blazing a trail down her stomach, her fingers tangled in his hair as he headed toward his favorite destination—her strong silky thighs.

He understood that she still felt guilty about that debacle that had put her lifemate and her friends in danger. But he refused to spend one more sleepless night with a woman that wallowed in self-pity, or who scooted as far from him as she could get until she practically fell out of the bed.

This new subdued Sort-of-Rhia that lay in his bed was not the woman he'd joined his life to, and she was no longer welcome in their home.

Just after dawn, a bare chested, royally irritated warrior rose and fastened a soft, saddle colored buckskin breech around his hips. Yanking on a pair of soft soled *moccs*, his actions didn't slow when Rhia mumbled from under the blankets.

"Wind Storm, where are you going? The sun's barely up."

"I'll return shortly, then I will not leave this room until one of us breaks. And know now, Rhia, I don't plan to lose this challenge."

Her head snapped up even as her mouth fell open. "Breaks?"

"Yes, breaks." He pinned her with a determined glare before the bedroom door closed solidly behind him.

Rhia wanted nothing more than to be alone and sulk in peace, but obviously RuArk wasn't having it. When he ducked back into the bedroom, she watched him climb the stairs to the bed, and set a chiller down in front of her. On top of it was placed a carafe of juice and a platter full of fresh melon, grapes, roasted and sliced lean meat, bread and cheese.

She sat up, holding the blankets over her breasts and looked over the goodies. Rhia reached for a piece of fruit. RuArk's voice stayed her hand.

"Don't touch anything," he demanded roughly.

"Okaaay? Did you bring all of this food upstairs just so I could look at it?"

Instead of an answer, he lifted a piece of melon to her lips and began to feed her. Mmm, now this was a sensuous undertaking. Her gaze strayed to his beautifully scarred, strong hands, while her body recalled how those fingers felt stroking her bare flesh.

On the last bite of melon wedge, her tongue slid over her top lip then deliberately wrapped around his fingers to lick the juice off of them. Grapes, cheese and a bit of bread were next, and she didn't pass up a single chance to suckle his fingers seductively.

Wait! She was supposed to be depressed and sulky, damn it, but the whole me-warrior-me-feed-you thing was really getting to her.

He finally allowed her to touch something—a small glass of juice. She pressed it to her lips and moaned. The liquid was sweet as it passed over her tongue, then a burst of flavor from the slightly sour pulp made her jaw clench just a bit.

Delicious.

As Rhia sipped, her gaze dropped to the supple suede of RuArk's breech. The longer she stared, the more it rose up to greet her. Suddenly, she wanted to push him back on the bed and do things that would make him call her name over and over as she rode him into the Wind.

The game was afoot and when he stood to take the platter from the bed she held on to his hand, more than ready to play.

"Wait. You haven't eaten anything. Let me feed you," she said. Her senses feasted on the sight of his bare chest and legs. The breech left nothing to the imagination, especially since what was under it was practically writing her name in the air.

Still holding the covers over her nakedness, she lifted a piece of melon to RuArk's lips. As his teeth sank into its honeyed sweetness, he grabbed the covers and slowly pulled them down to expose her swelling breasts. She kept feeding him as if nothing had changed, lifting another piece of fruit to his mouth.

This time, as he bit into it, his hands caressed one of her breasts and teased the darkening tip until it was stiff and screaming for satisfaction. He caressed and smoothed her sensitive skin before he slid talented fingers down and around her sides to brush lightly against the quivering flesh of her belly.

In short order, her breath began to slip away in swift gasps.

This time she didn't stop RuArk when he removed the platter from the bed. Their kiss began deep and slow, tantalizing her senses with the taste of honey melon, and the smell of musk and man. Her mind could only hold on to one word—delicious.

RuArk took his wife in his arms, gently cradling her body as he rained kisses across her beautiful face and throat. He moved gently over her fading bruises and continued a path down her throat. When her strong fingers clutched at his bare skin he knew she was beginning to allow the shell she'd erected around herself to crack. But a crack wasn't enough. He wanted it destroyed and would press her relentlessly until he'd reawakened her passionate nature.

RuArk laid her back on the bed and lowered his

head to nip at the flat planes of her stomach, then rolled her over and blazed a trail up her spine causing the flesh to come alive and shiver at his every touch. She began to writhe, ever so slightly.

The hot skin of her back scalded his chest as he rubbed against her body, sliding his hard cock back and forth between the crease of her lush bottom. Burying his nose in her hair, his words were hard at the back of her neck.

"I want my mate back," he growled. "That willful. Stubborn. Fiery. Woman." He nipped her soft skin with sharp teeth between each word. He knew she was hard pressed to get an answer out in between pants, but RuArk didn't let up.

He would have what he wanted and he would have it now.

"Where is my woman?" he asked, laying her on her back to plant a wet open mouthed kiss underneath her right breast. "Where is she?" he demanded.

"Here! Oh god, RuArk, I'm right here." Her body twisted wildly against his mouth, trying to scoot down enough to bring his lips into contact with her swollen nipples. Clamping down on his rising arousal, he continued to tease her unmercifully.

"Where is that self-pitying creature that's been in my bed these past weeks?"

"Never heard of her," Rhia breathed and reached down to pull him to her lips so she could lick and bite him. With every kiss came a hungry moan, and every breath became a gasp until she was completely wanton. He would not take her. Not yet.

Carnal, suckling kisses were planted along her inner thigh until she thrust her hips, begging to be tasted. RuArk wanted nothing more than to consume her.

So he did.

Teeth teased the sensitive flesh with gentle nips and laves of his tongue as his thumb brushed the little rosebud of passion at the juncture of her thighs.

"Taté Icamna!" *Wind Storm*, she screamed in Gaian, then exploded against his hand, her whole body trembling from the intensity of her release.

Slowly, he lowered his body over hers, coating his shaft in the honeyed juices flowing from her warm core as she spread herself, giving him perfect access. He wanted her so much it hurt. Full to bursting, his cock bucked wildly at her entrance but he gave her only the very tip. He felt her open for him, but the primal urge to slam into her heat did not override his true desire— he wanted to see her lose it. He didn't have to wait long.

She wrapped her legs around his waist and thrust her hips, impaling herself on his throbbing shaft. She pulled him deep. Urged him to fill her.

"Please," she gasped when he didn't move. "I want...oh RuArk, take me. All of me." Wild with need, Rhia wrapped arms and legs around him and held tight until he could scarcely breathe. She moved with him, stroke for stroke as he rocked into her, buried himself, and then retreated until only the large throbbing head was inside of her tightening sheath. When she reached for the peak of fulfillment, he slowed his strokes just enough to keep her release at bay, torturing both of them.

His words a rough whisper against her ear, he called her name. "Rhia. My woman. My Fire Storm, yes?"

"Yes!"

He slammed home until her honeyed walls clenched around him in spasms and pulled his own release from deep within. His seed rushed toward her womb and his name left her lips over and over again, and with it came the one thing he'd desired to hear since the day he'd pledged himself to her in the *Seeking*.

"RuArk, I love you." She continued to whisper those words as she ascended into the clouds. RuArk closed his eyes against the emotion that threatened to overwhelm his warrior's mind. The thought that his woman might possibly feel such depth of care for him almost caused him to stop moving in and out of her body as he rode her down from her orgasm. Did she realize what she'd said? Did she mean it, or was it just a reaction to climax?

No matter. She would declare it again. He would see to it.

They slept and loved until they were so bone-deep sated the thought of moving took too much effort. Much later, after a bath spent whispering endearments, dressed and refreshed, they left their bedroom for the first time that day.

RuArk, Rhia, Marth, Joan, Linc and Sharyn all reached the main hall at the same time. The women were all flushed and languid. The warriors all wore cheeky grins.

Tomorrow they would cross the river to Gaia for an overdue visit to RuArk's estate at Wind Song. He was sure his clansmen were preparing a huge celebration for them, given this would be Rhia's first visit to his homeland. Unfortunately, this visit wouldn't be all festive. A conversation with the Grandfather about their encounter with Bryan and Ricard by order of the so-called Dreadlord was definitely in order.

———————————

The household was abuzz as RuArk descended the steps and stopped at the wide open doors of the great hall. Where was their baggage for the trip to Wind Song?

"Lunis!" RuArk thundered, moving swiftly past the dining hall toward the steward's office. The man must have heard the bellow, along with the rest of the household, because appeared outside his door before RuArk got there.

"Lunis, we are to depart in half an hour. Where is our gear?" But Lunis wasn't looking at him, but rather at something behind him as a firm, familiar voice answered the question.

"There has been a change of plans."

RuArk turned and looked into the faces of the Grandfather and Azel Sholen. Greatly respected, Azel had been the Protector of the Realm until RuArk had come of age. Azel's Gifts had continued to develop and strengthen with age and over the years he moved from skilled blade wielder to a truly powerful Realmwalker. While any trained Gaian could walk the Dream, Azel and those he trained, were expert in their craft, able to do amazing things in the Dream that others could only 'dream' about. While their expressionless faces gave nothing away, RuArk knew that whatever reason had brought Azel and the Grandfather to his door had to be urgent. That didn't bode well at all.

Back in his apartment, RuArk encouraged the men to relax out on the terrace. His honored guests accepted an aromatic cup of steaming coffee from a slender young Houseman, but he noticed they waited for her to leave the room before either would open their mouths to explain their presence.

"Are you sure we are alone, Wind Storm?" Azel asked, setting his cup down on the marble and glass coffee table between him and RuArk.

"Yes, sir. My lifemate is asleep in the other room, otherwise we're alone."

The Grandfather sat his cup down with an easy grace, but his back stiffened with concern. "Fire Storm is asleep at this hour? It is well past dawn. Is she ill, grandson?"

"No, Grandfather, she's not ill. She rose early and went through her usual morning routine." His mate had dressed, went down for breakfast, packed her gear and all the rest of it before settling down on her favorite couch on the terrace. "She's prepped and ready for our trip, but she's a bit tired. I didn't have the heart to wake her again after she dozed off in the middle of a coffee. So I left her." He couldn't have kept the satisfied grin off his face if he'd tried. Rhia had been up all night and it was all his very smug, very satisfied fault. Azel nodded his understanding at his old student and then got down to business.

"We bring news on a taint we discovered in the magical Realms some time ago. The Realmwalkers have been following the aura of foul energy. It is that of a man who journeys through the Place Between Worlds and into the Realm of the *Dream*. Since one can appear as one wishes in that Realm, this man chooses to appear as a bright and glorious being to attract whatever person he seeks."

RuArk sat back, puzzled. A being of light? This certainly didn't sound like what Bryan and Ricard had described. He motioned to Azel to continue.

"Once he gains their attention, he transforms into a

dark, black clad creature with pale translucent skin, white hair, white eyes and elongated canines."

"Fangs? Noman," RuArk whispered, more intrigued than before.

"Yes, he appears as such. But in the *Dream*, we could not tell if he was truly a Noman or if he appeared as one to inflict fear into the hearts of the ones he wished to control."

Over the next couple of hours, RuArk learned more than he cared to about the unseen danger that dogged their footsteps. Now he understood the extent and limitations of this Dreadlord. Thankfully, an amateur in the use of the magick, he was not skilled enough to manipulate any person with innate Gifts, a person mated to a person with the Gifts, or anyone who was bound to RuArk through a pledge of loyalty.

He was relieved that all Gaian, along with Rhia, Joan and every Draeman soldier who'd sworn to serve him were all safe. However, the bastard could manipulate just about everyone else.

All this Dreadlord's prey needed to do to ensnare themselves was to accept him, either purposely or out of mere curiosity. It was all the invitation he needed to invade their dreams and control them with promises of glory or horrors so ghastly they were too afraid to resist.

Unfortunately, those faithful to Rhia could be used because she didn't carry the cord of magick tied to the title, Protector of the Realm. With so many people outside of RuArk's covering, how the hells would they ever know who to trust?

"Thank the Ancestors he is limited to controlling only a few victims at one time," the Grandfather said.

"But if those victims have authority to command

others, that introduces another problem." RuArk's head was beginning to pound with the weight of it all. Just when he seemed to get his mind wrapped around the danger to his lifemate, a new problem appeared.

Azel interrupted his thoughts. "This may explain why he chose the Draeman man, Bryan. He was a man of authority, his father a member of the Council of Seven, very close to the sire of your lifemate, yes?"

"Yes," RuArk ground out through clenched teeth, "And Ricard was the brother of Rhia's lifelong friend and companion, Brita." But RuArk had another question. "If this imposter Dreadlord really is Noman, how would one of their kind come to learn our ways? It has been lost to all but our people since the Breaking of the world."

"Yes, Wind Storm, but remember the Gifts were once common to all people. All those who have a Source have the ability to use it. It is the place from where our Gifts flow. If the High Counsel, who was taught to touch his Source and walk the *Dream* by the Fire Storm's mother, why would it be impossible for anyone else to learn such a thing?"

"I believe I am beginning to understand. Thank you, Grandfather. Thank you, friend Azel."

But in his mind all he could think of was Rhia's Draeman slang that summed up this whole situation.

Fucked all to hells!

CHAPTER ELEVEN

RuArk bolted out of bed, his stomach tied up in knots and a fine sheen of cold sweat covered his body. Sensing no immediate threat, he lay back and rolled toward Rhia, seeking the warmth and solace of her touch. It was still dark out, but she wasn't in bed. He snatched up her pillow, noting it was still warm. She hadn't been gone long, so why were alarms screeching in his head?

He threw himself into a pair of trousers and stalked out the bedroom door, all thought focused on Rhia. The second the life bond flared to life he felt her distress, but there was no sign of her in their apartments. Where the hell was she?

Halfway through the living room, a new urgency filled his heart almost to the point of physical pain. Rhia's curved dagger was one piece of steel she cherished above all else. It belonged to her mother, and she never left it behind, even if she were just going to the bathroom. But here it lay haphazardly in the middle of floor.

Out of their apartments, RuArk flew down the staircases on silent feet. No sign of her in the great hall, the kitchens, nor her sparring room. Without breaking stride, RuArk called out to Lunis, who was just entering his offices.

"Lunis! Rhia?"

Grimacing, the steward pointed toward the hall near the kitchens that led to the back of the villa. RuArk moved faster at the man's worried expression, and he was down the hallway, out the thick beveled glass doors, and down the steps into the rear courtyard in a bound. His heart dropped into the pit of his stomach as he took off at a dead run towards his mate.

Under his favorite tree was Rhia, her arms wrapped around its trunk, holding on for dear life as she heaved up her guts. As long as he'd known her, she'd never been sick, not even as a child. Knowing she had fallen asleep before eating the night before, she surely needed what little she had in her stomach this morning.

He frowned at her greenish pallor and ignored her gasp of surprise and miserable moans as he lifted her easily in his arms. RuArk took the stairs three at a time and had her back in their apartments and laid out on a couch in a flash.

Kneeling on the floor next to her, he took her hand and gently stroked the inside of her palm. "What is it, sweetheart? Why are you ill?" he asked, his voice hard with concern.

RuArk glowered when she lowered her eyes without giving him an answer. Something was wrong and he didn't particularly feel like playing games about it. She wanted to keep quiet? Fine, he'd get his answers somewhere else, but get them he would. He left her side and disappeared through the bedroom doors to return fully dressed, blade and knives secured and boots laced. In his arms, he held a set of clothes and a light cloak for Rhia.

"Lift your hips," he demanded, stripping off her robe and easing a pair of buckskins up her legs, covered by a gray sarand. RuArk tuned out her fussing, held out her cloak and said, "We will sail across the river to see the Grandfather. He will know what to do."

"RuArk, I don't think my stomach can take a trip across the river. At least not right now. Just give me a minute and I'll be fine," she said, looking down at her feet.

What. The. Hells? Rhia avoiding his gaze? It was both an odd, yet telling, move on her part. Why? Because it was fucking unheard of, that's why.

"Stubborn ass woman!" Unmoved at the comical look of surprise on her face at his choice of Draeman curses, he pointed toward the door. "I will not give you and your stomach one minute. Since you choose not to tell me what I wish to know, we're going. Now."

RuArk nudged her out the door and made her sit on the large patio at the front of the house while he sent a Groomsman for his horse.

"Oh come on," she protested. "I can certainly walk down to the stables."

"Not today. Not after what I just saw." She grumbled, but sat nonetheless.

A few moments later, with her tucked in front of him on his stallion's back, he settled them into a slow easy pace down to the low gates and out of the estate. The closer they got to the three-story building that housed the Society of Physicians, the more the woman fidgeted.

As they rode, she avoided conversation and wouldn't say a word. Rhia was hiding something and not doing a very good job of it. Fine. He would have his answers one way or another. Instinctively reaching for his Source to heighten his sensitivity to their life bond, the bond flared. He knew he had her attention when she craned her neck and practically yelled up at him.

"RuArk, no!"

"Then tell me what I want to know, Rhia." She blushed furiously. Her mouth opened, but nothing came out. Holding her chin firmly so she couldn't turn away from him, he practically snarled at her. Damn it, he couldn't protect her if he didn't know what was going on. "Tell me," he demanded using a hard-edged tone reserved for her most stubborn moments.

"It's nothing," she whispered with a wavering sigh. The tears gathered in her eyes before her spine went ramrod straight and she didn't utter another word. Enough was enough. RuArk stopped in the middle of the road and glared at her.

"Rhia, I do not like when my woman lies to me." In that moment, he let the reality of how much she meant to him flow down their bond. Rhia was more than a responsibility, more than a pledge of honor to her father. He hadn't ever told her, was just coming to terms with it himself, but he loved her more than life. If anything should ever happen to her...

No. He pushed the thought away, refusing to go down that path. He simply couldn't bear it.

He dismounted and led his mount over to a small park across the road and tethered him to a tree. He sat down in the thick manicured grass, and pulled Rhia down into his arms. Settling her in his lap, they cuddled beneath the shade of the broad branches.

"Rhia Greysomne Miwatani, you will share your concern or I will keep you here until the snows fall." He kissed the top of her head, taking the heat out of his words. No response. Even his threats of punishment weren't working? Tilting her head up for a kiss, he couldn't believe his eyes. She was asleep! Why was she so tired all the time? Yes, he was a demanding lover, but even RuArk couldn't take responsibility for this level of fatigue. After a gentle shake, her eyes drifted open to squint against the sun.

He absently stroked the thick cottony locks of her dark, flame-streaked hair. She looked up at him, tried to stifle a loud yawn and again he watched her choke back tears. This time, he allowed everything he felt to show in his eyes, in every line of his face. She had to know how worried he was for her.

"We don't need to go to the Physicians," her voice was so soft, he barely heard her. She repeated her words and stiffened in his arms. He went still and waited.

"RuArk, I said we don't need to go to the Physicians. There's nothing wrong with me."

"How can you say that? I know what I saw! You were clinging to a tree heaving…"

"RuArk, I'm pregnant."

"…up your guts! You have never been ill, and we will go find out what…" RuArk snapped his mouth shut. "What did you say?" he asked, his voice pitched low, part irritation, part disbelief.

"I said I'm pregnant, damn it. Look, I know we didn't plan to have children, but please don't be angry." He recoiled as if she'd kicked him in the groin. In fact, her words made his belly cramp. How could she say such a thing? When he opened his mouth, the words were cold, flat.

"You thought I would not want our child?" He was appalled. Not because she carried his baby, but because she thought him less than a man. Only a Noman would despise his own flesh and blood.

"Well, you've asked me if I wanted children someday, but we didn't plan for this. I-I just didn't know if..."

Her voice trailed off as his expression morphed into the most contemptuous that he could muster. How could she believe that he, a man who had sworn himself to her in both word and deed, would not want their baby?

But when her tears began to roll down her cheeks, he felt like a complete heel.

RuArk winced at the anguish in each sob. There wasn't anything he hated more than seeing Rhia cry. It wasn't something she did often, so when it happened he knew she was truly miserable. He wrapped her in his embrace, and tucked her head beneath his chin. Crooning soft words of understanding, he kissed her gently on the top of her head.

"I'm sorry, Ree. I'm not mad about the baby. I'm mad you didn't tell me, love." RuArk's anger melted as her tears continued to flow unchecked down her soft cheeks. Hell, perhaps he would bawl, too. And since when did warriors have such depth of feeling? Maybe they were both pregnant?

Then, it hit him. She'd had all the symptoms for weeks now. He thought on how tender her breasts had been. So tender, in fact, she couldn't bear to be touched. Even when he pressed her to his chest for a gentle hug, it had been too much. Not only had Rhia been unusually tired, her moods had traveled from happy to sad, and back again so fast, his head spun. And just this morning he'd witnessed the true evidence of her condition when he stepped outside to see her holding onto a tree, retching like a sick puppy.

Finally, he asked, "When are you due?"

Rhia sniffled. "Around New Spring. About six more months."

He took a deep breath and wished he could kick himself. How could he have missed so many clues? Some Protector of the Realm he was. Hell, he'd paid more attention to the way she dressed than her well-being.

"Rhia, love, I'm so sorry. I should have known. There is no excuse." He plunged ahead and let the words she most needed to hear tumble from his lips. "I love you, Fire Storm. You and our child."

"Y-You love me? Really? B-But what happened to the whole 'warriors don't love' business?" she asked with a watery tilt of her lips, using his sleeve to wipe her wet face.

"Rhia, you are my heart. This child is you and me. I am humbled."

She threw her arms around his neck and squealed, "Oh, RuArk, I'm so glad you're happy. We never agreed to have children so soon. We just don't do it like this in Draema. I mean, children are planned and there are so many other things I know you want to do. A child right now…"

"Rhia, all I want is to love and protect you, and care for our family. Before all else, that is my desire. It is every warrior's desire."

As they sat under that sprawling tree, pride welled up in his chest. Pride like he'd never felt. He was going to be a father. The Fire Storm was having his baby. *Their* baby. Suddenly, he couldn't contain his happiness. He jumped up, grabbed her by the waist and swung her around with a loud *whoop*.

A couple of warriors patrolling the park stopped and stared, their eyes wide with incredulity. RuArk didn't care that they saw him without his Protector's face plastered firmly across his features. He was going to be a father!

The gawking warriors quickly realized what they were doing, wiped the disbelief off their faces, and strode away. Suddenly, he needed to get her home, to see her cared for. Setting his lifemate on her feet, he took her hand and practically dragged her toward his horse.

"Wait, where are we going?" Rhia called, her shorter legs scrambling to keep up as he strode across the grass.

"Home. You need to eat something, and then you will rest."

She shook loose from his hand, her voice sultry and soft. "Wind Storm," she crooned, "I don't want to go home yet. Why don't we duck into the grove over there and, uh, spend some time together?"

Great Ancestors, the little warrior was trying to seduce him! He thought of all the times he'd set out to do the very same thing and his blood sang with the need to make love to her. But her body was tender and sensitive. Pounding into her on the hard ground or up against a tree was out of the question, whether she liked it or not. He slammed his granite mask into place and bit the inside of his cheek to hide a chuckle when she glared.

"We are going home. You will eat, then you will rest," he scolded. When they reached the villa's stables he wasn't surprised when Rhia stormed off, leaving him behind to care for his mount. He watched her go, too happy to care that she was annoyed with him.

Besides, he had plans for his little Fire Storm that involved lots of sweating and orgasms. Now that he was calming down a bit, he accepted that if Rhia wanted to roll around naked with him, there was no reason to refuse her. She knew her body better than anyone on the planet, so if she was up to it, then so was he.

His mind did a one hundred eighty degree turn, and with furrowed brow, he handed the reins over to a Groomsman and headed toward the building that now housed a central office for his commanders. There was no forgetting the fact that someone wanted Rhia, and from what he'd uncovered so far, they wanted her alive. But who? Why? And with a baby coming, it was more important than ever to solve this dark mystery.

Rhia awoke to a completely quiet apartment. She lay in their bed and listened. It didn't sound like anyone was around. She closed her eyes, reached for her Source, and thought on her husband to invoke their bond. Her heart warmed as she thought about how different her life was because of this man. She hadn't known about the Source or Gifts or much of anything Gaian, and now here she was, using the magick as if she'd known how all her life. After a few seconds, she felt him out in the living room. His back was to her as she tiptoed toward him looking curiously around their apartments.

Rhia's breath caught in her throat. Her warrior husband stood in the middle of the open glass doorway of the terrace with nothing on but a breech, which was basically two small pieces of leather tied around his lower body. No trousers, no buckskins. He was practically naked. The man was breath stopping, rugged and just damn beautiful. Bronzed skin stretched over rippling muscle that glowed with health under the bright sunlight pouring onto the balcony. Glorious dark hair hung loose, lifted every now and again by the warm breeze so that it floated across his back and gave subtle peeks at his broad back.

Rhia's tongue stuck to the roof of her mouth.

She took another step, growing just a bit nervous. It was too quiet. No one knocked on the door. No one ducked in or out with a report for the Protector. What the hell was going on?

"RuArk, where is everybody?" she asked warily.

He turned on her with a growl and a devilish grin, every mischievous intention written clearly across his face. She shrieked and turned to flee, but her catlike reflexes weren't fast enough. His arm shot out and caught her before she'd taken two steps. She squealed and laughed, feeling like a child who'd just received her favorite candy and a tickle on the belly.

RuArk allowed her to break away and run for their bedroom. He gave chase and caught her just as she tried to close the door on him. He tackled her gently, landing with her cushioned in his arms in a sprawling heap on the floor. She hadn't thought much about it when he'd suggested she nap in one of his large linen shirts that buttoned down the front. But now that he'd captured her, she understood perfectly. Buttons flew everywhere as he exposed her ripe round breasts and every inch of her skin from head to toe.

Instantly aroused, she was almost annoyed with herself when reason intruded. "RuArk, it's the middle of the day. What if somebody comes?"

He carried her up to their massive bed and tossed her into the middle of it. "The only person I want to *come* is you," he said slyly.

"But what if one of your warriors needs you? Oh." Her eyes closed as his strong, rough fingers closed over her tender breasts, testing, teasing.

"Then perhaps they will receive a lesson in the intimate details of how a warrior makes his woman writhe like a cat before he fills her with cream."

"You are so dirty."

The man's words were enough to melt her bones. His mouth came down on hers, hot and seeking. His touch was urgent, and kisses became rough and untamed. He was relentless in his pursuit of her lips and tongue, sucking them into his mouth and biting down. When she did the same, he became wild and desperate, laying a fire trail of wet, carnal nips from her lips to her cheeks to the sensitive spot behind her ear.

He nibbled at the cords of her neck and was rewarded with a gasp of pure pleasure. Oh yes, he knew what she liked. And Rhia knew he would give it to her until she couldn't take anymore.

He didn't leave a single patch of skin untouched as he made his way to her aching breasts, then laved and suckled the sensitive tips until they throbbed. RuArk moved from one full mound to the other as if he couldn't get enough. Finally, he took the full crown into his mouth and sucked hard until she writhed and panted harshly.

"Oh god!" she cried as he moved down her rib cage. He rubbed his face back and forth across her belly and the rippling cage of her stomach, inhaling her scent. Mmm. It felt so primal. Natural.

"Tell me what you want, Fire Storm," he breathed

raggedly, his lips and tongue warm against her skin.

"I want... Oh, yes. I want you to touch me. Please."

"I love to do just that. I love the scent of her arousal, your skin. He planted a kiss on her slightly rounded belly and smiled, surely thinking of his child who slept peacefully inside her. She grabbed him gently by the hair and pushed him closer to her dewy wet center.

"Taste me, please. I need you to..."

She let out an unsteady gasp as his thick silky hair spilled across the sensitized tips of her swollen nipples. He liked that she loved his hair, soft as feathers and long as a horse's mane. He noted her reaction, and gathered the thick mass in his hands. He caressed her sensitive skin with it, tickled her navel and slid it all along the inside of her thighs.

He sent her over the edge when he dropped his hair over her stomach like a sensual curtain and buried his face in her moist coral folds. She arched her back on a scream, bowing so hard she practically buried the top of her head in the thick, plush bedding underneath her.

"Oh RuArk. Yes." RuArk continued his sweet assault. He made her fly until she was flush against the hot summer sun. And just when she couldn't take anymore, he hummed against her swollen clit and she exploded in a spectacular show of brilliant sparkling lights.

Soon she was a boneless, writhing, aching mass of strength in femininity.

As her second orgasm became to release its grip, RuArk loosed the leather thongs that held his breech in place. Rhia stared in wonder as he tossed it across the bed.

Then he was on her, and it was magnificent. Every

part of his body, including his velvet-covered cock, was hard and taut, corded with sinew and muscle. And when he entered her, he was so big, so hard. And so *there!*

They both let out a cry of urgency as he pushed inside. RuArk gritted his teeth against the sensation of her wet folds closing around him, squeezing him, milking him. Rhia's legs wrapped around his waist, and he sank deeper. One stroke, and then two. She was coming, her body bucking and thrashing.

This new release was swift. Hard. The pleasure so complete, she was oblivious to everything except the hot steel of her husband moving inside her. Taking her to complete satiation. She yelled his name, and then chanted it. A litany of praise and awe on her lips as wave after wave of sensual pleasure washed over her.

RuArk joined her in the dance, responding to the tightening of her sugared walls. He lurched forward with a roar, releasing his seed deep within her. Like a storm of lightning and thunder, his warlike cry shook the very foundations of their bond. Rhia might have been startled at the intensity of it had she not been floating outside of her own body in sensual awe.

Later that afternoon, Rhia stood out on the terrace, as was her habit when she needed some quiet time. As she watched RuArk head down the hill, he stopped and looked back toward her. He raised his hand and waved. While he usually kept himself clamped down tight, right now his side of their mate bond was thrown wide open. He let flow through all the things he couldn't say right now, and Rhia let it fill her until her heart overflowed with awe.

The man was thrilled about her pregnancy. He was even more thrilled that he'd made a baby with *her.*

She waved back and he turned away. She watched him pass through the courtyard and beyond the trail that would have taken him to the soldier's barracks and stables. Rhia's eyes remained on him until he'd made it all the way out of the low gates and out of sight toward the center of town.

She stood beneath azure blue skies until the sun began to sink from its highest point. Thinking on her current situation, she rocked back on her heels.

"Guess becoming a mom does that to a woman," she mused to herself.

But it was more than that. Much more.

Her life had taken a huge turn long before her father had ever summoned RuArk to the High City to investigate the plot against her life. She just hadn't known it yet. Had it always been her destiny to be here, in this place, with this man, these people?

She couldn't say whether she now believed in fate, but she knew when to take a step back and reassess her situation. Life was one big strategy session. Sometimes things went as planned and sometimes they didn't.

As she sat, Rhia's thoughts turned to Sharyn. Sharyn Miwatani was as bad ass as any soldier she'd ever trained or met. The woman was second to no one, yet never needed to steamroll her way into, or out of, any situation. Sharyn was an alpha, no doubt about it, yet she didn't wear it like a warning sign. Most impressive was that she was an expert at choosing her battles.

It was something Rhia had been trained to do in true warfare, but she hadn't had a clue how to be wise in an intimate relationship. A conversation they'd had when they'd first met came to mind. *"You could have so much more from the Wind Storm if you bend but a little,*

Rhia. Bending branches do not break. If you give your mate what he wants by wearing the sarand and learning the ways of the Gaian, what have you lost by doing so?"

Rhia now had her answer. Nothing. She'd lost absolutely nothing at all. Giving her mate, her husband, what he'd asked for had made her no less of a soldier, no less of a woman. In fact, he'd given her plenty without her even asking, including things he'd already known she needed, even though she hadn't had a clue herself.

And now, here they were. This wasn't a crossroads, or even a point of contemplation. This was an acknowledgement of the fact that some of her old ideas were no longer relevant. Period.

The against-all-odds need to prove herself to RuArk was a fallacy. In fact, the man had never asked her for such a thing in the first place. No, that was baggage she'd brought all on her own. And now it was time to cut it loose.

Would she morph into some other person? Not a chance. She was still First Heir. Still a Blademaster. Still Rhia Greysomne Miwatani. Yet, she was more now, not less — a lifemate, and a mother.

The latter thought almost sent her into a panic. Like her first foray into her relationship with RuArk, motherhood was something she had no idea how to do. Thoughts of her own parents brought a jumble of joy and pain. Fulfillment and utter loneliness. Love and loss. Fear.

Facing all of it head on, Rhia made a decision.

I'll learn to be a mom just like I've learned everything else. But without the giant hole in her soul that used to be filled with nothing but her own ambition. Now it carried new hopes and dreams. A new family. New friends. New places to call home.

Rather than strive, perhaps she'd finally reached a point in her life where she could simply... be.

Surely she and RuArk would still bump heads about things, but bumping heads for the hell of it? Nope. No more exercises in futility. No more almost losing someone to a permanent death before realizing how much they meant to her. No more stubbornness just 'because'.

Oooh, I'll need to work on that one. This calls for emergency reinforcements.

She sucked in a fortifying breath and headed to Joan's for a cup of strong spiced chocolate.

CHAPTER TWELVE

As the months slipped by, Rhia bloomed with good health, her body lush and ripe. RuArk took every possible chance to make her feel like the most desirable woman he'd ever seen. Though large with child, she wouldn't hear of him leaving their bed even though he only wanted to make sure she was comfortable.

On her last check-up to the Physicians, she'd even asked if it was normal for abstinence to be the last thing on her mind. The further along she got, the more she craved RuArk's cock. She'd even taken to teasing him by walking around their apartments naked. All. The. Time.

Just last night she'd stretched out in front of the fireplace in the living room on the plush carpets and palmed her breasts until he'd pounced on her. Hells, he walked around with a perpetual hard-on. The fact that it was her fault only made her grin wider.

New Spring was around the corner and Rhia was more than ready for some raucous frivolity, über pregnant or not. While it was a legal holiday in the province, the history behind it had been lost long ago. All her life, it had been something she'd indulged in for fun simply because it's what they'd always done.

Now, thanks to Sharyn's history lessons, Rhia knew exactly how the celebrations originated. For the Gaian, who were participating in the fun this season, it symbolized renewal, growth and birth, demonstrated by thanking the Ancestors and the exchanging of gifts, which symbolized new beginnings.

Rhia and Sharyn spoke very little about the Foreknowledge of RuArk's brush with death and focused instead on preparing for the holiday.

After all, what she'd seen had clearly happened in summer, and that season had come and was long gone. There'd been no more attacks or attempted kidnappings. No strange dreams. No odd messages from home. Nothing. She hadn't seen anything like that bloody scene since then, so why dwell on something she'd obviously mistaken. Perhaps it had all been a fluke that came with learning to use her new Gifts?

With several weeks left to prepare, and Lunis's help, all of the public spaces, town centers and Society buildings were prepped for decorating.

Outside the villa, the courtyards and walks were cleared. Inside, the linens and wall hangings were washed and aired, and the walls, floors and carpets scrubbed.

An emissary from the High City's branch of the Society of Historians arrived with a few reproduced pages from an old culinary book. Joan jumped right in and planned menus for the feasts. RuArk then selected the meats that would be smoked with the special wood he had brought across the river from Gaia.

After the main meals were planned, including some of the typical Draeman dishes for those who couldn't quite get used to non-synthetic food, the kitchens were thoroughly scrubbed and buzzed with activity.

Sometimes, she was still amazed at the turn her life had taken, even with something as simple as food. Ever since she'd been truly immersed in the culture, Rhia had to admit, the stuff was damn tasty.

Next to conquer was the list of treats for all of the children—a fun, but monumental task in itself since there were so many.

After the abduction by Bryan and Ricard, Rhia had reassigned several of her former, fully-vetted students from the High City to Province Springs. They, along with Gaian warriors and their families, had poured into the township. The place was fabulously overrun with little ones.

When presents from across the river began to arrive prior to the scheduled festivities, Rhia was so excited that RuArk had threatened to send her up to bed if she didn't relax a bit. His threat failed miserably, especially after he'd had the men fell a huge evergreen and drag it into the main hall. When they'd settled the Festival Tree into place, he'd given up trying to keep her calm when she'd pretty much flipped with joy and then waddled off on a quest to find decorations to cover it.

That same night, the first gifts they'd opened together were from the High Prince of Gaia, RuArk's older brother. Away visiting the eastern provinces on the other side of the world, he'd taken the time to make sure the presents arrived in time.

The enclosed note read:

To my dearest brother, the Wind Storm and his lifemate, Fire Storm. Congratulations on your joining. May the years bring you prosperity and happiness beyond measure. Mother contacted me to tell of your celebrating the Draeman holiday of New Spring this year and I thought it only fitting to send something worthy of you. My only regret is that I cannot be there to deliver these gifts in person but please accept them as tokens of love and care.

Sincere regards,

Your brother,

Rogear

Wrapped in the softest doe hide had been a pair of eastern-styled swords, double edged and etched with gold. The sigil of the wind danced across RuArk's blade from the razor sharp tip to the hilt and the pommel was highly polished ebony inlaid with onyx stones. Rhia's sword, a smaller version of RuArk's, held the symbol of fire while her pommel was a solid chunk of polished ivory with red gems inlaid in the top.

Suddenly she slipped into a bit of melancholy as thoughts of her blood kin danced through her mind. RuArk's family and friends were fully engaged, yet, neither Rhia's father nor brother had arrived.

RuArk's firm hand had settled on her belly as he sat next to her in the main hall among their people. His presence wrapped around her consciousness like a warm blanket as three simple words quietly filled her head. *"I am here."*

A smile had bloomed and lit her from the inside out as she'd locked gazes with her mate. A moment later, Drefan had hauled a huge package in front of her.

"We are to open these now. The rest will wait until the actual celebration," RuArk had whispered.

It turned out that Queen Mila had sent bolt after bolt of fine Gaian silk in every color imaginable. After removing what seemed like endless bundles of greens, oranges, pinks, blues and more, Rhia had called for help and several tables were piled with a mix of vibrant and soft hues as the hall rang with laughter and good times.

She had immediately put the Society of Tailors to work making both traditional garb and sarands for the women of the township since many, to Rhia's surprise, had taken to occasionally wearing the wispy garb to imitate their lady.

RuArk's father had sent a small cache of antique weapons for his son. These weren't just old, but original, well preserved articles carried by the first Protector of the Realm appointed immediately after the Breaking. These weapons were several hundreds of years old and had been lovingly restored.

When RuArk had come in from patrol the next evening, he had been simply undone to see them polished and hung on the walls of the main hall along with his other blades, maces, long knives and bows.

With only a few days before New Spring, the greatest gift of all had shown up last night and now poked his graying head through a partially opened door.

"Rhia?" She was greeted with a magnificent smile by none other than Grey Greysomne, her father, also known as "the complete wreck".

His arrival the night before had almost thrown Rhia into labor, she'd been so shocked. The High Counsel and RuArk had conspired to surprise her for the holidays, but RuArk hadn't told her father about her pregnancy. He'd waltzed into the main hall in the middle of the evening meal, got one look at her oversized belly and went pale as a sheet. That was quite a feat given how dark his skin was. And there he'd stood, rooted to the spot as she'd waddled across the room to greet him properly.

Hugging was not something Rhia and her father had done often, but she'd been so glad to see him that she hadn't hesitated to reach out to him, bumping bellies, unable to suppress her giggles.

Then the questions had begun.

"Are you eating enough? Are you resting enough? Have you seen the Physicians? What did they say?" And on it went as he'd given RuArk the evil eye as if the pregnancy of his only daughter, with the largest baby in all creation, was his fault.

As far as Rhia was concerned, New Spring hadn't even arrived yet but her father's appearance last night was more than she could have hoped for.

The High Counsel of the entire province of Draema, commander-in-chief of the Society of War, was the epitome of the anxious grandfather.

Shaking her head with a wry grin as he stepped into her apartments and settled in next to her on the couch, Rhia poured him a cup of coffee.

"I'll be going with some of RuArk's men for a ride in the groves. If you want, I can stay with you. Did you have breakfast yet? Is there anything you need? How are you feeling?"

"Father, I'm fine. Really. I've never felt better in my life." She absolutely glowed and was bursting with energy regardless of the constant pressure in her lower back.

"Well, if you're sure that you're all right?"

"Have a nice ride, Father," Rhia smiled. He took one final swig from his coffee cup, rose and headed out. Rhia waved as he closed the door behind him.

Now that he'd finally stopped clucking long enough to leave, Rhia headed to the tub. Her back was aching and good soak would do her good as long as she didn't stay in the warm water too long.

As she slid down into the silky suds, Rhia fought the panic that threatened to overtake her as thoughts turned to her mother. That wonderful lady wouldn't be here to see her first grandchild take his first breath. Rhia's mind screamed warnings about surviving the birth. What if she died while the child was young? She was scared to death of having this baby, but physical pain had nothing to do with it.

She shook away the dread. Everything would be fine. RuArk's mother had promised to come. And Brita, Sharyn and Joan would be here. And her husband was so stubborn he wouldn't let her die if he had to follow her to the next realm and drag her back by her toes. She stilled and cocked her head to the side.

Blink. Blink.

When had she developed so much faith in the man? Well, whenever it had occurred she was glad for it. He was her rock. Her gravity. Her...

A sound in the living room startled her.

Rhia looked up. RuArk stood before her as naked as the day he was born. She would never get used to the way he moved. So stealthy and quiet, always catching her off guard. She let out a gasp of surprise and raised her hands over her breasts, suddenly self-conscious of her burgeoning shape. Her anger flared when he chuckled at her last attempt at modesty. She knew she looked ridiculous trying to cover her breasts while covered up to her shoulders in water.

"What are you doing here?" she whispered, failing miserably at being annoyed that he stood before her, showing off every inch, and she meant *every inch* of his beautiful body.

"Is that any way to greet the man who has slipped

away from his duties just to make love to you?" he asked. "And you're not supposed to be in the bath. What if you lost your balance and hit your head?"

"Oh please. I already have one crazed and worried man. I don't need another. Besides, both the healers and the Physicians have said the buoyancy of the water helps relieve pressure. As long as it's not too hot, and I don't stay in too long, I'm fine."

Rhia lowered her lashes and tried to hide the smile in her eyes. So, she'd made him skip out on his duties, eh? She'd never even dreamed it would be possible to make love in the middle of the day when she'd still been home at the Citadel—too damn busy. But RuArk taught her to balance those duties, relax into her new life and enjoy it, enjoy him.

Shamelessly, she admitted to herself that she'd do the same as he—lay down her duties to invite a bout of hot sweaty sex with him, anytime, anywhere. But he wasn't supposed to do that kind of stuff. He was the blasted Protector, yet here he was, playing hooky. She laughed out loud with a few snorts thrown in.

"I'm sorry, RuArk. It's just that I didn't expect you home," she managed to squeeze out between giggles.

"I am glad, because if you had, you'd be dressed right now."

"As you can see, I'm bathing. If you'll excuse me, I'll join you for a late breakfast in a few minutes. I'll have Lunis send up your favorite." She sunk lower into the warm suds. There was no mistaking he wanted her, but she hadn't bathed yet, and Rhia would not allow him to touch her until she was clean.

She'd been particularly fussy about her appearance lately, as well as everything else about the house. She was forever directing that something be cleaned, dusted, repaired or replaced, even if it didn't need to be done for New Spring. Must be that nesting thing that women were said to have when they were close to having their baby?

Instead of leaving, RuArk climbed into the tub behind her and nuzzled the back of her neck. "I have every intention of bathing every inch of your beautiful body." His voice was husky with desire and a deep tremble stole over her as he tipped her favorite bubbling oil into his hands. Spreading it over her shoulders, he massaged the muscles before moving over her breasts to work the oil into a sweet lather. Over and over her nipples, underneath the heavy globes, back up and around. *Oh, so sweet.* The ultra-sensitive peaks stood at attention as a new dampness began between her legs that had nothing to do with the water in which they bathed.

"Ooh, yes." She arched against him and was almost annoyed when RuArk turned her toward him. Instead of fussing, she automatically went up on her knees. The water was now down around her middle, exposing her stomach and breasts. He cupped his hands to sluice the water over her, rinsing the lathered oil from her skin then taking a puckered nipple into his mouth. His free hand rubbed slow, gentle circles over her distended belly.

"Mmm..." God, he made her feel so luscious.

"Oh, RuArk, more." His fingers smoothed over her stomach and down to the heat between her legs. She was already on the verge of exploding.

"Come for me, my sweet Fire Storm," he breathed into her ear.

"Yes. Mmm, yes... Owwww!"

"What?" He stopped cold. "What's wrong?"

"I-I'm not sure, but... Oooowwwww!" She stiffened then doubled over not sure whether to grip her belly or her back as a sudden sharp pain knifed through her from both directions.

"What is it? Did I hurt you?"

"No. It must be the baby. Gods, is it supposed to hurt like this?"

"How the hell am I supposed to know? I have never had a baby before. I have been too busy being a warrior, gods damn it. What does it feel like?" he snapped.

"Don't snap at me! And what do you mean, 'what does it feel like'? It hurts like hell!"

He lifted her from the tub and toweled her off.

"How long have you had the pain?"

"I don't know. I've been having a little bit of pressure for the past couple of days, but it didn't bother me much so I just ignored it."

The tilt of his gorgeous dark head and the disapproving downturn of his mouth told her he wasn't buying it. Silence stretched between them, but when RuArk's side of the bond flared she knew he was going to get the truth one way or another, so she may as well spill it.

"Okay, fine! I had some really bad cramps and my stomach got all hard, but RuArk ..." He'd gone from stern set of his mouth to a full on scowl as he picked her up and headed out of the bathing room.

"The cramps, Rhia?" he ground out through his teeth. She knew he'd be furious if she had indeed been in labor for two days.

"I... I'm embarrassed."

"Get. Over. It!" Wow, he'd never yelled at her before.

"All right, already!" She yelled right back. "I'm scared out of my mind at the thought of having a baby. Your mother promised to be here, but she hasn't come yet. I started having cramps and thought it was nothing. I can take a lot of pain, RuArk. After all I am a soldier. I've been injured plenty of times and..."

He set her on her feet in the walk-in closet, grabbed a clean gown out of a drawer and yanked it over her head. Lifting her back into his arms, he carried her toward the bed.

"Hey, I don't want to go to bed now," she snapped.

"Get to the point, Rhia. The pains?"

"Impatient much? As I was saying," she huffed partly from anger at having to tell him of a fear she was ashamed to have, and partly because it was getting harder to speak with the incredible pains tightening her stomach. "It started a couple of days ago, but they've just begun to get worse over the past twelve hours or so. I thought it might be the baby, but until your mother gets here I'm not having a baby. Do you hear me? This baby just can't come now, period."

RuArk shook his head and she cringed as disappointment flashed through their bond, uncontrolled. He couldn't believe that she hadn't trusted him with her anxiety. That she'd rather suffer alone for two days than tell him about her concerns, hurt him. On one of the happiest moments of their lives... and she'd hurt him. Again.

"RuArk, I'm sorry, I..." He hadn't quite made it to the bed yet. "Oh! Oh no!" Her waters broke. All over her mate.

"RuArk, I'm so sorry. This is..."

"Rhia, this is what happens when women have children. It is nothing to be ashamed of."

She stood stiffly as he quickly stripped off her soiled gown and replaced it with a warm clean robe. As she was shuffled underneath the covers, his concern rose as she tried and failed to suppress a moan as her breath came in shorter and shorter gasps. He ripped off his wet shirt, moved to the closet and grabbed the first thing he saw, which happened to be one of her workout shirts. The thing was way too small and ripped at the seams as he tried to yank his arms through the sleeves.

With the thing in tatters, he returned to Rhia's side and pressed a kiss on her forehead.

"You will not move, woman."

"But…"

"No, you will remain here while I get someone to assist in this. Do you want me to send Brita to you?"

"Yes, but, no. Wait, RuArk…" Her moans were quickly becoming snarls and she wondered herself just how far along she was in the birthing.

"You have held off your labor for two days? Stubborn, stiff-necked, bone headed…" he muttered as he made for the door, not bothering to close either the bedroom or apartment doors behind him.

RuArk caught up with Lunis in the main foyer at the front of the villa.

"Lunis, send someone for the Grandfather and my mother right away."

"What is happening, sir?"

"The baby is coming. Move it."

"The baby is coming? The baby is coming!" Then another man gave a startled yelp as the front doors flew open.

RuArk couldn't help but roll his eyes as he turned toward that voice. Just what he needed. Rhia's father would choose this precise moment to walk into the front hall. He was approaching a state of barely controlled hysterics himself and he didn't need any help from Rhia's father.

It was amazing what women and babies did to a man. RuArk had known the High Counsel all his life. He'd never, ever seen him with any expression on his face that wasn't confident, cool, or humorous. Now, he was completely undone. But RuArk was in no position to point fingers.

The doors banged open again, causing all three men to turn with a start. He'd reached for the hilt of his sword before realizing that he'd taken it off in his chambers before joining Rhia in the tub.

"Mother! Thanks gods!"

The High Counsel and Lunis were visibly relieved to see Queen Mila sweep into the front hall with her entourage in tow. Then came old Aunt Leena and a couple of RuArk's twin cousins, Elana and Elaina, both about Rhia's age. They'd brought their sons. They were like bookends, these boys. Matching in almost every way. Two sets of twins. Elana's sons were a mirror image of her, while Elaina's boys looked just like their Gaian father.

"Grandfather said this would be the day to come. Have the pains started?" Mila asked.

"Yes!" yelled RuArk, Grey and Lunis all at the same time.

She looked at the High Counsel wringing his hands, moving from one foot to another. It seemed that he didn't know whether to go or stay. Mila made the choice for him.

"Hello. I am Mila, Queen of Gaia and mother to Rhia. You must be Grey, Rhia's father?"

He nodded his head dumbly, while still trying to look like a statesman. He didn't pull it off very well.

Finally, he said, "Yes, I'm Grey Greysomne. Rhia is my daughter. I'm worried about her. What if something goes wrong? I couldn't stand to lose her like I lost my…"

"You will cease such talk." He didn't respond fast enough so she took a step closer. Queen Mila would brook no nonsense from him, High Counsel or not.

"You were married to a warrior woman of Gaia, were you not?" At his somber nod, she continued. "Then you know better than to speak such things. This is not the time for negative words, actions or thoughts. Rhia needs your positive energy. The Great Spirits of our Ancestors will care for her. See to it that you send your strength to her. She will need it before the night is done. Understand?"

The High Counsel took a deep breath, and said, "Of course."

"RuArk, please go and help your father with the presents. He is having some of your men load the carts."

"Carts?" RuArk wondered aloud.

"Yes, carts. We had your harbormaster bring two carts down to the docks so we could unload the presents for the baby. But later for that. I have a new mother to take care of. Off with you now."

"Lunis, get my mother anything she needs. And mother," he turned to take her by the hand to place a thankful kiss on her cheek, "she's been fighting the labor for days."

"That's good to know. She can be quite stubborn at times." But it was said with a fond smile. "And I would not have her any other way if she is to deal with you."

RuArk appreciated his mother's humor just now as he stepped outside and noted how cool the breeze was. Like a late season snow was coming.

"RuArk, get going. And please take the High Counsel with you. Your father is waiting. And Rhia is waiting for me. Lunis, please have our things taken to our rooms. If I need assistance I will send word."

"What about the children?" RuArk called back as he started down the front steps. He looked back at the four well-behaved boys standing calmly watching the adults take care of the details.

"They can help you," called Elana and Elaina, almost in unison. They looked at each other and smiled. Turning those smiles on RuArk, he nodded his consent. He helped the boys get their coats back on as the group of women swept up the stairs, leaving a befuddled Lunis in their wake to deal with the mountain of baggage sitting just outside the front doors.

CHAPTER THIRTEEN

RuArk, the High Counsel, along with every warrior that could fit inside the main hall, sat and waited for word on Rhia's progress. She'd truly won the hearts of his men and already held the love of her own people. Judging from the number present, there would be no shortage of guardians of the child.

"Joan, what is happening?" Marth called after her as she and Sharyn flew past them on yet another trip with their arms full of linens and towels.

"Not now," she said irritably. "We're busy!"

"That I can see," he muttered to himself. "Women."

"Here, here!" came the good-natured agreement of the warriors who'd been close enough to hear him griping.

RuArk wondered about some of Rhia's concerns and figured this was as good a time as any to get some answers. He turned to his father-in-law.

"Sir, would you join me?" He led the High Counsel out of the main hall, down the hallway to the foyer so they could have a bit of privacy.

"Tell me what happened between you and Rhia after her mother died? She is deathly afraid of having our child, but says the pain of the birth has nothing to do with it."

"What happened after the death of her mother? Basically, my life was shattered, ruined. I was so numb with grief that I just closed in on myself and locked out the world."

"And you locked out your daughter, too?"

"Yes, her and her brother, Sean," the High Counsel admitted honestly and without hesitation. "I just couldn't seem to function, think, or care about anything. That great woman was my whole world, my everything. I grieved for years. By the time I came out of it and realized life had gone on without me, Rhia and Sean were well on in years. While I saw to my duties as High Counsel, I did it in a bubble of sorts. Functioned, but wasn't really aware of much going on around me. Almost like a waking dream.

"Rhia had gained First Blade and taken on the running of the Society of War. She stepped into her role as my first born and heir, even gave direction to the Council of Seven. Sean had earned the appointment of Harbor Master, obviously without any help from me. Rhia, as First Heir, had approved the appointment and my only son had been gone to Harbor Station for almost two years."

"Do you realize she has been trying to walk in her mother's footsteps since that time?"

The High Counsel sat up considerably straighter as he took in that bit of news. "But that's ridiculous. No one could fill my wife's shoes." The High Counsel lowered his head as understanding finally dawned in his downcast eyes. He suddenly looked so...old. "I hadn't realized. She seemed to be willing to learn what was required as First Heir and she could out-do most of the men. So I let her take on as much as she could handle. I simply thought she was ambitious."

"Yet, where was her father?"

"I was right there! I was…"

"Perhaps you lived in the same building as her, worked in the same Society of War, even ran the Province with your daughter's help. But were you *there* when she'd scraped a knee?"

RuArk knew that Brita had seen to her.

"Or when she needed to talk to someone about a problem?"

Joan, no older than Rhia, had been her confidante.

"Or when she was trying to decide what she wanted in life?"

Silence.

Finally, Grey spoke. "Perhaps if I'd paid more attention she would have never been engaged to that blasted Bryan Collaidh all those years ago. She would have never been in danger or in a position where he could beat her senseless like he did. I stepped in, but I never comforted Rhia, nor did we ever talk about what really happened that day, or any other day. I just left her to herself thinking she needed to grieve alone, like I did."

"What you needed as a man was not what she needed as a young woman. She has spent all these years trying to get you to love her."

"But I do love her. I've always loved her."

"But did she know that? Did you tell her? Show her?"

"I tried to show her by letting her be herself and do as she pleased."

"By piling duties on her? By making her think that if she worked hard enough, if she ran herself from sun up to sun down that maybe you would love her like you loved her mother?"

"How dare you judge me!"

RuArk was getting angry now, and so was the High Counsel. But this should have been handled long ago, almost the whole of Rhia's life, to be exact.

"I do not judge you, sir, but I tell you what I have learned as Rhia's lifemate, what I have seen in her every day. Until I literally made her delegate her responsibilities and forced her to take time away from duties, the woman pushed herself from dawn until she crawled into bed at night. She used to challenge my warriors, Grey. Warriors! Just to prove she deserved their respect, not realizing she had it already simply because of how honorable a woman she is." RuArk shot to his feet and tried with all his strength to keep his voice down and his hands at his sides.

"At first she tried to give me only her body, not wanting to let me into her heart. Do you know why? It was because she could not stand to love."

"What? Why?" the High Counsel asked, angry, but genuinely confused.

"Why? For fear of losing the one she loved as she lost both her mother *and* her father. Now she is afraid of having our child because she does not want to die and leave the child alone without love. Without care."

"Oh gods," the High Counsel sobbed. "What have I done to my daughter?"

"You have done nothing that cannot be undone. It is your Draeman New Spring, and the Gaian season of rebirth. It is your holiday of giving, yes? Legend says it is a time of miracles. Perhaps you will have one. Or perhaps, if you choose to, you will *make* one."

With that, he patted the High Counsel on the shoulder and bounded back up the stairs toward the main hall, leaving him to think on all the time and opportunities between he and Rhia that had been lost.

RuArk had had enough of waiting. As he approached the doors to the huge dining area, he took a sharp left and ran upstairs to their apartments. He'd put a hand on the door just as another woman flew out with a basin of bloodied water and even bloodier linens.

Rhia's blood curdling screams stopped him cold, and then mobilized him. He had to get to her, had to help her. Nobody would scream like that unless they needed help.

Once through the apartment door, Elaina met him at the threshold of the bedroom, barring the way.

"Sorry cousin. You cannot go in just yet."

"That is my woman, this is my house, and I will go where I bloody well please!"

"Not today." Elaina refused to back down. Rhia screamed again and he was driven by something that twisted deep in his gut. He was going to get to his lifemate no matter what. He reached down, caught Elaina underneath the shoulders, and lifted her straight up into the air. She remained undaunted.

"You may be a gigantic Gaian warrior, and you may be Protector of the Realm, but that room is full of women who won't hesitate to tear you to pieces if you intrude on their domain. Now. Put. Me. Down."

Just then, he heard a loud squalling hiccupping sound. He turned his head toward the bedroom door, still holding Elaina three feet off the ground. The hiccupping turned into a mewling, and finally an all-out yell to the rafters. And it wasn't Rhia.

He set his cousin on her feet and reached for the doorknob just as his mother opened it and stepped out.

"May I present your son, Taté Icamna." She held the little bundle with the large lungs out to him and disappeared back into the bedroom. To RuArk's surprise, the babe immediately quieted and began to observe his father just as his father was observing him. The little one was perfect in every way, from the little black and reddish tufts on his head to his charcoal gray eyes, and skin like sweet cream.

His son. *Their* son. He looked down at the newborn held in one of his massive arms and his eyes filled with wonder that something so small could hold him in thrall so completely. He thought he heard another wail. The bedroom door opened again.

"And your daughter, Relaina Grey."

Another child? A girl, who was the spitting image of her father. Dark midnight curls, and slate gray eyes with the intelligence of her mother shining through.

Two babies?

Elana stuck her head out the door a few moments later. "You may see her now."

Everyone cleared the room, leaving RuArk, Rhia and the little prince and princess to spend some time alone together.

He climbed the stairs to their bed as Rhia stirred.

"RuArk, aren't they beautiful?' she asked with a yawn.

"Yes, they are beautiful babes. Just like their mother."

He lay down next to Rhia and placed the babies between them.

"I never thought in a million years I would have twins. Even when I felt them kicking from all different directions I still never imagined I carried two babies," she said happily, though sleepily. "RuArk?"

"Yes, love?"

"Are there any other twins in your family beside Elana and Elaina?"

"Elana and Elaina both have twin boys. I am also a twin."

"What?"

"Yes, Rogear and I were born several minutes apart. He is my older brother, though not older by much."

"You have a twin brother and you never told me?"

"I told you I have a brother, Rhia. But twins are common in our clan so it did not occur to me to mention it."

"And he looks just like you?"

"So we have been told."

"It isn't true, RuArk."

"What is not true?"

"He can't look just like you. There couldn't possibly be another man like you on the entire planet. Certainly not one as handsome. You are a god."

"Do you really think so?" he said, with all the arrogance he could muster, but inwardly he was humbled to the bottom of his heart.

"Rhia, I know you were afraid. To be honest, I was worried for you as I guess all fathers-to-be worry." Unable to keep the awe from his voice, he said, "Look what you made."

"Look what *we* made." She began to doze.

"You're tired. I'll leave you to rest."

"No, not yet. I need to feed the babies first."

"Shall I call my mother or my cousins to help you?"

"No, sweetheart, I want you to help me. Do you mind?"

Mind? He'd expected to be excluded from this part

of the birthing and was touched that she would ask him. She was a proud woman and he, being a proud man, knew how difficult it could be to ask for help at times. He helped her sit up a bit more and fluffed an extra pillow behind her back.

"So, was the pain so bad?"

"Do you want me to lie?"

"No."

"It felt like someone had taken a sword and run me through. And every time I had a contraction it felt like I was being run through all over again. Oh, blazes, it was awful. It was like trying to push a melon out of something the size of a lemon...twice. I mean could you imagine trying to push an orange out of your cock and then..."

"Rhia!" The images she'd painted would never leave his mind.

She started laughing. "Um, you're turning an awkward shade of green. I didn't know a golden god could get so pale in the face!" She winced.

"What's wrong?"

"Laughing hurts. My stomach muscles are tender, but I just can't help it."

While she nursed the babies for the first time, RuArk marveled at how perfect they were, all fat cheeks and chubby fingers. And so wonderfully greedy, they fell asleep with Rhia's nipples still in their little mouths.

Not long after, his mother came in, reached for Tate and handed him to Sharyn, who was soon joined by Grey, Joan, Linc and Marth. Joan took Relaina Grey and began to croon to her. The thoughts on her face clearly read by all—what would it be like to have a child of her own?

Now that their friends were here, Rhia asked him to help her down from the bed for just a little while. RuArk gently picked her up and settled her into a plump cushioned chair while everyone who wasn't holding a child freshened up the room.

"Where is Brita?" Rhia wondered as her eyes closed on a contented sigh.

"She is somewhat out of sorts," Sharyn answered noncommittally.

"Is she ill?" asked Rhia.

"I don't think so," said Joan lowering her face to rub against the soft cheek of little Relaina Grey. "She just seems to walk about in a daze. It kind of comes and goes for what seems like forever now. Physically, she's as healthy as one of those trees out in the courtyard as far as her body scans say."

Joan didn't sound concerned so Rhia let it go. She was thankful they had an oversized bedroom. Even without Brita it was getting pretty crowded. She was exhausted and slipped into a light sleep as their family and closest friends cooed over the babies. She came wide awake when she heard Joan telling of how she cursed RuArk in a couple of different languages as she'd pushed the first baby out.

Rhia actually tried to get up off his lap with threats of choking Joan when she began the story of how she'd stood up in the middle of their bed and announced that she wasn't having a baby today.

Joan stuck her tongue out at Rhia and kept right on with the tale. "In fact she stood in the middle of a pile of sheets, doubled over with a contraction and told us that she wanted us to pack her things so she could go home to the High City. Oh, and Queen Mila was informed that Rhia had in fact changed her mind about this whole business so mom-in-law could go back home because there weren't going to be any grandchildren. Ever."

Even RuArk laughed at that one before kicking them all out so Rhia could get some rest.

She slept as he lay the babies down together in one of the gifts from his parents that had come off of the carts this morning—a large, beautifully carved cradle with the sigil of the Wind overlaid in gold. It was full of delicate swaddling and blankets done in a shimmering soft gray, in the color of their houses—Miwatani and Greysomne.

He left his mate to her dreams as he quietly closed the doors to their apartment and went down to the main hall where his men still waited for news.

"I'm a father twice over!" he shouted as he descended the staircase. A great cheer went up complete with clanking mugs, congratulations and good natured thumping on the back.

RuArk had never celebrated New Spring in this manner, but he was familiar with the Draeman custom. It was supposed to be the season of extraordinary things. It must be true because he had three miracles upstairs asleep this very moment.

Rhia awoke to a soft knock on her bedroom door.

God she was tired. Fighting labor for two days and then surviving that intense pain for so many hours had her completely exhausted. Yet, there was an inner strength and energy she had never experienced before. Strange contrast, for sure.

While exhilarated in her spirit, her body felt like

someone had spent several days rolling her up and down the cobblestone walks through the courtyard.

She smiled, opened her eyes and gazed across the room to the cradle that was the temporary refuge of her new son and daughter. They weren't there.

They're out on their first adventure.

She lay there and stretched without a worry in the world. Their father was RuArk Miwatani, and she knew without a doubt that absolutely nothing was amiss as far as those particular children were concerned.

Closing her eyes, she lay still in the huge bed and reached out to her husband through their bond. She felt him nearby. He had the babies with him and was bursting with joy. And uncertainty? Hmmm, she'd have to ask him about that.

The knock sounded again just as softly as before. Whoever it was really didn't want to disturb her, of which she was grateful, but she had to get up sometime and there was no time like the present.

She tried to sit up and fell back heavily against her pillows with a sharp gasp. *Holy fuck that hurt like hell.*

Determined to rise anyway, she rolled over onto her side, pushed herself up to a sitting position and swung her legs over the side of the bed so her feet rested on the top step of the platform.

"There is no way I am staying in this blasted bed," she grumbled to herself. She was a warrior woman, a soldier and Blademaster. Surely, she should be having an easier time than most?

Not wanting to keep her guest waiting, she called out, "Come in."

Mila whisked into the room and came to a dead stop. "What are you doing?" Impatient and clearly annoyed, the woman was up the steps and at Rhia's side in an instant to tuck her back in.

"I was just going to get up for a while."

"You will do no such thing. If you need help to the bathing room, I will help you. But other than that you will rest at least two full days before you rise. After that, you may go down to the dining hall and maybe walk a bit, but nothing further, Rhia. And that is the end of it."

This was the Queen of Gaia, a woman more stubborn than herself. Why bother trying to persuade her, Rhia thought. But the thought didn't last long.

"Mila, women have babies every day. This is no big deal, right? Why can't I get up now?"

"It is true that women have babies every day, however, Ms. Fire Storm, they do not usually fight their labor for two days then give birth to two children at once."

Well she couldn't dispute any of that. Crap.

"And second, your children were quite large. After you were asleep, Sharyn used her Gift of Healing to assist, but you must rest and eat in order to regain your strength. You know as well as I, that the person receiving the essence of the Gift gives their energy just as much as the person giving the Gift.

"There will be some swelling and you did hemorrhage some, which caused you to lose quite a bit of blood. If you stand on your feet right now, I would not be surprised if you tumbled from that monstrous bed of yours. Yes, from the first step all the way down to the floor. And I am not sure I would be inclined to help you up again should you decide to be stiff-necked about this." Mila finished calmly. Then she stood there and waited with that blasted super-patient, you-know-

I'm-right expression.

Finally, knowing she wasn't going to win this particular battle, Rhia grumbled, "Fine, I get the picture."

"Good. Now, I have come to help you change your packing."

"Aw, man. Seriously."

"This is not the time to be embarrassed, Rhia. Besides, I saw all there is to see considering I brought your children into this world."

Rhia blushed furiously but knew she was being ridiculous. Draema wasn't the most modest of places to begin with and Gaians didn't get squicked out about typical bodily functions.

Mila took in her stricken expression.

"Did you learn nothing in Draema about having children?"

"Of course. We have sex education, but it wasn't something I spent much time on. Other than fighting, I mostly studied finance and diplomacy. When it comes to sex all Draeman learn how babies are made, but I didn't bother with the *having* part since the *making* was much more interesting." She grinned insolently at her mother-in-law and began laughing only to immediately regret it. It made her belly twinge.

Instead, Mila laughed for her and offered to help Rhia from the bed to the bathing room. She got to her feet on her own, but after that most of her weight was on Mila's shoulders.

Rhia silently acknowledged that her mother-in-law was quite correct in regard to her state of health considering it even took energy to take a pee.

Mila helped her wash up, showed Rhia how to care for her stitches, then dropped a bomb.

"No sex for at least thirty days."

"Wait, what? Even with our advanced technology, I can't bump uglies for thirty blasted days?"

Mila laughed again. "It has nothing to do with technology, but with common sense. Give your body time to recover naturally. Blood does not regenerate overnight."

Good grief, what a disappointment. "Does RuArk know?"

"Of course he does. He is Gaian. Our men may not quite get the labor part, but they are well schooled in aftercare."

"Really?" Draema had pretty much done away with the whole natural birthing thing. Tech was king, and in this case, Rhia kind of liked it that way. Suddenly, she could almost see him, his presence so near she could have reached out and touched him. What was he doing? Was he wearing one of those skimpy little breech things that showed his fabulously muscular ass? No, too cold outside. Perhaps a pair of wool-lined leather trousers instead, the buckskin ones that fit so perfectly and outlined his backside and calves? Damn, even after all that ungodly pain she was ready to do the thing that made babies all over again.

I must be crazy to want him already.

Mila kept talking, not noticing the somewhat vacant expression in Rhia's eyes as she thought on her husband. Releasing the bond, Rhia tuned into her mother-in-law's words, then wished she hadn't. There were so many suggestions, traditions, rules and advice that Rhia decided to simply take what she needed from the conversation and leave the rest on the table.

The journey back to the refuge of her covers took forever. Winded and very relieved that Mila had insisted on helping her, Rhia settled back in bed. Propped up on pillows, enjoying a spot of coffee, light toast with winterberry jam and her favorite eggs with spicy sausage and peppers mixed into the fluffy dish, Rhia didn't think she'd ever been so content. Mila kissed her on the cheek and went to answer a faint tap at the door, tidying as she went.

"Would you like to join me, father? I could have Lunis direct Cook to send something up here to you?"

"No, thank you. I had breakfast with the little ones this morning," the High Counsel said, beaming.

"How did you have breakfast with the babies? I didn't nurse either of them yet this morning."

Queen Mila answered, "We brought a nurse with us. She recently gave birth, but her babe was born too early and did not survive. She has offered to help with the nursing of the little princelings so you can rest at night."

Rhia felt sorry for the woman's loss of her own child, but that did nothing to quell the fire that erupted behind her eyes. She was immediately jealous.

"I don't particularly like the idea of anyone else feeding my babies."

"Rhia, I know you slept very little last night. Between both children you were awake almost every hour to feed them. If you wish to double your recovery time, then feel free to feed them yourself and you can stay in bed until…"

"Never mind, already." *My husband the tattletale.*
I heard that.
RuArk.

She grimaced, then blinked in wonder. "Mother, is it possible that having kids can make your bond with your lifemate stronger?"

"Strong in what manner?"

"I just heard RuArk in my head, clear as day. It was like he's standing right here."

"It would take an incredibly strong bond, but yes, it is very possible. And that means you'll have to practice keeping your naughty thoughts to yourself."

"Mother!"

"What? Do you think I was any less, as you say, *horny* for my mate than you are for yours?"

"Oh god, I don't even want to imagine that! And I'm glad you're having such a fun time laughing at my expense. Both of you." She glared at her father, who'd settled on the steps of her bed as Mila continued.

"Her name is Rose. She is a bit older than you, but she has a kind spirit and is very easy to get along with. She'll help you in whatever way you require. And by the way, she is sweet, but she is no pushover. I believe RuArk called her a 'veritable dragon' or something along those lines," Mila grinned. "She stands guard over the little ones, not letting anyone get too close. You know, germs and all."

"Fine, she can help, but I won't have anyone trying to replace me as their mother."

The High Counsel exchanged a telling look with Mila. Rhia felt immediately foolish, knowing that she was being a bit too possessive. Mila rubbed some good natured salt into that little wound before she left the room chuckling, leaving a disgruntled Rhia to tear her toast into little angry pieces.

"On second thought, I'll have a cup of this coffee. It smells delicious," her father said, helping himself to the carafe on the night table next to Rhia's bed.

He sat back down near her, propped an elbow on the thick mattress and appeared to take his ease. The quiet soon became a bit uncomfortable. Rhia could tell he wanted, or rather *needed* something. In fact, she needed to talk to him, too. But how to begin?

With a deep breath, the High Counsel jumped into the silence and began a long needed cleansing.

"Rhia, I'm afraid I haven't been a very good father." Plate forgotten, she snapped to full attention.

"Excuse me?"

"I grieved deeply after your mother died. But you were hurting as well. You threw yourself into your duties, I guess to take your mind off of losing your mother. And I let you bury yourself in those duties. I realize now that I rejected you. It may have been unintentional, but rejection is rejection no matter the reason. After a while you stopped asking any questions about her or her people, *your* people. And in my selfishness and grief, I didn't volunteer any answers. I am so, so sorry Rhia."

"Father, you don't have to do this."

"Yes, I do, Rhia. I love you more than anything or anyone in this world. I love you because you are my daughter, not because of anything you do or have done for this province. I do not love you because you filled your mother's shoes, because that simply is not possible."

The words stung. Rhia's spirits flagged. Lowering her lashes in an attempt to hide the pain, she took a sip of coffee, but didn't taste the sweet brew. It settled like bile in her stomach and it was all she could do to keep from throwing up.

It had all been for nothing. She'd become the most skilled warrior in her province, worked herself to death learning and executing the laws of her people. She'd run the blasted place, dammit. And all for absolutely nothing. Her father still didn't see her as the warrior her mother was.

"Rhia, your mother was a magnificent woman, an amazing wife and caring lifemate. She was an unmatched warrior, not only in Draema, but among her own people. Like Sharyn, you know? It's rare for a Gaian female to choose that path, but she was who she was. And you are who you are. You never had to match the image of your mother. You've created your own legacy, your own accomplishments and your own feats of greatness. For lack of better words, you don't need to fill her shoes. You've made your own and you're just as great as the fabulous woman who gave birth to you."

Hugs had never been the High Counsel's preferred method of affection, so it was something Rhia hadn't been the recipient of on a daily basis until she'd joined with RuArk. But those walls had long since crumbled from around her heart and disappeared altogether. RuArk had started the assault on those walls, and now her father had completed it. Rhia reached out for him now and for the first time in almost twenty years he was there for her to touch in body, mind and spirit.

"I love you father."

"And I love you, my little red fox."

"You haven't called me that since I was five or six years old."

"It was because your hair had all those red streaks in it, and your skin as brown as the rarest cinnamon spice. Intellectually, you were pretty sharp at a very young age. But now I should remember that you are not my little red fox anymore. You've grown up into the Fire Storm. You're pretty damn amazing, Rhia Greysomne Miwatani.

"You know, I was proud when your brother Sean

had his children, but Rhia I must say that I am most proud that I was here to greet the new First Heir of Draema, who is also a prince of Gaia. And his baby sister, a princess of both realms. I am so very proud of you."

His expression morphed from relieved to alarmed when a tear slipped down her cheek. "Father, these are tears of joy. I'm just so happy that you and I understand each other. I felt so alone for most of my life thinking that you didn't love me because I wasn't... Well, enough. I do believe I'm the happiest daughter in the world."

"Well, you have your husband to thank for that." Head cocked to one side, Rhia's eyebrow shot up, clearly questioning him on what in the world RuArk had to do with any of this.

"He took me aside when you went into labor and set me straight on a few things. I had to really sit down and think about what our relationship has been like over the years. The more I thought on his words, the less I liked what I saw. I shouldn't have abandoned you to your grief, Rhia. I wasn't there for you and I realize now that you were very much alone. You had Brita and Joan, but that is no replacement for a father. And now that's one thing I'll never worry about."

"What's that?"

"I'll never worry about whether RuArk will be there. I have no doubt he'll take care of you whether you wish it or not. You've met your match, and I'm grateful for that."

"Thanks father," she chuckled. "I think."

CHAPTER FOURTEEN

It just so happened that Rhia's third day of rest, post-partum, fell on New Spring's Eve. At noon, she was up and about after promising, of course, to nap when she needed to rest.

The townsfolk had arrived and the vast courtyards that surrounded the villa were brimming with revelers. There was nothing quite like a New Spring party, but this one had a few *very* special twists.

The first of which, were the two receiving lines—RuArk sat at the head of one for the men, and Rhia sat at one for the women. It was wholly Gaian and nothing she'd ever seen before at a festival of any kind. She was relieved when her mother-in-law accepted an invitation to sit with her.

Besides, it was only proper since Mila was in residence, that she personally present the beautiful sarands Rhia had commissioned from the vast amount of silk the woman had sent over weeks ago. Sitting beneath a large sun sunshade in the middle of the largest courtyard, Rhia greeted every woman, whether Draeman or Gaian, with a genuine smile.

Her heart filled with warmth as one after another expressed gratitude to the Queen of Gaia, who winked as each held the colorful garments up to their bodies. Rhia knew they were imagining what they would look like once they put them on, because she'd done the same on several occasions after receiving one of the lovely outfits.

RuArk presented each man with a well-made dagger and a tunic with the sigil of the Wind embroidered over the left breast—a symbol that they were, indeed, under his Protection. When RuArk had first arrived, the Draeman accepted him because he had the blessing of the High Counsel. Now they accepted him because he'd shown himself to be a man worthy of respect, and they would serve without question.

Rhia shook her head at the strange, yet wonderfulness of it all. These people were Draeman citizens on the edge of their province. Their Council of Seven rep hadn't been through in so long, many didn't even remember what he looked like. Yet here were the elusive Gaian, again showing their hospitality.

The kitchen had outdone itself providing relaxed, but substantial meals for everyone, even those who preferred Draeman engineered synth protein meals. The Houseman had managed to spice up the blandness of the foodstuff, which put the staff firmly in godlike territory as far as Rhia was concerned.

The acres of gardens RuArk ordered installed a cycle ago had yielded abundantly, so there was no need to send to Gaia for all the ingredients they needed. As a result, the feast was the most lavish and decadent the people had ever experienced. They were getting used to seeing some rich Gaian food, but only those who resided, worked, or reported to RuArk in the Protector's home had the fare with any regularity.

Fish from the lake were now freshly baked and

laced with ginger butter. Roasted wild hare and water fowl had such a variety of sauces to choose from that it was impossible to select just one.

The sweet orange-colored squash preserved during the winter had been taken out of the stores, baked and then garnished with mint sprigs and fresh berries. Several roasted yearling calves turned over a spit in the center of the courtyard were constantly surrounded by merrymakers urging the cooking staff to slice the succulent meat faster.

There were loaves of hot crusty bread still warm from the baker's ovens, rolls with honey were piled high on huge platters. Next to them was as array of colorful, fresh greens, crispy and sweet, smothered with a tart and creamy dressing. Pans of crispy noodles tossed in a kind of sweet and sour spice sat next to trays of meat pies filled with duck, chickpeas, carrots, potatoes, onion and savory broth.

Rhia had deferred to Joan on the desserts, and the woman's choices were beyond addictive. She'd had the bakers deliver fruitcakes soaked in lemon liqueur, shortcake drizzled with hot butter and a dollop of winterberry jam, and Gaian coffee laced with dark chocolate rounded out the desserts. The children received hot chocolate and sweets of hardened spun sugar made into little trees, animals and tiny sigils of both Draema and Gaia in every color imaginable. They quickly became a favorite of the kidlets who wished to be just like their Protector and First Heir.

The warriors stationed inside the township rode to the outer walls and delivered goodies to their comrades on guard duty so no one was left out of the festivities.

All the townsfolk mingled together with no care that some of them were Draeman and some were from the land of Gaia across the river. Celebrating well into the night, the courtyard emptied slowly, each person returning to their home with high spirits and a lighter, though somewhat wobbly, step.

The following morning was the traditional exchanging of the gifts. Rhia rose early, threw on a morning suit and robe and after their feeding, scooped up the twins. RuArk was already breaking his fast, standing in front of the fireplace near the high table when she arrived. He sipped a steaming cup of coffee and held another out for her.

RuArk relieved her of their daughter and rubbed his face against a chubby cheek. Gurgling in response to her father's attention, Relaina Grey grabbed a fistful of his long black hair and promptly stuffed it into her mouth. Rhia smiled at the tender scene. RuArk dropped a kiss on Taté Icamna's forehead as they turned both babies over to their caregiver, Rose.

Sharing a plate, they sat at the high table. Speaking quietly to one another, they watched their friends and family make their way into the hall. Almost every one of them headed directly for the coffee carafes to pour a healthy cup and not bothering with sweetener or crème.

"I think there may have been a bit more liqueur in those desserts than expected," RuArk whispered with a wicked grin.

Rhia snapped her gaze to her husband's. "Did you…?" He winked. She gaped. "You did that on purpose? Seriously?" He said nothing. Instead, he simply raised his cup with a wink and took a sip of the steaming brew.

Marth plopped down in the seat opposite RuArk.

"I believe I should have left my head upstairs with

my lifemate," he groaned, took a gulp of his coffee, and then rested his forehead daintily in his hands.

"Marth, I don't believe I have ever seen you with elbows on the table, head in your hands and utterly miserable," RuArk chided.

Marth grumbled. "Your voice is as loud as that bloody train that runs through the eastern Neine."

RuArk laughed even louder and Rhia stifled a giggle as Marth lapsed into a round of pitiful groaning.

"Perhaps you should give up your swords and take up gardening. Flowers are nice and quiet," Rhia said. Marth turned toward Rhia and tried to scowl, but he couldn't get his facial muscles to cooperate. He settled for a low growl instead.

"Speaking of life mates, when is Linc going to join with Sharyn?" RuArk asked.

"Your cousin, Sharyn, is the most stubborn Miwatani alive, and that includes you, RuArk."

"Well," Rhia chimed in, "he's been wooing her relentlessly."

"Hopefully Linc's gift is impressive enough to move her to say yes. Finally."

"Speaking of gifts, isn't it time?" Rhia asked.

"Indeed." RuArk stood and signaled to Lunis, who then signaled to a Houseman closest to the door. A moment later, a loud gong-like sound filled the room. Rhia knew the same sound was ringing throughout the villa. It usually rang five minutes before main meals, but today it signaled gift giving time.

Moments later, the last of their family and Household, with their mates and children streamed in and took their seats. This was a very private affair. Rhia knew that across the river, the rest of their family was doing the exact same thing — honoring one another with gifts of love.

Linc escorted Queen Mila and Sharyn, along with Joan, Brita, Drefan, Dalmore, Osgar and several other bleary-eyed folks.

When the Housemen brought in box after box, Rhia sat…and sat, and sat as her eyes got wider and wider. Her father, who had come in and taken the chair next to her, winked devilishly.

No wonder there weren't any goodies for me in the things that arrived weeks ago.

There were endless packages and containers to open and every single one was for her and the new babies! The notes and little tags showed that the Grandfather, numerous aunts, uncles, cousins and other members of Clan Miwatani had all sent their love.

She received several sets of linens for summer and warm soft silks for winter. She crooned over leather leggings with matching tunics, boots and vests — some silk-lined and some fur-lined to accommodate the weather. And the cloaks with special pockets in the lining for her weapons to be concealed were to die for. Now who had thought of that?

The gifts for the children were just as amazing. Not one cradle, but *two*, hand carved, polished and engraved with their sigils. There were beaded soft leather shoes, tiny buckskin leggings and shirts in all shades of soft blue, yellow, white, green, gray and pink. Then came the tiny silk undershirts, tightly woven cotton bibs, warm hats, wraps and such. There were so many outfits, clothes and toys for the children that Rhia wondered how she would get them to wear it all, play with it all, and chew on it all before they were ten cycles old. Rhia turned to her mother-in-law in awe.

"How did you know we were having two babies, a

girl and a boy?"

"The Grandfather told us."

That should have been no surprise. The man knew everything.

Marth gave Joan a pendant of the clearest, most beautiful pink diamond set inside a loop of cleverly intertwined silver and gold strands, and hung on a thin rope of gold.

In true suitor-in-pursuit-of-warrior-mate fashion, Linc gifted Sharyn with a new bow, wrist guards and a quiver of arrows designed especially for her. The bow was carved of spirewood, a rare tree found only in the northernmost forests of Gaia. It was light and pliable, but incredibly strong and durable. The bowstring was crafted of the thinnest, most flexible steel cord Rhia had ever seen. This would eliminate the need for concern if caught fighting in wet weather.

The quiver was fashioned from oiled leather. It was full, but still somewhat smaller and lighter than the one she presently carried. They all wondered why until Sharyn began to remove the arrows—they were made of hollowed, brushed Draeman steel and were thinner and shorter than her traditional wooden arrows.

Remarkably, these arrows could fly a much farther distance and she could carry more of them. The vivid burgundy feathers set into the ends, the colors of the house of O'dann, were coated with a clear, almost undetectable finish to protect them from the elements.

The most unexpected present was Marth and Linc's parents who'd arrived just in time for the exchange, along with Joan's parents who'd come from the High City to surprise their daughter and meet their new son-in-law.

Rhia nervously presented RuArk with his gift—a

hand sewn white buckskin shirt, with beadwork done in the traditional blue hues of Clan Miwatani, along with the subtle grays of his house.

"I understand the time and effort it takes to make something like this. So I have one question, Rhia — between running the estate, learning the Gaian customs, and training any and all who wished to learn the skill of the blade, when in the world did you have time to do something like this?"

"A woman has her secrets," she mused. Then he kissed her soundly in front of all their close friends and family, which caused a raucous cheer.

"Well, one good turn deserves another," he said with a wink and a devilish smile.

From the warrior who had once forbidden her to wear anything but the sarand, she now received the finest and most beautifully made fighting gear and workout clothes done in a cross of the Draeman and Gaian styles. Her man had style and she recognized the quality that went into each and every piece.

And it was all for her.

By the time he placed the final two packages in her hands she was in tears, overwhelmed by the generosity of this fierce, yet tender man. One box contained a finely wrought gold ring with an ancient Gaian blessing engraved on the inside. On the outside, instead of the sigil of the Wind Storm, RuArk had created a swirling combination of lines and symbols that brought together the Wind Storm and the Fire Storm to create a new sigil symbolizing the gathering of the Storms.

He slipped the ring on her finger and waited. Rhia sat down heavily in a chair and just looked at her hand for long moments.

"It's feminine, yet sturdy, just like you. Do you like

it?"

When she could take her eyes off the ring, she stood and kissed her husband on the cheek, but still said nothing. There were no words that fit what she was feeling—the piece symbolized the intertwining of their lives. Her father had been right from the very beginning—she would never be alone as long as RuArk had breath in his body.

"I'll take that as a yes?" he queried.

She nodded dumbly as he took her hands and placed the final gift into her trembling fingers.

This last box contained a dagger wrought of the finest hardened black steel. At first glance, it looked identical to her mother's, which she always carried. When she looked a little closer, the saw that the forging and style of the weapons were unique enough that she could tell them apart.

"This was made for you, my love. While you may look like your wonderful mother, you are not her," RuArk said. "You are yourself, your own woman, and I love everything about you. I hope that you can leave the past behind and move forward into a future of your own making."

She looked up, throat clogged with tears, and whispered, "No. A future of *our* making."

She got it. She truly knew what he'd been trying to show her all along. She was Rhia. No one else. There was no need to try to emulate anyone else. She was respected and loved simply because she was herself. And that was enough.

She removed her mother's dagger from the little sheath that was always strapped around her thigh. She held it up to the light and examined the expertly crafted blade. The hilt, beautifully inlaid with gold and silver, was somewhat worn now. She stood and turned to her father with shimmering eyes and a watery smile. She took his hand and presented her mother's blade to the High Counsel.

"She would want you to have this, Father. For a long time, it was my link to her, my way of reaching out to her so I wouldn't feel so alone. But I'm not alone anymore. She would want you to live again. As you begin to do so, remember her with fondness. Not with grief."

Wrapped in her father's arms, hot tears ran down her cheeks—a mix of her own and his. It was a bittersweet moment that she would remember forever.

Once back in her seat, RuArk took her hand and gave an affectionate squeeze, but in his eyes were unspoken promises of things to come as soon as her time of recovery from the birthing was done.

At the calls of cheer that circled the room, Taté Icamna would not be left out of the festivities. From their cradle near the high table, Relaina Grey slumbered but her brother let out a rafter-shaking wail that declared a feeding would happen *now* and the rest of New Spring be damned.

The three-day celebration had gone off without a hitch and, once again, everyone headed home. Thankfully, the weather was cooperating nicely for those who had to travel. Though it was somewhat chilly in the early hours, there was very little wind. A late night rain had fallen and morning dawned with clear blue skies.

Evidence of the new season spread quickly. Lush

green fields and newly budding trees were abundant, just as they'd been when they'd arrived at this same time last spring.

Marth and Linc's parents had instantly loved Joan and they'd all gotten along splendidly. Now, all the Gaian in-laws were packed up and ready for the trip across the river to RuArk's private home at Wind Song. From there, the King and Queen would go to the high seat of Miwatan to the east, while the O'dann's would ride for their home in the Plains to the northeast.

The High Counsel and Joan's parents headed for the train depot in central Draema Neine for their ride back to the High City. RuArk sent two fireteams with them to make sure they cleared the passes down out of the mountains safely. New Spring may have been a fabulous affair, but he had not forgotten the threat that loomed over Rhia's life. While it had been strangely quiet for months, he didn't believe for a second that the danger had simply faded to nothing.

CHAPTER FIFTEEN

The main hall was full of early risers eager to get about their daily training exercises. RuArk enjoyed his, and now Rhia's, favorite breakfast of fresh, light, honey-soaked rolls, fluffy eggs and spicy poultry sausage.

As he dined, his mind drifted back to the woman he'd left sleeping upstairs.

A powerful squall had blown through and it seemed as if the very sky had opened up and decided to drown them all. For the past several weeks, there had been nothing but deluge after deluge. Strange, considering that the transition from spring to summer usually brought storms that were short and mild.

He'd been sensing something with his Gift, but couldn't pin it down. Something definitely niggled at the back of his mind. As much as he longed to see his wife and children, he hoped that they were already asleep so he could step into the Dream and seek out the Grandfather. Perhaps his elder could give him some guidance in this situation.

RuArk climbed the staircase dead tired after helping his men clear the roads and trails of numerous fallen trees. He thought on Rhia as he opened the door to their apartments and stepped silently into the darkened living room. It was amazing having a bond with a woman as complex as she was loving. Though she was still stubborn as all creation, she hid nothing of herself like before.

He knew when he'd unwittingly hurt her feelings or pleased her without her saying a word. At times, he could literally hear her. He also knew if she was engaged in something that she probably shouldn't be... like taking Drefan's boat across the river to Gaia when she had no idea how to sail it. He shook his head and grinned at that one.

Weary and in need of a bath, he leaned against the door to their apartments, his back resting against the solid threshold. Eyes closed, he relaxed for a moment as his thoughts filled with Rhia. Though he considered her his own precious jewel, just two months ago, she'd given him the most wondrous gift – a son and a daughter.

Suddenly the bond flared and RuArk physically jerked away from the door as if he'd been scalded. A rush of blood flooded his cock as lust fired through the synapses of his brain. Rhia was far from asleep. In fact, she beckoned him now with the most seductive thoughts she could muster and he felt every one of them.

RuArk stripped as he moved toward the bathing room, leaving a trail of soaking wet clothing in his wake.

"Come to me now. I'll warm you up."

Changing direction, he dropped his breech at the bedroom door. The Grandfather could wait until tomorrow...

Suddenly a commotion echoed in the hallway, yanking him out of his more pleasant thoughts. Damn it.

"I must see the lord of the manor right now! Out of the way, you blasted tree! I'm a Draeman soldier and can go where I please!"

The voice was unfamiliar. Several gazes left their breakfast and eyebrows rose, along with quite a few bodies. RuArk had no need to rise, but his lip did lift into a proud grin as warriors and their Draeman counterparts, who were almost a foot shorter than his men, made their way out of the hall side by side.

It immediately grew quiet. Too quiet.

He had an appointment with the Grandfather that couldn't be missed. First, he had to get to the little spot he'd found where Rhia wouldn't walk in on him. If she knew he'd been walking the *Dream* in pursuit of the Dreadlord, she would try her best to string him up for not including her.

Whatever was going on just now might make it difficult to get where he needed to be, unseen. Growling inwardly at the thought while watching the time, he waited.

Moments later, Ewan, Osgar, Dalmore and Drefan entered. Between them was a Draeman soldier who appeared somewhat pale.

RuArk remained in his seat until the man stood before him. He looked like no Draeman RuArk had ever seen. The province had been a safe haven of people after the Breaking with a population that had mixed so much, they long ago began to look as if they were one race rather than several.

According to the histories, hair and eyes in a wide variety of browns was the norm for the last two hundred years. This man was all flaming red hair and a beard to match, with vivid green eyes that stood out in his smooth, fine boned face. No scratches or scars made RuArk wonder if the boy had ever been in a fight.

"What is your name?" asked RuArk.

"My name is Larel Kohn. What's yours?" snapped the young man. "Better yet, Gaian, stop asking me questions and get the Council of Seven rep for Province

Springs."

"Council of Seven?" RuArk asked quietly, not bothering to hide his surprise. "Who?"

"Yes, Council of Seven. I was given no name and no details on who was to receive the High Counsel's message. I was only given a title and told that he was the husband of the First Heir, Rhia Greysomne."

RuArk went still as stone. Setting his napkin down on the table, he met Larel's gaze and let the cold anger simmering just beneath the surface, shine brightly. "I believe I can help you with that, Larel."

"Good. This business is urgent, so if you could move a little faster, I would appreciate it." The little whelp's insolent roll of his eyes said otherwise. Who the hells was this man, and what did he *really* want? The High Counsel would not send such an ass to engage RuArk. And what was this Council of Seven rep business? The rep didn't have a residence here in Province Springs anymore.

Then again, a new soldier might be less likely to be in on a plot to remove Rhia from her rightful place. So just maybe…

"What is your rank, Larel?"

"I have just made First Blade three days ago. This is my first assignment for the Society of War in the High Counsel's service."

Ah, well that explained the arrogance. All young men believed themselves invincible at this age. He should know given the number of times he'd attempted to fly when he should have still been crawling.

"As you say, I'm Gaian…"

"You don't sound Gaian."

"I'm well-traveled," RuArk said, and then let silence hang in the air a moment. His men followed his lead and kept quiet and alert. "As I was saying, I am Gaian and while I'm familiar with your province, I've never seen features quite like yours before."

The young man's hair was such a fiery shade it looked as if it were on fire.

"My parents came from the northeast, across the sea, when I was just old enough to start kinderschool. I have no Draeman blood in me, but thankfully, Draema welcomes all." The last was said with a nasty snarl.

Larel obviously had more on his mind, so RuArk took a sip of coffee, sat back in his chair and crossed his ankles. "Please, continue."

The men who'd previously surrounded Larel dispersed, some to strategic points around the room and others back to their tables to continue eating.

"History says that the Gaian wouldn't share their knowledge with us. The best and most experienced of Draeman Blademasters were turned away when seeking to learn from them. It's hard to admit, but I'm having a difficult time dealing with the fact that Province Springs is overrun with...*your* kind."

So, they'd come to the crux of it—good old fashioned prejudice. The young soldier's gaze traveled from Gaian warrior to Draeman solider. Each word had been said through a sneer, as if they all reeked of horse shit.

The Gaian were often misjudged, their desire to keep to their own, except for trade, often seen as arrogance rather than a true commitment to their ways. Although Rhia's mother was Gaian, she'd left her homeland to join with the High Counsel. Right here in Province Springs was the first time since the Breaking that there was truly a blending of Draeman and Gaian. Not just a joining in marriage, but scores of different people actually living, working and training together.

RuArk's people were already familiar with Draeman customs, or lack thereof. Though unbending in their beliefs and practices, they shared with those in Province Springs freely. It was an extension of their own home simply because the Protector was here.

Okay, so maybe his people were a bit arrogant, but they were second to none in any case.

RuArk hoped that this boy's disdain for all things Gaian was not so ingrained that he wasn't willing to learn about those he had come to hate.

"My kind?" RuArk stood, slowly and with grave purpose. "Interesting choice of words. But while we're in a sharing mood, I am RuArk Miwatani, second son to the King of Gaia and Protector of the Realm. Some call me Wind Storm." Larel's jaw dropped. "Others call me lifemate to Rhia Greysomne, and the man to whom the High Counsel has sent you."

The blood drained from the young man's face. He blushed until his face was as red as his hair.

"But the High Counsel said Council of Seven rep..."

"Did he now?" RuArk asked.

"Well, no. But I assumed... I-I apologize, sir. I truly meant no disrespect."

"Of course you did. I will be sure to inform the High Counsel of your lack of courtesy and common sense. Or... Perhaps I should summon the First Heir? I am sure she can give you a lesson or two in manners. Oh, wait, she's not good enough to teach you anything. I'm sure you despise her."

The fire returned to Larel's eyes as he said, "Of course I don't despise her. She's one of the greatest commanders the Society of War has ever seen. I've observed her classes. She's magnificent! I haven't had the privilege of stepping into the circle with the First Heir. No one ranked lower than First Blade is even allowed to participate in any of her training. Still, I just don't see why she couldn't marry one of her own."

"Yet she is half Gaian, so I *am* one of her own. Do you despise her now? Your answer should be interesting considering you are not Draeman either, yet I doubt there would be a problem if she'd married *you*." Words deceptively calm, RuArk seethed, just waiting for this pup to say one disrespectful word about Rhia.

"No! I mean yes. That's not what I mean. Why would we give an entire township to the people who've refused hospitality to the Draeman since the Breaking?"

"We have refused hospitality, you say? Were you awake during your history lessons in kinderschool? How do you think the High Counsel himself was able to marry a Gaian woman? Did she miraculously appear in the High City? Did the Sensuan you enjoy, who are all Gaian, just *poof* themselves into Draema?

"The nonsense you spout gives proof of your lack of knowledge of the customs of the Gaian, therefore your feelings are understandable. However, they do *not* excuse your conduct toward me or my men. Our cultures have never had a strained relationship, simply one that respects my people's desire to walk the ways of our Ancestors.

"Friendship has always been solid between our leaders. The house of my Fathers has been in covenant with the High Counsels of your land since before the Breaking of the world. Perhaps you should spend more time studying and less time running headlong into stone walls. It causes brain damage."

Larel's mouth opened and closed, but nothing

came out. Good. He'd said enough for one day as far as RuArk was concerned. He only wanted one more thing from Larel. "Now, my young asshole, deliver your message and we will see about 'hospitality' after."

Larel stiffened his spine, his mouth compressed into a thin line. For long moments, he said nothing.

Finally, he took a long, deep breath and released it on a slow, even sigh. "I will accept whatever judgment you deem fair. It was wrong of me to allow my personal feelings to interfere with my duty. I will accept the consequences of my actions, sir."

RuArk nodded sternly as he held Larel's gaze. He allowed his anger to seep away, knowing typical young male ambition and hot headedness when he saw it. Other than his fine features and slim build, young Larel reminded RuArk of himself when he'd just received his first rank of significance—overconfident and amazingly naïve about himself, his people and the world around him.

Larel reached into the inner pocket of his traveling coat and retrieved a small metal-looking case. He handed it to RuArk.

"It's encoded. The High Counsel said to simply say *'matted hair'* to you and you would know the password.

RuArk chuckled. *Good one, Grey. Very good indeed.*

He took a few steps away from Larel, flipped open the little tablet and tapped in the code—*bird shit.* The screen flashed bright blue then faded to a steely gray as words began to appear.

"It's from the High Counsel," Larel said. "I rode as fast as I could. I even took the train to the Neine border, then rode by..."

RuArk raised his hand for silence, reading the High Counsel's note

His expression grim, mouth and brows tightly drawn, he turned to Linc and Marth who had quietly joined him. "So it begins. We ride at dawn," he said, striding away, handing the High Counsel's note to Marth as he headed out of the hall.

He stopped at the threshold and turned. His tone was stone cold. "None of you are to tell Rhia about any of this. It is for her safety and nothing comes before the safety of my woman. What you heard here stays here. All of you will meet me in the pasture on the other side of the township on the far side of the lake. Pack to ride fast and light. Even your fellow warriors are not to be told. Am I understood?"

Every man in the hall nodded, even Larel who couldn't possibly be sure what had just happened.

"Osgar, send word across the river to the men patrolling our southern borders. Have them quietly cross into Draema to the east and meet us on the western border of the High City. I will meet with you later to take care of the issue of my mate."

Osgar gave RuArk a lopsided grin knowing that Rhia would probably be more of a challenge than whatever he'd seen in the High Counsel's note.

"Lunis and Brita will have to be told, as we will need their help in gathering supplies. We must know what we can take and what must stay here. Swear them to secrecy. And neither Joan or Sharyn can know." The O'dann twins looked at each other then back at RuArk. "Look, I know what I'm asking of you, but if either of those two women have any idea of what's being planned, Rhia will know mere moments later."

Turning to his unexpected guest, RuArk said, "Larel, I will ask my questions of you in private. Ewan will bring you to my office in one hour. You will dine with my mate and me tonight, however, in the meantime, have some breakfast. Ewan see to our guest, please."

CHAPTER SIXTEEN

RuArk ran up the stairs two at a time, stopping on the third floor to check in on Rhia. Thankfully, she was still asleep. He left their apartments as quietly as he'd entered.

After the Noman attack that had almost taken his life, RuArk had poured over the architectural designs of the various structures in the township. He'd learned of some interesting little bolt holes in the villa, and he made his way to one of them now. On the fourth floor was a small room at the very end of the hallway. He ducked inside and strode quickly through another door at the rear of the room, closed it firmly behind him and armed the wall lock.

He retrieved a tall, sturdy ladder that had been tucked in a closet and propped it against the doorjamb, and then climbed quickly to the top. He pushed against one of the large tiles on the ceiling, but it didn't give way. Putting more of his strength behind the shove, the tile creaked loudly, showering him with a fine coating of dust. Finally, it gave way and revealed a dark entrance to a safety room—a place where one could go if the villa came under attack and there was no way out of the building.

Climbing up quickly, he pulled the ladder behind him and slid the tile back into place. He then lay down, closed his eyes, and settled in to wait for the Grandfather to summon him into the *Dream*.

"Grandfather, a messenger arrived from the High City not long ago. Rhia's father calls for aid. Councilman Rama Collaidh is behind the treachery against Rhia and himself."

"What has become of Collaidh?" asked the shimmering form of the Grandfather.

"The High Counsel says that he escaped Draema only to return with an army of mercenaries from the east. Noman are also with them. How Collaidh can control packs of Noman, I have no idea. Grey doesn't know if others are aiding Collaidh from within Draema Proper."

"We believe it is the Dreadlord that both Ricard Shae and Bryan Collaidh mentioned before they died."

"Perhaps, but I do know that the High Counsel is in danger of being overthrown and expects the City to come under siege any day now. Somehow he's managed to keep the situation quiet. Even the rider who delivered the message was unaware of the danger."

"What will you do?"

"I'll answer his call. Things are already in motion."

"I expected nothing less of you, grandson. What of Rhia?"

"She doesn't know, and I will keep it that way if I can."

"Something does not feel right about all of this, grandson. Are you sure the message was from the High Counsel and not another ruse?"

"I am sure of it. He included phrases that only he and I have shared. No one else would know the meaning of them."

"Keep in mind that if the High Counsel is under siege, someone may be coming for Rhia as well. Or the little princelings. You must keep them safe at all costs, RuArk."

"Rhia would try to go with me. This is why I have not, and will not tell her that I ride for the Citadel at first light. I would send her and the children to you, but she would want to know why I wasn't coming with her. And to her, I cannot lie. Not only because it is not honorable, but because our bond would tell her."

"Your mother's Gift of Foreknowledge showed her that she must come for your twins, but she learned nothing else. She only saw little Tate and Relaina Grey in her arms. She was sitting in the Hall of Miwatan next to your father, the King, and knew that your children were with her there. The Gift impressed upon her an importance that it be so, yet did not reveal the reasons. She does not know why she must come to you, nor does she know that you are in danger; only that it is imperative that she do so. She left Miwatan from the harbor at Wind Song early this morning. She is on her way across the river now, and will be there by midday."

"What reason will she give Rhia? My woman will not simply pack up our children to go across the river to Gaia with no explanation!"

"She will simply say that she missed her grandchildren and has come to get them so Rhia can have some rest for a few days. Now, as for your bond with your lifemate, I am sure it is quite strong by now."

"It is. What can I do?"

"There is a way to conceal the bond for a short while. However, if she concentrates on the bond at the correct moment, she will know that you have gone."

"Not if I leave while she's asleep. The children have been keeping her up late, so it's no surprise for her to rise a couple of hours later than usual." RuArk began to seriously plot. *"I*

can also leave instructions that she is to work with the men on weaponless fighting. She will believe that I am simply busy with duties. And now that she's received permission from the Physicians to get back to her regular schedule, she'll be happy for the opportunity to throw warriors around the courtyard that she probably won't think of me all day."

"You had better ask the Ancestors to help you when she finds out you've gone without her."

"Trust me, Grandfather, I have already asked them. Now, what of this Dreadlord?"

"Listen, grandson, he is involved with this plot. I can sense it when I follow him through the Dream. If Collaidh has Noman with him, it is possible that this man is controlling them as part of the bargain."

"How? It's unheard of?"

"They will follow him simply because he is one of them. They are a wild, untamed lot and because this Dreadlord is somehow learned, it is enough to make him appear almost a god in their eyes. Listen closely to what the Realmwalkers have learned of this dark anomaly who, believe it or not, appears to be half human."

"What?!" Shock was too tame a word to describe the explosion in RuArk's brain. Half human? Impossible. Yet, in the past cycle he'd been in Province Springs, he'd learned of plenty of other impossibilities, so perhaps… "How do you know?"

"Azel took a Healer who specializes in detecting energies, into the Dream with him. This Noman who walks the Dream has no shields to speak of."

"Ah, now we get to the heart of the matter. He knows just enough to be dangerous. He can walk other Realms, like the Dream, but has no idea how to protect himself from other Gifted."

"Exactly," the Grandfather said. "This Healer has

studied Noman over the cycles."

RuArk nodded at his Elder's words. *It was well known in Gaia that Noman were often caught outside of their territory while hunting. It wasn't unheard of for a warrior to bring a wounded or dying Noman to the Healers for study. It's how they knew their enemy's weaknesses and strengths. It's also how they knew it should be impossible for one to touch the Source.*

"This Healer slipped into the Dreadlord's consciousness undetected and discovered this man's brain chemistry is just a bit different than other Noman. He is, as it was explained to me, 'wired' more like a human, which means his depth of emotion and spirituality are greater than his kin."

"So what are you saying, Grandfather?"

"Touching one's Source requires a bit of faith as well as the ability to direct one's own energy and accepting that of another. The typical Noman brain is too chaotic for such things. However, this particular Noman, the Dreadlord, is a perfect mix of feral madness and brilliance."

"So," RuArk replied, *"like I said, just enough to be dangerous."*

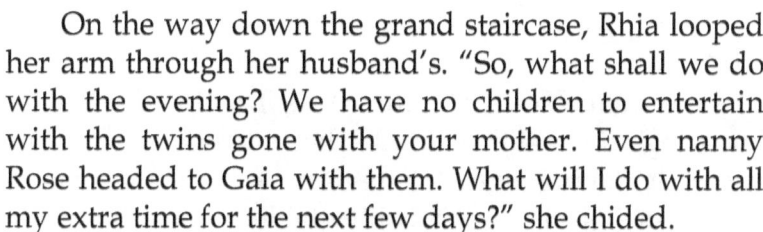

On the way down the grand staircase, Rhia looped her arm through her husband's. "So, what shall we do with the evening? We have no children to entertain with the twins gone with your mother. Even nanny Rose headed to Gaia with them. What will I do with all my extra time for the next few days?" she chided.

"Would you like me to start by telling you all the places I plan to kiss you, or shall we skip the meal altogether and find out right now?" RuArk stopped dead and reached for her. There was no way to miss the familiar stormy seas that began to churn in his gorgeous gray eyes. If he got his hands on her, they would indeed miss dinner.

That's what you get for teasing a wolf.

His hand shot out to pull her into a strong embrace, but she'd already turned and fled down the last few stairs. She looked back at him and grinned as she stepped over the threshold of the main hall.

Shortly after being seated, Rhia was introduced to a new graduate of the Society of War, Larel. He'd just arrived from the High City this morning to begin his first assignment in Province Springs. The man looked at her with an expression of adoration and awe. He even sank to one knee, kissed her hand, and proceeded to stutter all over a simple "honored to meet you."

Rhia stifled a giggle at her husband's attempt and utter failure to not roll his eyes.

"Perhaps I should have taken an ugly duck as lifemate. Then all my men would still be loyal to me rather than in love with you," he said under his breath with a smile.

"Yes, but if you'd taken an ugly duck as lifemate you would have a mouth full of prickly feathers to kiss instead of my silky thighs."

"And you have let your inner-witch out to play, eh?"

She chuckled at RuArk's frustrated breath, knowing that she caused the current discomfort currently taking over the region of his cock. Just to make sure he was as uncomfortable as possible, Rhia boldly reached under the long tablecloth to find the bulge in his trousers.

"Just wanted to make sure you were all there, *dear*," she said with a smile so sugary sweet, it was enough to season a month's worth of confections. RuArk growled and moved her hand away. She grinned some more.

Through the meal, Rhia noticed that when Larel was asked about how things were in the High City, he deftly, though nervously, stole a quick look at RuArk before he halfway answered her questions.

Tonight, the children had the honor of singing to the Protector and First Heir during dessert in honor of the Solstice. She whispered to her husband as they filed silently into the great hall.

"Larel seems quite nervous, RuArk. Have you threatened to eat the young man?"

"I actually prefer Cook's sour sprout rolls to eating poor Larel. However, I did threaten to make him spend the night with the warriors in the barracks all by himself if he said anything to upset you."

He was smiling at her, yet his expression seemed somewhat strained. She'd barely noticed it at first, but it was there, just around the eyes.

"RuArk, is everything alright?"

"Yes, of course."

She didn't buy it. Instead of pressing him for an explanation that she knew wouldn't be forthcoming, Rhia looked away.

Wish I could read his blasted mind sometimes.

Ready to relish a scorched-caramel pudding, the spoon stopped half-way to her mouth. Rhia had invoked their bond, but nothing happened. Forcing herself to hide her utter shock, she forced the treat past her lips, but didn't taste the sweet creamy dish one bit.

This time, she enhanced the bond with her Source, opened herself to it and… nothing.

She concentrated so hard it seemed as if her insides sweated, as though she was zapped with an iozene charge. Yet, there was no RuArk in the little corner of her mind.

"What the hells is going on?" she whispered through gritted teeth.

He tilted his head, appearing perplexed.

"Rhia? What's wrong?"

She opened her mouth to ask RuArk if he could feel their bond, but changed her mind. It wouldn't do to let him know that she'd been probing in the first place.

"Rhia?" he repeated.

"Uh, nothing."

Even after she'd stopped trying to invoke her lifemate bond and released her Source, the little hairs on the back of her neck danced wildly and the skin on her arms began to prickle. It was a sensation she knew well—someone very close to her was touching their own Source.

She looked around at who was near. RuArk chatted with Lunis, who had come to make sure that all was well with the meal. Sharyn stood in her typical spot at RuArk's back. Marth, Linc, and the rest of the high-ranking warriors and soldiers were seated around the large table enjoying coffee, wine, dessert or whatever suited their fancy.

What reason could any of them possibly have to use their Gifts during dinner?

She looked toward RuArk again. His attention was firmly on the little children who had come to sing for them. When he turned, her questioning gaze clashed with his concerned one. She glanced away and wondered what in the hells was going on.

RuArk felt Rhia reach for their bond even as she attempted to pass discrete glances his way. He hated making her worry, but he had to know if the Grandfather's instruction on how to hide the bond worked. As he touched his Source, he appeared to be fully engage with the children singing so beautifully. Yet if someone had asked him what they sang, he couldn't have answered.

He hadn't realized how strong Rhia had become. He must remember to thank Sharyn for her consistent lessons to his mate. It took a considerable amount of effort to keep the barrier in place as Rhia pushed against it, concentrating with all her strength to get through to the bond.

The Grandfather had said that it would get easier with practice, but right now all of RuArk's energy went to his shields.

After a few minutes she appeared to give up, but he didn't release his Source just in case she decided to try again. All of the men leaving at dawn were hiding their bonds as well. Their mates must believe their bonds were broken or at least faulty if they were going to get out of Province Springs undetected.

RuArk stood and held out his hand to Rhia and bid their comrades goodnight. He looked down at her as they climbed the staircase to their apartments.

Amazing. I'm the Protector of the Realm, a warlord of Gaia and Draema, yet I must tiptoe around like a boy sneaking a sweet from underneath Rhia's nose.

He laughed out loud. An image popped into his head of himself, almost seven feet of speed, power and solid muscle, sneaking through the halls in the dark, with a sweet in his hand. He laughed harder, just couldn't help it.

"Do tell," Rhia said dryly.

Rather than attempt to skirt around a question he couldn't answer, RuArk swept her off her feet and covered her face with lavish kisses as he moved quickly toward their rooms.

CHAPTER SEVENTEEN

Rhia awoke and stretched languorously. Eyes still closed, she sighed contentedly and thought back on the ferocity with which she and RuArk had made love the night before. She had been her usual untamed self, while RuArk had been wild and feral–almost desperate. Taking. Demanding. Driving her to madness. She must have fainted–she certainly didn't remember falling asleep.

Where was RuArk? She reached out for the bond again, hoping that she would have better luck than last night. Still nothing. Just a strange mist-filled void.

She rose, broke her fast and headed for Sharyn's apartments only to be caught first by Osgar. He handed her a list of things RuArk wanted her to do. As she read it, her eyebrows rose higher and higher as her mouth dropped open.

Her mate wanted her to work out with the warriors on weaponless fighting? He hated it when she insisted on working out with those giants, so why would he change his mind? She turned to Osgar who had an answer at the ready.

"Ewan has been training the warriors, but he has

gone with RuArk and cannot instruct them today. You are the best at the business so he wishes you to take over for today."

"Really?" She eyed him suspiciously. "And exactly where is RuArk?"

"He has duties outside the walls, in the buffer zone." With that, Osgar nodded smartly, turned and walked away, leaving an open-mouthed Rhia to stare dumbly after him. Her surprise didn't last long. She tore back up the stairs to change into her workout clothes and meet the men in the courtyard.

The day began and ended with a flurry of activity. Rhia had been so busy she'd missed her daily lessons with Sharyn and Joan.

A nice hot soak before dinner was just the thing. Hoping RuArk would join her she lingered awhile and let the sweat and tension of the day melt away. She awoke in a pool of chilled water, shivering as she climbed out. Why hadn't RuArk awakened her? Surely he'd made his way to their apartments by now? It was full evening and her stomach rumbled, reminding her that it was time for dinner.

Wrapped in a cream and pale gray sarand, Rhia's brow furrowed. It had been a busy day, indeed, but not so busy that she shouldn't have seen RuArk at least once.

Sitting at the head table alone, Rhia motioned to Lunis to join her.

"Where's RuArk? I know he was outside the walls, something to do with the land bridge. But he should be back by now."

Lunis' feet began a slow sideways shuffle as he looked over every minute detail of his slender fingers, inspecting them down to the quick for any sign of dirt.

He didn't meet her eyes when he said, "Sorry, my lady. I'm afraid he hasn't sent word. Please excuse me. I need to check on dessert." He hurried away.

Strange.

Surely her failure last night was a fluke. Perhaps she'd just been tired? Besides, she'd never tried to touch the bond while RuArk sat right next to her. Maybe it didn't work when the person you were bonded with was so close? She knew she was reaching, but there had to be some kind of explanation.

Okay, it's bond linking time.

She tried. And tried again. Nothing. The awareness of her husband was simply gone.

Rhia was alone—something that both RuArk and her father promised she would never experience again as long as RuArk had breath in his body. Had they been wrong? If so, what else had they been wrong about?

And why did the absence of awareness of her warrior bother her so, when she'd gone without it all her life? Why did RuArk's absence from the evening meal make her feel like a widow who would spend the rest of her days bereft?

This is ridiculous. I've taken care of myself far longer than I care to remember. Have I become so dependent on that blasted man that I can't get through one day without knowing where he is?

But Rhia knew it wasn't dependence on RuArk. It was love—love for the man and the comfort and companionship he offered. He was her stability, her gravity. Her mate, plain and simple.

Could she do without him? Probably. But did she want to? Hells no.

Inwardly scolding herself, Rhia tried to relax. After

all, RuArk was a busy man. He was responsible for the protection of all of Gaia as well as this part of Draema Neine. It was not uncommon for him to spend days away with his men, checking in with those across the river and rotating troops.

So why did she feel so miserably apprehensive about his absence?

What if the Noman had attacked him while outside the walls? What if he couldn't call to her because something was wrong? What if...? No, there was a reasonable explanation and she absolutely would not think the worst. He was, after all, the Wind Storm.

The hall was half empty tonight. She wondered where the other warriors and soldiers were who usually dined at this hour. Dinner was typically a light-hearted, raucous affair, yet Rhia finished her meal in silence, not bothering to say goodnight to anyone.

She did, however, manage to catch Lunis in the hallway. "Where are Sharyn, Joan and Brita?"

"They decided to eat in their apartments tonight."

"Is something wrong? Are they sick?"

"No, they're just tired."

"Speaking of tired, that describes me pretty well. I'm going to bed, Lunis. Let RuArk know that I've already eaten when he comes in, alright?"

"Uh, sure. No problem. Goodnight."

"RuArk's already out this morning. Let's go to the stables and work the horses." Rhia took another sip of cool orange juice and nibbled on a piece of flat bread.

"Work the horses? No way, Ree." Joan yawned, held up her chin with one hand as she sipped her morning brew with the other.

"Working horses is your most favorite thing in the world. Well, after making love to Marth and sleeping, that is."

"It's midsummer, Rhia. It's too damn hot to run around outside, getting all sweaty and grimy. I wouldn't do that to the horses or myself." The last was said with a classic Joan snort.

Wait, something Joan said triggered a thought, but Rhia couldn't quite grasp it. "What did you say, Joan?"

"I said, it's too hot…"

"No, the first part."

"What? It's midsummer and…"

"It's midsummer!" Her fork clattered to the floor and glass shattered on the tile, coating it with frothy orange pulp.

"So what?" Joan inquired, putting down her own fork. "What's the big deal? Midsummer comes every cycle, Rhia."

"Midsummer, Joan. Dammit, dammit, dammit!" Rhia jumped from her seat and left her full plate of food behind. Running from the main hall at full speed, she headed for the meadow behind the huge villa where Sharyn practiced with her bow. Joan was right on her heels.

"Rhia, what's wrong? What's the matter with you?"

She didn't answer, just kept running until she reached Sharyn.

"Sharyn! Where's RuArk?"

"He, Linc and Marth went patrolling outside the walls yesterday."

"All of them? All together? And without you as part of RuArk's fireteam as a First Commander?"

Sharyn didn't answer, letting one of her steel arrows fly to hit a target dead center a good hundred paces from where she stood.

Eyes narrowing, Rhia pressed. "Doesn't that seem a bit odd seeing that they've never left you behind before?"

"Well, perhaps, but..."

"Sharyn, it's midsummer. Something is wrong here. I can feel it. We've got to go to your place. You have to help me." Rhia's voice rose with each word as sheer panic gripped hold of her guts and pulled hard.

"What is wrong with midsummer, Rhia? I don't get it," Joan snapped. "You're scaring the shit out of me, Ree."

But Rhia didn't answer. She held Sharyn's gaze until she saw understanding dawn in the other woman's eyes.

Finally, Sharyn whispered, "Foreknowledge?"

At Rhia's nod, they both shot forward on swift feet back to the villa as Rhia's heart lodged itself in her throat.

In the middle of the floor in Sharyn's living room, Rhia assumed her usual position, closed her eyes and reached for her Source. Touching the sweet energy was becoming second nature and almost effortless, but now she was so nervous and unsettled that she had to fight to keep herself focused enough to reach it.

Finally, she began to see snippets of images flash before her eyes. Then the snippets became scenes. Familiar ones.

"They're the same images I saw last cycle when we

discovered I had the Gift of Foreknowledge. I saw RuArk covered in blood and in chains being sentenced to death. Just like before."

"I remember now because you fainted."

"Yes," Rhia shouted, "and it was..."

"Midsummer." Sharyn finished Rhia's thought. "But surely Linc and Marth will protect RuArk?" But even as she spoke, foreboding dawned in her dark eyes.

"Sharyn, you and Linc are developing a bond, right?"

The other woman nodded.

"Try to reach it," Rhia instructed and immediately felt the hair at her nape dance.

Sharyn's eyes narrowed as she said, "It's not there. I cannot feel Linc at all."

"I can't feel RuArk either. I haven't been able to invoke the bond since the night before last."

"What in blazes is going on here? Rhia's foreseen something bad happening to RuArk, none of our men are within the walls and neither of you can touch the bond?" asked Joan, hands on hips and eyes blazing.

"Can you touch your bond, Joan?" Sharyn asked.

"You've been teaching me, but my bond is not as strong as yours and Rhia's. So, when I tried to touch it last night when Marth didn't come to bed, I just figured I wasn't doing it right."

"You know what this means, don't you?" Rhia asked, looking at both her friends.

Yes, they knew. Their warriors were gone. And Rhia's vision was coming true. If RuArk was in danger, then those with him were in danger as well, for there was no way that RuArk would be taken without a fight to the death by him and his warriors.

"Someone else had to know about this. Someone

had to help them prepare," snarled Joan, her brown eyes flashing in anger and fear.

"Yes, and I have an idea who. But first, I want Sharyn to link with me while I try to use my Gift. I have to be sure of what I'm seeing." The two women joined hands and steeled themselves for what they were about to witness. Again.

All three women swept into the main hall just before mid-day. It was empty except for the household staff who were laying out pitchers of icy water and clean dishes for luncheon. Rhia called to Shaw, a tall, dark warrior headed to the kitchens. His hands might have been full of glasses and trays, but the blade strapped around his hips didn't look the least bit out of place.

"Shaw, please have Lunis come into the hall."

He nodded and disappeared through one of the side doors that led to the kitchens. When a confident, snappy Lunis appeared, he didn't look happy to see any of them.

"You wanted to see me, my lady?" he asked, trying to sound much too busy to be having this conversation. Rhia wasn't moved in the least.

"Yes, Lunis. Where are our husbands? And no half-truths." Rhia held her temper in check as she painted on her stone, I-will-not-be-moved face. She held the Houseman's gaze, unwavering as her eyes blazed with anger.

When she and Sharyn both reached for their weapons, the blood drained from Lunis' face. They weren't the least bit satisfied with his discomfort. Rhia took a single menacing step forward.

Finally, he replied, "I'm sworn to secrecy. I promised the Protector that I wouldn't tell."

"And I promise you'll lose a lot of blood if you don't tell me." Those words were followed with a loud *schwing* as Rhia freed the katana from the harness strapped to her back.

And once Lunis started talking, the whole tale gushed out. He told them about the note delivered by Larel from the High Counsel, as well as how he and Brita helped the men with their secret plans to leave Province Springs.

"They were well armed and well provisioned, my lady. The Protector took a whole pack of warriors with him. And some of the Draeman soldiers, too."

"That's great and fine, Lunis, but it's a damn trap. They're walking right into a blasted ambush."

Eyes wide with alarm, Lunis gasped, "Surely not! What do we do?"

She took a deep breath and ran a hand through her already wild mane of dark fire-streaked waves. "I'll think of something. Just be ready. I'm sure I'll need you." Dismissing Lunis, she turned back to Joan. "At least the babies are safe," Rhia said, thankful that her mother-in-law had come two days ago and taken them back to Gaia for a visit. Now that she thought about it, she realized the babies had gone to Gaia the same day Larel arrived.

Was Mila's arrival linked to the fate that RuArk had gone to meet? How she wished she'd pressed RuArk into teaching her how to walk the *Dream* so she could seek out the Grandfather. She thought about trying to enter the *Dream* anyway, but circumstances and common sense prevailed. She simply had no idea how to go about it. The only thing she could do was send a note to the Grandfather asking him to help her, or at least give her some information.

Joan paced back and forth, then stopped short in front of Rhia, obviously flustered. "Well, what are we going to do?"

Features schooled into her First Commander's stoic mask, Sharyn said, "In RuArk's absence, I am in command of our warriors. It is my responsibility to defend Fire Storm, my lord RuArk's mate, as well as protect the township."

Rhia rounded on her with a snarl. "What? Defend the township? Defend me? What about your lifemate-to-be, Sharyn?"

"I must do my duty, my lady."

"My lady? Who have you just turned into, Sharyn?"

But she continued as if Rhia hadn't spoken.

"I will not forsake my duties. I am a warrior of Gaia and I am sworn to do as the Wind Storm would wish in this and any other situation. As for Linc, I trust him to return to me. He is a great warrior."

"Woman, listen to yourself. I happen to trust my husband, Sharyn. However, I know what I saw in that vision."

"It was Foreknowledge."

"What-fucking-ever! I know what I saw and when you linked with me you saw it, too. I trust RuArk, but if I don't go to him and figure out a way to free him, he and all our people with him are going to die. That includes your great warrior, Linc O'dann. For once, stop looking through warrior's eyes. You're not just a warrior, you're a woman, Sharyn. A blasted woman who ought to love her man enough to do something more than worry about blasted duties."

Rhia stormed out of the hall and immediately began calling orders to Lunis, a disgruntled Joan stomping right behind her muttering hotly.

"Wait until I see that Marth. Going off to get caught in an ambush. Blasted Gaian, I'll kill him myself."

In minutes, the two women had the entire place in an uproar.

"Osgar, you knew that RuArk was leaving to aid my father?"

"I did."

"And do you know that he's walked into a trap?"

"I do not think so."

"Well, whether you think so or not, it's true. Ask Sharyn, if you like." He started to protest, but was brought up short. "I don't have time to argue with you. We must go to RuArk's aid, as well as my father's."

"I am sorry, my lady, but I have strict orders."

"Look, you blasted hard-headed Gaian giant. You pledged your sword to me on the day RuArk and I were joined in the Gaian way, didn't you?"

"Yes."

"Well then, I suggest you make plans to fulfill that oath."

Osgar resisted of course, spouting the same nonsense as Sharyn about protecting Rhia and Province Springs. Rhia reminded him that if he wanted to protect her, then he would have to go wherever she went. And since RuArk himself had not confined her to the township, then Osgar would just have to protect her on her way to the High City. There was no getting around Rhia's logic. Osgar was now gathering those who would go with them.

While the horses were being readied, Rhia sent

word to the women of the township who had been taking swordsmanship and combat lessons from her. They were to report to the main hall to be informed of their duties. Some were Draeman women who'd lived in Province Springs all their lives. Some were Gaian ladies who'd migrated over from across the river to settle in the township with their warriors.

Rhia refused to lie to them, and held nothing back. Turned out that Rhia, Sharyn and Joan weren't the only ones who hadn't known their warriors had gone to do battle. By the time she finished her tale, they were all livid.

After the rancor died down a bit, Rhia relayed all she knew about what the warriors had gone to do and the dangers of their mission. If these women were going to do what she asked of them, they must understand the seriousness of the business.

Lunis, Brita, and the household staff were scrambling to gather light supplies for their trip while Rhia and Joan hurried up to their own rooms to pack their duffels.

Sharyn went up to her chambers alone. She sat on her balcony looking out over the mountainous countryside, catching the occasional sparkle of sunshine off the river in the distance. Her mind went back to the day RuArk had saved her life.

She'd been riding along the eastern border, barely a stone's throw from Draema. She remembered resenting who she was—daughter to the brother of the King of Gaia. A noble woman who never had a moment alone simply because of who she was born to.

Forever surrounded by servants, companions, and the women of her family, while the men could go where they pleased, do what they pleased. Thankfully, her cousins Rogear, RuArk and Drefan were of an age with her and good comrades who treated her as if she were no different than them, but only when they were alone. They'd even gotten her out of some of her household lessons to teach her how to ride and swim when she was little.

As most other Gaian women of her station, she'd spent her time learning the duties of a noble woman of her clan—how to run a smooth household. She was to leave the duty of protecting herself and her family to whatever warrior she eventually joined with. In the meantime, her male relatives saw to her safety. The only problem was none of them had been riding with her that day.

She'd snuck out of to enjoy the day alone. It hadn't been the first time she'd done so. But it would be the last.

Three unknowns had come upon her while she'd been swimming along the river's edge. She was so engrossed in what she was going she hadn't even heard them approach.

She squeezed her eyes shut recalling the ghastly images of that day, yet all she could remember was the panic and fear that had swamped her senses. Sharyn could almost smell the damp grass close to the bank as she lay on her back with a blade pressed to her abdomen. Rough hands on her body. The sound of her own screams. The blood that ran down her side into the grass that caused her to still immediately, knowing that these detestable men would slip the blade further into her flesh if she continued to struggle.

Suddenly the blade that threatened to skewer her, was gone. The rancid breath against her cheek disappeared. She heard screams, but they were not her own. Then she was being lifted into strong arms.

RuArk had come. He had been riding to Draema Proper for a visit with the High Counsel and had seen her horse tethered to a sapling. Wondering where she was going without an escort, he'd followed her trail. Even then, though RuArk was just coming into manhood, he'd already proven he was ready to take on the title of Protector of the Realm, and the responsibilities that went with it. He'd protected her that day. She swore her service to him on the spot, and he'd sworn to teach her to fight. She would never be helpless again. Ever.

Opening her eyes, Sharyn pushed the memories away and admitted to herself that her past had dictated many of her actions.

But that was then, and this is now.

She stood and paced under the warm sun and considered where she stood. What did she believe now? Where did her loyalties lie now? A wry smile played about the corner of her mouth as she thought on Rhia.

She'd taught Rhia how to bend a little to get a lot from RuArk, and Rhia's reward was that she'd gained more than she could have ever hoped for. Yet, unbeknownst to her charge, she'd been the stubborn, prideful, stiff-necked jewel of a woman who'd taught Sharyn that there was more to life than following orders. Life was to take chances. To pull against the reins at times. To lay down your past and allow yourself to live. And love.

Now, who is the teacher and who is the student?

Since that fateful life-changing day when RuArk had been near enough to save her, every moment of every day had been dedicated to loyalty, duty, orders, training, fighting, riding. And she'd loved every minute of it. She'd never thought anything was missing from her life. Until she met Rhia Greysomne Miwatani.

Stripping off her sarand, Sharyn made her choice. And for the first time in many years, she felt truly free.

CHAPTER EIGHTEEN

Still issuing orders from the center of a large ring of people, Rhia turned to answer a question. Her mouth snapped shut when she spotted Sharyn striding boldly her way.

All of the men stopped talking and followed Rhia's line of vision, watching as Sharyn shoved her way past several gawkers to reach Rhia's side.

She wore one of Rhia's gray tunics, leggings and mid-calf leather boots. Rhia thought she looked incredibly sexy in the sarand, but this form-fitting garb was almost too much. Any enemy that looked on Sharyn in the Draeman-styled outfit would surely drool himself to death.

An exquisite onyx handled dagger was strapped to Sharyn's left thigh, the near-black blade gleaming dully in the iozene light. As always, her bow was strapped across her back, but her sword was sheathed in a shoulder harness that hid the blade behind her so well that all anyone could see was a bit of the hilt sticking out just under Sharyn's right arm. With a fully closed cloak, no one would have a clue that the woman carried a two-foot-long piece of death.

"I see you helped yourself to some of my clothes,"

Rhia said, as a wide toothy grin spread across her face.

"We are sisters, are we not? I am entitled to steal your clothes on occasion." Though sober-faced, Sharyn couldn't hide her smile for long. The two women clapped each other on the shoulder in camaraderie as they'd done countless time before and got back to business.

RuArk's life was in mortal danger, which was absolutely unacceptable because if anyone was going to kill him, it would be her.

After a busy day of planning, all three of her best friends retired early and joined Rhia in her living room after dinner.

Joan spoke first, barely able to wait until they could get the door closed. "So, who's behind all this?" she asked impatiently and with an expression that said she'd skin the bastard personally if she could just get a name from Rhia.

"I don't know. I didn't see him in the Foreknowledge vision. But we have one good thing going. Something is wrong with the bond between RuArk and me so he won't know that we're coming after him. It could be a disaster if anyone found out."

"The warriors will tell no one of your plans. They are sworn to protect their lord," Sharyn said quietly as she poured herself a glass of chilled red wine from the tray of beverages Lunis had sent up.

Just then Joan turned toward Brita. The woman seemed to be somewhere else, her eyes clearly telling that she wasn't listening to a word they were saying. She'd gone deathly pale and was trembling slightly, causing the contents of her teacup to slosh about a bit. She seemed to be fighting something.

"Brita, what's wrong?" Joan asked, taking the cup from the woman's now badly shaking hand.

"I'm not sure. Perhaps I'm just tired. It's so hard to focus on anything. My mind keeps running away from me."

Sharyn took a deliberate step toward the woman Rhia considered one of her sweetest friends and asked, "Are you sleeping much? Perhaps you should go to bed now."

"No, I don't want to go to bed. I've been having the most horrific nightmares. I'm in no hurry to close my eyes tonight," she said through a watery smile. She was trying to keep her spirits up, but she wasn't convincing anyone in that room.

Rhia felt her blood run cold at the mention of nightmares. Sharyn urged the older woman to tell of the dreams. Joan and Rhia shared a look that spoke volumes as Brita began to recount the horror that waited for her every time she closed her eyes. Rhia had indeed had a similar experience until the Grandfather had begun to watch over her dreams right before she and RuArk had become reacquainted. She hadn't had a bad dream since.

Sharyn spoke first into the silence that followed Brita's retelling of her dreams.

"Grandfather and the Realmwalkers say there is a taint in the *Dream*. Someone is misusing their Source. They discovered it some time ago and have been surveilling it ever since."

"But I don't have any Gifts. I'm just a plain old Draeman."

"Those without the Gifts are vulnerable to those

who have them. The Gifts protect those who carry them, protect them from others who would attempt to manipulate or control them through things like the *Dream*."

"But Rhia had nightmares, too, and she has Gifts," said an even more pale Brita who seemed to become more terrified as the conversation progressed.

"Rhia may have been visited in the *Dream*, but she could not be manipulated because of her latent ability. There is a great difference. Now she is twice protected, joined to the Protector of the Realm with the protection of his bond as well as her own Gifts. We must know if your nightmares are true, or an intrusion. If they are an intrusion by this dark, strange taint the Grandfather has spoken of, we must cut all ties to it. We do not know what kind of damage may be done."

Sharyn moved from her seat to stand in front of Brita, who had risen and began to pace. Joan and Rhia joined her, placing their hands in Brita's to offer their support.

Sharyn lay her hands on either side of Brita's head, probing with her Gift of Healing for damage or a dark presence in Brita's body or mind, just as she and Rhia had searched inside of RuArk's body the night he'd had his shoulder hacked open by a poisoned Noman blade.

The taint was very subtle but Sharyn was able to find it quickly. It had only taken a few minutes, but Brita fell into unconsciousness, and Rhia and Joan found themselves holding her up, then easing her down onto the long couch. Suddenly, eyes still closed, she began to slap at Sharyn's hands, trying to get away.

"The taint is there," Sharyn exclaimed, still trying to keep hold of Brita's head, trying to isolate and unwind the tendrils that were wrapped around the woman's subconscious. "It is resisting my Heals, as if it knows I am trying to remove it." Brita began to thrash in earnest. "Rhia, Joan, restrain her! Now!"

Joan and Rhia flipped Brita over on her stomach and pressed her face into the cushions of the couch. Rhia put her knee and all her weight in the middle of Brita's back, holding her down. Joan wrapped both arms around Brita's legs, trying to keep her lower body still. They managed to subdue her. But just barely.

"How is she so strong?" Joan yelled over Brita's muffled screams, which soon mixed with chilling howls and growls.

"It is more than just her that is fighting me," said Sharyn, struggling to hold on to Brita's head. The smaller woman had indeed become incredibly strong.

Brita went rigid, yet the howling went on and on. They could almost hear the darkness in her voice. It was enough to make Rhia silently vow to kill the person who had done this to her friend.

Finally, Rhia ripped off a part of her shirt and stuffed it into the woman's mouth, still resting all her weight on Brita's back as Sharyn continued her healing.

Afterward, a relieved, weeping, upset and exhausted Brita lay resting on the couch.

"Brita it is not your fault," snapped an impatient Rhia, who was handing Brita yet another cloth to wipe her tear stained cheeks as she blubbered on about the consequences of being visited in the *Dream*. "You didn't know anything about the *Dream*. I didn't even know and I'm part Gaian."

"I know, but it doesn't change the fact that I may have betrayed you to some unknown enemy. I don't know who it is, and I can't remember what any of the dreams were now. I can't even tell you how to stop this maniac, which makes me feel pretty fucking useless!"

"But I can." All eyes turned to Sharyn who lay in the middle of the floor resting to regain some of the energy sapped out of her from healing the damage done to Brita's mind.

"While I was touching Brita with my Gift, I saw what was done to her, how she was manipulated. I saw the one who violated her mind. And I now know what information was taken by him. Thankfully, she has not slept or napped today so our plans are still unknown to him."

Rhia reached out a hand to help Sharyn up off the floor and settled her into her favorite chair.

"The knowledge was taken directly from Brita's subconscious mind and she would have had no knowledge of what was being done to her. It was the same man who RuArk threw out of your apartments, the same one who kidnapped you with Brita's brother, Ricard. Yet, at the same time, it was *not* him. He was somehow...different, almost another man completely. He looked like Bryan Collaidh but he looked like Bryan if he had been something else. Like a Noman."

"But how could that be possible?"

"Remember, the Gifts are Gaian alone, but it was not always so. Perhaps this other Bryan has found a way to touch his Source and walk the *Dream*?"

Perfect platinum brows furrowed in equal parts question and concern, Joan asked, "But without a Gaian to help him, how could he possibly learn such a thing? And if the Gifts aren't natural to him, then how would he be strong enough to use them in such a way?"

"Well put, Joan. Unfortunately, I have no answers," Sharyn replied.

"And," Rhia spoke up, "why would Bryan look like a Noman? And how is it Brita was still being affected even though Bryan is dead?"

"No idea, Rhia. But I do know that this Bryan-who-is-not-Bryan is aware of RuArk's plans. He knows when RuArk departed for the High City, who accompanied him, and anything else that Brita knew of the journey since her last dreaming."

"How long was Brita subject to this violation of her mind?"

"We cannot know, however it would explain how Bryan happened to appear in Province Springs and spirit you away the last time RuArk was out of the city. It would also explain her tendency to walk about in a daze. Her spirit was fighting the invasion, yet her mind could not resist. There was no way she would know how."

Brita, still in tears, blubbered, "Then perhaps my brother was forced to help Bryan. Perhaps he wasn't a willing partner in all this after all?" One could always hope, but her hopes were soon dashed upon the rocks.

"From what I saw in your mind, the Bryan-who-is-not-Bryan was in league with your brother."

"But how can you know this if all you saw was what information was taken from me?" Brita was yelling now, almost hysterical at the implications, as well as what could still happen because of her.

"I did not say that the only knowledge I gained was what he took from you."

A light illuminated brightly in Rhia's mind. Suddenly, she knew. She understood.

"Sharyn, you saw this counterfeit Bryan's plans, didn't you?"

"I saw some of his plans, yes. When you link with

someone using the Gifts, it is not a one-way conduit. Yes, knowledge was taken from Brita. But knowledge was also left behind. The only reason she did not realize what was happening is because she does not have the Gifts herself. If she had, she would have felt the invader's presence as soon as he had reached out to her."

"So you're saying that this invader left behind information on his dealings with my brother and his plans?"

Sharyn nodded.

"But why? Why would my brother do such a thing? Why would he join forces with someone like that?" Brita asked.

"Because he was promised something."

All three of the women asked in a shout, "What?!"

Sharyn took a deep breath, turned directly to the older woman and said, "Your brother was promised Rhia."

"What?" Rhia was beside herself with anger at the audacity that she could be promised to someone without her knowledge or consent. She was even more pissed off that Sharyn had just confirmed what Ricard himself had told her before he died. And all of this by a man she didn't even know.

"Rama Collaidh promised Rhia to this white haired *other* Bryan, as well as to Bryan himself. Then this *other* Bryan promised Rhia to Ricard. Their plans are to rid this world of the High Counsel and RuArk. They are waiting for them to arrive in the High City. With your father and mate out of the way, it leaves Rhia as High Counsel of Draema province and free to marry either the Councilman, Rama Collaidh, or the white haired Noman-Bryan."

Brita promptly fell into a dead faint. Unfortunately, Sharyn was too tired to aid her and Rhia and Joan were too stunned to catch her. She landed in a heap with a solid thud on the thick carpets.

This whole thing was a fucking nightmare, even in their waking hours!

CHAPTER NINETEEN

Their party disappeared into the deep darkness of the trees and allowed a lone rider to pass.

Rhia signaled instructions. *'Oh my mark, draw blades. I'll approach first.'*

One of the warriors signaled back. *'No, we will surround him and...'*

'When RuArk leads a fireteam, does he ever sit back and let you take point?'

'Well, no...'

'Didn't think so. Now shut up and let me do my job.' With that, Rhia was the first to burst through the branches to confront the rider. She skidded to a halt.

"Mannon? What are you doing out here?"

"My lady! I knew I would find you," he gasped, clearly relieved even as he slumped from his horse and landed in the thick foliage in an unmoving heap.

Mannon slowly opened his eyes, squinted up at the night sky and wondered how much time had passed. With the thick clouds and no moon, he could barely make out the outlines of the thick tree trunks all around him.

The last thing he remembered was the ground coming up to meet him as Rhia stood ready to slice his head off. In all his years of serving the House of Greysomne, Mannon had never been so happy to see anyone in his life. He lay on a thick pallet, still wearing his boots and trousers but his shirt had been replaced by a single, soft blanket.

He'd been gravely injured and feared the worst even though the scent of blood was absent. This was going to hurt, but he had to know how bad it was. So he held his breath to keep from crying out as his fingers sought the spot where he'd been sliced as he fled the High City.

Instead of a raw, bloody gash, he found a bandage laid neatly over the site of the deep cut. The surrounding area was sore and achy but somehow the wound felt as if it were a few days old rather than just a few hours.

A moment later, Rhia quietly announced herself as she came and knelt next to Mannon.

"Hey, Manny. Glad you're awake."

"That makes two of us," he said.

"Can you sit up?"

"Yes, sir," Mannon replied. "A bit stiff, but I can do it." Ignoring the twinge of pain that radiated across his stomach and ribs, Mannon sat up. The blanket pooled in his lap as Rhia helped him scoot back a bit so he could lean against the nearest tree. Images of the terror he'd faced, the death that he'd been sure would find him, filled his head.

Feeling exposed, he pulled the blanket around him like a cloak and huddled beneath it. Although the night was balmy enough to need no covering at all, Mannon shivered uncontrollably.

"Be right back." Rhia retreated, only to return a few minutes later.

Mannon was grateful that she slowly eased into his space and made no sudden moves. "Here, drink this," she said. "It's thick Gaian coffee laced with anise and honey."

At his puzzled expression, she said, "Licorice, Mannon. It's good. And there's some calming herbs in it to help with the shock of whatever sent you fleeing the High City on a horse."

"Thank you." He took the cup from her fingers, sipped and closed his eyes on a sigh of contentment. She was right—it was delicious. Given his circumstances, he felt lucky indeed. He could have fallen from that horse before ever meeting up with Rhia and bled to death. Or worse, become food for the animalistic Noman overrunning his home.

One thing was certain, he preferred his nightmares to stay in his dreams. Instead, he'd seen monsters running around his City, his home. Draema hadn't been attacked in too many years to count and nobody saw this coming. In this case, even the laser cannons atop the walls were of no use—they faced *out* towards wild terrain, which did no good when your enemies were already inside.

Opening his eyes, Mannon forced himself to meet Rhia's concerned gaze. He didn't bother pretending to be calm or 'okay'. He let all of his emotions play across his face, hoping it conveyed what he couldn't quite form the words to say just now.

Wait. Something moved in his periphery, he was sure of it. Peering past Rhia, Mannon tried to distinguish the shapes moving in the darkness. They were quite close now, but made no sound. It was times like this he wished he had Noman sight in this fucking pitch blackness!

Eyes grew wide as they were slowly surrounded by a formidable wall of raw muscle with an energy that buzzed around him until his hair felt as if it stood on end.

"Don't worry Mannon." Joan—another person he was so glad to see—stepped into view and moved directly into his line of sight. "They're with us."

"They" turned out to be scores of huge Gaian warriors and even some Draeman soldiers, all fully armed. The closest ones wore the colors and sigil of the Wind Storm. *Thank god.*

"Can you eat?" At his nod, Joan handed over a small plate of cold fowl, bread and hard cheese, and then settled on her knees next to Rhia. "Sorry the food is cold. We had to travel light, so we don't have cooking equipment that can accommodate all of us, and we're way too close to the city to risk a large enough fire. But thanks to Draeman tech, at least we have coffee courtesy of a few iozene powered heat elements."

"Coffee," Rhia chuckled. "Gotta have it. Survival 101."

Still a bit unsure of his surroundings Mannon noted how quiet the camp was. None of the men made a sound, though most of them looked much too large to possibly move so quietly and gracefully. So caught up in his observations, Mannon accepted the plate with his left hand and momentarily forgot about the wound on that side. He instinctively winced at the wicked pull, and then realized there was no true pain. Even the soreness that he'd felt upon waking just a few moments ago was diminishing.

But how?

As if reading his thoughts, Rhia addressed the

questions swirling around in his brain.

"Sharyn used her Gift of Healing to help mend the injury. She is sleeping now to recover from the drain on her energy, but in a few hours both you and she will be good as new. Luckily, the blade that made that wound of yours wasn't poisoned. That would have taken the both of us. And you would have been on your back for at least a good seven days."

He nodded, though he didn't truly understand at all. He'd heard tell of magick and Gifts, but only in the old histories that read more like Gaian fairy tales. Reading of a culture and experiencing a culture were certainly two different things.

Mannon's mind snapped clear as he realized something else. Sure, he shouldn't be sitting here, alive and drinking the most delicious beverage ever, but more amazing was that he shouldn't be sitting here *with Rhia.*

"Wait a minute, Rhia. What are *you* doing here? When I set out from Draema Proper I expected to travel for days before finding you."

"Well, you traveled for less than three hours. My father sent for help from RuArk and the story goes downhill from there." She told a horrific tale about the danger to RuArk and the High Counsel, and a mad dash from Province Springs in pursuit days earlier. Mannon was less than pleased to confirm that the City was indeed overrun.

By Noman and traitors.

"All is lost."

"All?" she asked, her expression filled with pain and anger. "Is that a fact, or a guess? You rode for three hours from the High City, but it takes six just to get to the outer wall and into the buffer zone between Proper and the next colony West of here."

True, but thinking was hard and relaxing was out of the question.

No, no, no. This is no time for emotional bullshit. Suck it up, do your job and give a proper status of what the hells happened, Mannon. You are First Assistant to the Commander in Chief of the Society of War. Fall apart later.

After several deep breaths, Mannon sat up straight, pulled his responsibility around him like a shroud and spoke. "I withdraw the suggestion that all is lost. You are right, we are still technically in Draema Proper and I have no idea if any of the close-in colonies, such as Draema Salone or Draema Porto, are taken as well. The High City gates are secured and no one is getting in or out. I barely made it myself, but I had to try. I did not know what else to do but try to find you and tell you what happened. To warn you not to come here."

"Fire Storm," an agitated man interrupted from a short distance away. These were some of the most disciplined people he'd ever interacted with. Stoic. Still. The epitome of calm. In all his years of dealing with Gaian who came into the High City for trade, Mannon had never seen one shift from one foot to another. Though the movement was slight, this kind of behavior from a warrior seemed downright giddy.

"Fire Storm, it is urgent."

She motioned for the man to join them. "Mannon, this is Osgar. Osgar, this is Mannon. Mannon has been my father's right hand for a long as I can remember. Mannon, Osgar is a high ranking warrior, one of RuArk's most trusted."

With the pleasantries dispensed with, she said, "All right, Os, what's going on?"

"Before the Wind Storm left Province Springs, he

had me send word to several of our men across the river."

"So…"

"They were to quietly cross into Draema and meet him here to aid him in the battle."

"Get to the point, Osgar."

"Rhia, their forces were delayed by a summer storm and they could not cross the river. It was high and running too fast. By the time they reached the meeting place, the Wind Storm had already gone into the City."

Even as dark as it was, Mannon watched understanding dawn in Rhia's eyes. In fact, she seemed to grow more and more thrilled by the second. And so did he, but he refused to jump to a conclusion. No, he would let this man say what he was thinking before allowing himself to actually get happy about it.

"Our scouts came upon them while patrolling and brought them back to our camp. Those fireteams from northern Gaia are here. *Right here*," he whispered hastily.

"How many, Osgar?"

Just then another warrior walked into the circle and answered Rhia's question.

"Five hundred, Fire Storm."

"Five hundred?" she gasped.

Five hundred seasoned, ruthless, armed-to-the-teeth warriors? That large a force, combined with those who'd accompanied Rhia from Province Springs would be enough to take any city in the world. Hells, a single Gaian warrior to ten typical soldiers was almost unfair. And Mannon was thankful for it. Perhaps fate was with them after all…

———➤——————◄———

After Rhia returned from meeting the forces that had snuck into Draema to help RuArk, she was restless. They needed to rest and bed down for the night, but more than that, they needed a new strategy and more intel. Signaling to Osgar and Shaw, they joined her next to Mannon. Sharyn and Joan came along without being asked.

"Okay Mannon, we need more details. We need a new plan now that we have more men, and we need one now if we are to ride out of here with any chance of success.

"I will lead you, Blademaster."

"No, Mannon. You're injured and should get more rest."

"That is not possible while I know the High Counsel is in danger. My wound is a minor irritation now, nothing more. I will not be left behind."

"Mannon, you're kind of short, but I swear you sound like one of these bone-headed Gaian warriors." Osgar snorted. Joan laughed and Rhia smiled as she clapped Mannon lightly on his uninjured side.

"Thank you for the compliment." Mannon inclined his head and then turned a bit to wink at Sharyn, who immediately blushed.

"What can you tell us of the City, Mannon?" Sharyn asked.

"It is full of those nasty Noman creatures. They seem to be everywhere."

"What of my father's soldiers and the Society of War?"

"Captured. The Noman came into the City, somehow unseen. Before we knew what was happening, they had overrun your home at the Citadel and were fully engaged with your mate's forces there. Our men closed the City gates to keep anymore from coming in, but all we did was lock our people in."

"I have never been to the High City. I do not understand how it is arranged," Shaw said.

Rhia squatted down and drew a quick diagram in the dirt. "It's like a bunch of rings inside other rings. Here's the Citadel, right in the center of the High City. The Citadel is a military facility, which includes my father's home, barracks, stables, training facilities and the like. It's completely self-sustaining and sits on a hundred acres. There are low walls and gates around it, just like our villa in Province Springs. The High City surrounds the Citadel and there is a higher wall around the High City. Outside that is the rest of Draema Proper. You don't see another wall until you get to the edge of the colony, and that wall's gates lets into a buffer zone, which is a few miles of open space between Draema Proper and its neighboring colony. Got it?"

At Shaw's nod, the man turned back to Mannon. "So what happened after the capture of the First Heir's father?"

"They used him as a bargaining chip with a promise that the High Counsel would be kept alive if all the Gaian warriors and Draeman soldiers within the gates surrendered. RuArk signaled to his men to lay down arms. The Society of War followed suit. It was a complete coup in no time at all."

"And the rest of our forces would have no idea what happened because they're out patrolling the buffer zones, the rivers to the north, and the seas off the southern coast." Rhia knew this because she'd been the one to set the schedules for the rotation of their troops for years. Damn it, damn it, damn it.

"Precisely, my lady."

So... There was no way into the City, and no way out? As a strategist, she knew a piece of this puzzle was missing, but she couldn't think of what it was. At the same time, it had been so long since anyone had attempted a siege on the City, she wondered if they'd simply become lax.

Clenching her jaw, Rhia reined in her temper even as an idea flashed into her head. "Wait a minute. Mannon, if the palace is overrun and the gates are closed, how did you get out?"

"Do you recall a certain old man who promised to keep the secret of the Lady Rhia when he found her playing in the passages within the walls of the palace?"

"Holy hells, I forgot all about that little incident. I was so young at the time I don't even remember how I got into those tunnels or how you found me."

"One of the exit doors is close to a seldom used gate that the Noman had not secured. I hid in the passages hoping things would be chaotic enough outside that I could slip out. I got out of the Citadel unseen, but getting to the wall of the City was another matter. I slipped into one of the thick groves between the Citadel and the City wall. I don't believe they discovered how I did it because they didn't notice me until I was almost in the trees."

"But you fell off a horse? Where did you get it from?"

"I had no way to get to a hover, and I would not have been able to take one into the cover of the trees anyway. Luckily, the attack happened before the Groomsmen brought the last of the horses in from the farthest pasture near the City wall. I grabbed one and did not look back, even though I was wounded."

"So why wasn't I told about the passages?"

"They were built in the days of your forefathers during the re-establishment of the rule of law after the Breaking. Upon the death of the High Counsel, the knowledge is passed from the dying ruler to the next High Counsel. They are only known to the High Counsel and me but you would have been told when it was time for you to ascend to the title."

"If the location of the tunnels is only passed from one High Counsel to another, then why do you know of them?" Joan asked, her brow arched skeptically.

"I have been the steward of those passages for almost forty years now, and sworn to secrecy by the High Counsel himself. He did not think it wise that he be the only person in Draema to know their location. He wanted them in good working order, which meant someone had to maintain them. If he hadn't confided in me and made me the keeper of those passages all those years ago, I would not have been able to save you when you were a child. And I would have had no way to get out of the City today."

"Why wouldn't you have been able to get me out? I was certainly yelling loud enough." In spite of the gravity of the situation, Rhia laughed.

"Yes, you were quite vigorous about the business," Mannon chuckled. "But sounds made within those passages can only be heard from inside those walls."

"Sound proofed?" Rhia asked, incredulous. "Seriously?"

"Yes. I only entered once every week or so. If I hadn't happened to be inside at the time, you might have starved to death. I would have come upon you eventually, but you had ventured into a part of the passages that is farthest from the Citadel and leads under the City itself and exits across the river."

"So nobody else has been in those tunnels?" Rhia asked, wanting, *needing* reassurance that there was at least a glimmer of hope.

"There are two others."

"But, I thought…"

"One of them is here; the other is your husband."

Rhia knew her mouth hung open, but closing it proved impossible. She hadn't seen any of this coming. After a few steadying breaths, she said, "Somebody here has been in those tunnels? Who, damn it?"

He turned slowly to Sharyn, who simply stared back. She said not a word, and neither did Mannon. It simply wasn't necessary.

Finally, Sharyn spoke. "When we first came to Draema Proper summoned by your father, we met Mannon at the stables before we were well off our horses. He said your father did not wish for us to be seen, as the matter was one of life and death. Most urgent. Mannon escorted RuArk and me to a door at the back of the Citadel, then through the tunnels and directly to your father's offices where he awaited us."

"And you never told me?"

"I am a woman of honor. It was obvious that the knowledge shared with RuArk and me was not to be revealed. Besides, was there a reason to disclose such knowledge before now, Rhia?"

"So," Joan jumped in, "we have a couple of things to worry about here—getting into the Citadel unseen, which we seem to have an answer to, and second is finding RuArk and the High Counsel and getting them out of there."

"Yes," added Sharyn, "but we do not know who else is involved. We cannot simply walk in there not knowing who to trust."

She had a point.

Joan spoke. "From what we know, Collaidh helped the Noman gain entry to the City. We also know that this Not-Bryan is controlling them somehow. But Sharyn is right. We don't know who else is being manipulated. What if other Council members are involved?"

Rhia had the answer to their most pressing question. "We won't trust anyone. Period." She rose from her spot beside Mannon, determined and focused. "Our family is in a hot place, so whatever we do we *must* get to Collaidh and either capture or kill him if we hope to get them out of hell."

Actually, it was more like the east side of the seventh level of Hell…in summertime.

CHAPTER TWENTY

They waited until almost midnight. The horses were left in the grove outside the walls of the City and soldiers and warriors moved in as close as they dared. They had to know who manned the walls and how many of those 'who's' patrolled the Citadel grounds.

The scouts reported a half hour later with dismal news. Mannon had been right. The Noman were everywhere. Several were up on the high inner walls that overlooked the High City as well as the key entrances and exits of the Citadel grounds. It would be a risky undertaking getting to the tunnel entrance unseen. After all, Noman hunted at night, their eyes made for the darkness and their sense of smell amazingly keen.

The smell they could take care of. The company of warriors took strips off of the horse's saddle blankets and tied them around their waists underneath their clothes to mask the smell of skin and hair. Noman had long since ceased feeding on animals, so the men and women were at least safe in that regard. But they didn't look like horses and the dark was when a Noman's sight was sharpest.

There was nothing they could do about it except be

smart and not get caught.

Splitting up into two teams, one headed north and the other south, around the City. Rhia, Osgar and Mannon led their group while Sharyn, Shaw and Joan took the other. They all quietly made their way from the shelter of the groves and met up again at a small, non-descript, vine overgrown gate in the Citadel's rear wall.

Interestingly, all of the gates Rhia knew of could be opened and closed automatically from several communications centers and command posts within the City or the Citadel. But this one was manual. She didn't recall seeing it on any schematics either. No wonder it was overgrown. And she couldn't have been more thrilled, in spite of the fact she thought she knew all there was to know about her home's defenses.

It was, in fact, the same gate Mannon had fled through without detection. He reminded he hadn't been seen until he ducked out of the very groves they hid in right now and tried to run for the High City wall.

Rhia held her breath as Mannon slipped through the gate first. She watched him duck behind several bales of hay stacked high and wide enough to hide his approach. Next, he made his way from the wall to the entrance of the passageways.

The door blended so well with the stone, Rhia didn't see it at all until Mannon actually opened it. The thing was impressive and made no sound at all as it slid open.

Mannon entered with Rhia and Osgar on his heels. They took a quick look about and listened as Mannon suggested several points where their people could gather until they were all inside. Unable to turn on any light until they could shut the door behind them, it took several tension-filled hours to get all of the warriors through the wall and into the passages without making a sound—an amazing feat considering there were hundreds of them, all bristling with weapons.

Finally, Mannon secured the entrance so it could only be opened from the inside. It simply wouldn't do to have a pack of bloodthirsty Noman sneaking up on them from behind.

Rhia was as much impressed with the state of the passages now that she'd seen them, as she'd been when Mannon had described them. They were extremely large with high ceilings, polished floors and iozene lamps that illuminated every step. They were so wide that ten of their weapon clad warriors could walk abreast comfortably.

The floors were sparkling clean, covered with silver-veined, smoothed stone tiles. Intricately carved woodwork graced the walls.

"Mannon, do I smell lemons?"

"Yes, sir. I polish the woodwork with lemon oil."

Rhia ground to a halt, eyes wide. "By hand?"

"Of course," he said. "The Protector thought it was quite well done." The man's smile was full of pride, and it should have been because the place was spectacular. Rhia was still amazed that she'd grown up here and hadn't a clue about this place.

The main hallway they'd squeezed into was lined with endless unmarked doors, each with a wall lock, but no signs or symbols to tell what was inside. But Mannon remembered them all. Moving as swiftly as they were able, they reached a fork in the passages with a hallway running off to the left and down some stairs, the other was off to the right with its stairs going up.

Pointing to the left, Mannon said, "This is where

we part. That passage runs directly down to two exits. One takes you to the dungeons and holding cells. The other is a passage that leads across the river."

"Is the river an option for escape if we can't win back the City?" asked Rhia.

"Yes. The exit across the river is well hidden, but would take us hours on foot. We would also have to leave our mounts in the grove."

"Is it dark down there, Mannon?" Sharyn asked, peering toward the dungeon's direction.

"These passageways are well lit, but further down the light is dimmer on purpose. At the end, take the heavy black wooden door on the right. It opens to a small room that serves as a sally port. Go into the room, close the door to the passages before opening the door to the dungeons. There are too many of you to fit into the sally port so be sure to turn off the iozene lamps in the passages or they will give you away when you attempt to pass out of the passages into the dungeon hallways."

"I understand," Sharyn replied. "Osgar, you and half the men come with me. We will go to the dungeons and free our people. Rhia, where shall we meet up with you?"

"Make your way to the Council Chambers in the observatory on the first floor. Mannon will bring you there from the dungeons. The room is shaped like a big old-fashioned key. It's one wide, long hall that ends in a large circular meeting room. That's where the judgments are rendered. Both sides of the hallway are lined with dark screens where the spectators sit. Bring your team around to the right and I'll bring mine around to the left. Also, the entire judgment circle rotunda is darkly screened as well so we'll be well hidden. If I were a Noman, that's where I would scout out the place. And that's where they are going to bring RuArk for sentencing."

Mannon drew Rhia a map that showed the fastest passage route to the observatory quickly. With that, they split up and moved at speed toward their destinies.

Silently opening the door that let out into a pass-through room, Rhia, Joan and Shaw secured the passageway door, and then proceeded to another that let out in the back of her father's large bedroom closet.

Holy shit, we're in my father's bedroom?

Warriors remained in the clothes closet, more in the small pass-through room between the passages and the walk-in wardrobe, while the rest waited in the passages themselves. If the coast was clear they could make their way to the Council Chambers quickest from there.

Thankfully, the bedroom was empty. Shaw took the lead and sprinted through the rest of the apartment before coming back to the bedroom to signal the all-clear.

Joan went back into the closet and returned, followed by most of their men. Once out of the passages, none of them stood still. Instead, they moved over every inch of those apartments looking for intruders and traitors in places Rhia would have never thought to look.

Her chest swelled with pride. Her husband, the Warlord of Gaia, the Wind Storm, Protector of the Realm, had trained these men. And they were most efficient at their business.

Shaw lifted his gaze toward the ceiling as if searching for something in the very air itself. He flashed a quick hand signal and the entrance to both the clothes closet and the secret passages snapped shut from the inside, and every Gaian warrior in the chambers disappeared behind a bookcase, tapestry or underneath a table or desk. Shaw pulled Mannon and Rhia into the long drapes that hung on either side of the floor to ceiling windows. In mere seconds, all were hidden.

Just as Rhia was about to ask what was going on, she heard the outer door to the apartments open.

"It smells like horses in here," said a whiny, scratchy voice.

A deeper, growling tone answered, "We do not care. We cannot feed or hunt until we have finished checking this floor. Let us do it quickly and move on."

"Everyone in the City knows the High Counsel and that huge dark haired warrior are being held in the upper towers. Why must we check these rooms?"

"Because we were ordered to," said the growler, who moved closer to Rhia's hiding place. She heard a quiet *click* and knew he was checking the locks on the windows.

Scratchy was not content with the answer. He moved into the bathing room and yelled back at his partner, "I grow tired of his ordering us about, as if he is better than us. As if he is not Noman himself."

"Yes, but he has the magick. Somehow he has regained the Gifts that were lost to all but the Gaian," said the growler.

"Yes," said scratchy, moving toward the main door, satisfied that they'd found nothing. "He has found the lost magick and it is the only thing that keeps me from bleeding him dry."

"You speak boldly, but know you would never

challenge him."

"You are right, but I might choose to cross his father, that Collaidh filth. Filthy Draeman traitor. If he would betray his own people, he is a fool to believe we would ever trust him. The idiot believes he is controlling Behn. I want to be there when he finds that he is mistaken."

Chuckling they left as quickly as they'd entered. Rhia breathed a sigh of relief as their voices drifted down the hall and away.

One by one, the warriors appeared, their faces hard with resentment at what they had heard. So it was true. There was a Noman in charge. Skin crawling with disgust, Rhia stepped out of her hiding spot.

Barely above a whisper, her voice hard and her expression harder, Rhia spoke. "They are holding RuArk in the towers two floors above this room. There are only two chambers up there. And one of them is mine."

When they reached the tower rooms, Rhia quickly entered her code into the wall lock. All they found were torn strips of dry bloodied cloth and bonds.

But they'd learned something important by her lifemate's absence — the Noman didn't trust Behn... and Behn didn't trust them right back.

Linc closed his eyes and mindlinked with Marth in the next cell.

"Marth, did you hear that?"

"Hear what?"

"A faint gurgling of some sort. I cannot tell what it is. Oh, and Sharyn is here."

"What! Sharyn? Bloody hell."

"Yes. I stopped blocking our bond some time ago, and I can now feel her. She is near and she is quiet... unhappy."

"As are we all." After a few seconds, Marth said, *"I can now sense Joan somewhere close by. What the hell are those women doing here in the High City?"*

They sat in silence waiting, then, after what seemed like a lifetime, they finally heard something worth listening for.

CHAPTER TWENTY-ONE

Sharyn alone exited the passages and stepped silently into the common hallway that led to the dungeons. With a quick peek around a corner, she saw that the hallway was the only way in or out and led to a huge room with two alcoves off to either side.

There were at least thirty Noman simply lounging in those alcoves. The edges of their fangs could be seen gleaming under the dim lighting as some fed off dying men and women. Others were asleep after having obviously gorged themselves into a stupor.

But at the rear of that room was a single door. And that door was actively guarded by ten more of the creatures.

Sharyn stepped back into the passages so cleverly hidden inside the walls of the Citadel. With a hand signal, she instructed twenty of their warriors to clear the alcoves. Three others would help her take care of getting to the central door that no doubt led to their friends.

The Noman were caught completely off guard. The last thought they had was confusion at smelling horses in the dungeons. The fight was vicious. Merciless. Swift. The Gaian's superior swordsmanship and fighting style ended the confrontation quickly, silencing the Noman with a clean slice or huge fist to the throat before they even had a chance to scream.

Sharyn and Mannon stripped the key tags from their dead quarry, activated the wall lock to the main entrance, and raced quietly down yet another hallway lined with archways. The first few had chains hanging from the ceiling. From the layers of dust on the floors and grayish tint to the white stone of the walls, it was apparent that these alcoves had been there for some time. However, the lack of rust and smooth fitted links of the metal chains was a clear indication that they'd been recently used.

Finally, they came to a section that appeared to be cut right into the earth. The iozene lamps here weren't bright enough to see where they were going, and it could very well be a trap. With determined, but silent steps, they moved into the darkness together and found the arches no longer led to open alcoves. These were dank, musty, gated cell-like rooms that could only be described as gloomy.

Sharyn's heart sank. All of the rooms were empty.

With mind and heart focused on her mate-to-be, she invoked the bond and almost screamed with relief.

Farther. They had to go farther into the darkness.

"Linc," she called quietly. "Are you back here?"

"Yes, here. Keep coming. All the way to the back." She'd never been so happy, and so pissed, to hear his voice.

It was a relief to find each cell packed with their men. Both Gaian and Draeman were locked inside and crammed together so tightly, there was barely room to move about or sit.

In minutes, they were freed as the key tags were

passed around so they could unlock and snatch open the cell doors as quickly as possible before moving on to the next one.

Sharyn found Linc stuffed into a cell at a dead end. He and his comrades' expressions were proud, unyielding, and determined. Heads held high, their stances belied what had been done to them in these dungeons, and their eyes silently vowed vengeance on their captors.

Linc and Marth were the last to walk out of the formerly guarded door and into the large room. They noted the number of Noman who lay where they'd been cut down and nodded their approval.

"We must get to the observatory. Rhia, Joan, and some of our warriors are there searching for RuArk and the High Counsel. Where are your weapons?"

"In a locked room at the entrance to this place," Linc said calmly.

Wave after wave of Linc's admiration—along with utter shock—flowed through their newly forming bond. On one hand, she wanted to throttle him for leaving Province Springs without telling her. To yell that she should leave him in this cell until he apologized for his reckless attempt to protect her. To jump into his arms, hold him tight, tell him how afraid she'd been at what she would find back here in the dark.

There would be time for tenderness later. Right now, they were First Commanders and they had a job to do. RuArk and the High Counsel were missing.

They piled all the Noman bodies into one of the far cells and covered them over with moldy straw taken from long-unused pallets.

Sharyn, Marth and Linc joined ranks and left the

dungeon with their men rallied behind them.

Just as they reached the sally port door, Marth silently called a halt. It was a moment of quiet chaos. The Draeman soldiers who'd been training with RuArk had a good grasp of the Gaian hand language and understood what Marth was doing, while the soldiers from the High City did not. They ran into the backs of their fellow soldiers and began grumbling and questioning.

Sharyn let out a somewhat loud 'Sssh!' They all fell silent and their gazes followed the direction of the hand she held up that pointed to the huge green-eyed warrior who had called the halt.

"What? What is it?" Mannon whispered. Marth again motioned for him to be quiet and listen. Whatever, *whoever* it was, made a muffled yet urgent sound, and it was very near.

"Mmmmfffff!   Mmmmfffff! Aawwwaawaaahhhmmmf!"

Linc moved toward the noise, which appeared to come from a solid wall. Drawing his weapon, he tapped the wall with his sword. It was hollow.

"Move," Mannon demanded and began to search the wall for a hidden lock. He found it behind an iozene lamp and quickly engaged it. The door slid open to reveal four hidden rooms, one of which held the High Counsel. Bound and gagged, he lay on the cold stones of the dark cell. His clothes were torn and his skin scraped in places, but otherwise no worse for wear. Needless to say he was glad to see them.

And he knew exactly where to find RuArk.

Soon they were all off at a dead run praying that the Ancestors would help them reach RuArk in time.

Rhia eased out of the hidden passage into a small closet sized room with a single door. According to Mannon's directions, on the other side of that door was the observation area in the Council Chambers.

She eased it open and peeked out.

There were usually soldiers on patrol in this building, whether council was in session or not. It was eerily quiet. Not one guard, friend or foe, to be seen. Strange.

She looked around, hoping she'd been quiet enough, knowing that it was a good fifty feet to the main door to her left, and another fifty feet to the front of the room where she could hear the Council of Seven already gathered.

Backtracking to the passageway, she signaled the all clear. Silent as death, the warriors entered the observatory and ordered themselves into a strategic line, three men deep from end to end.

Leaving Joan and Shaw to command, if needed, Rhia exited the screening room through a back door and hid behind a pillar close to the Council's judgment circle. She stilled, listening intently to the Councilors raised voices.

"I am most qualified to be High Counsel," yelled an impatient Collaidh.

"No, Collaidh. You have shown that you are most qualified to bring the filthy Noman into our midst. You are supposed to be the Council representative of Draema Major, not the Noman vermin!" the Councilman from Draema Porto yelled at the top of his lungs. His round pie-shaped face was as red as a freshly picked apple. Hand and voice shook with anger, which was something Rhia had never seen from the man in all her dealings with his colony.

"Yes, and what of the First Heir? Isn't her claim legitimate and to be considered prior to *your* claim?" This from the Councilman of Draema Seine. Her dark brown eyes glittered with anger. "You've called a meeting in the dead of night. Why?"

"The High Counsel is dead!"

"Perhaps Collaidh, but the First Heir is not dead," the Councilman of Draema Salone jumped in angrily, but was cut short by the Councilman of Draema Minor.

"Or are there any other surprises you have for us? Are you going to tell us that Rhia Greysomne is dead as well as the High Counsel?"

Collaidh glared at his esteemed colleagues and his expression said that he wished them *all* dead! He was losing ground here, and quickly. The dismissive wave of his hand at the Councilman of Minor's statement didn't gain him any.

"And this is not a legal council meeting by our laws, Rama! The High Counsel or First Heir must be here to represent Draema Proper and render final judgment. Not to mention, the man you claim to be a criminal is the only authority in Draema Neine since the High Counsel gave him Province Springs and did not name a new Councilor," said the Councilman of Draema Minor. Nods of agreement came from all of the other members, including the female from Draema Shivna, who had not yet spoken.

Rhia's mouth fell open. In the cycle-and-a-half that she and RuArk had been in Draema Neine, a council spot had opened and her father hadn't filled it?

That was huge news. *Huge.* It meant that Collaidh had moved against a member of the Council of Seven,

even if RuArk was only the acting authority. Such a thing was punishable by a good long stint in the iozene mines, along with being stripped of all titles, lands and property gained through the position of councilship.

With that, all of the council members took their seats as Collaidh grumbled about their lackluster cooperation. This was, after all, a most unprecedented gathering. They had no jurisdiction to condemn a non-Draeman person in a court of law, and certainly no authority to hold a trail at night.

Not only was it pre-dawn and fully dark outside, but they were without the traditional witnesses or observers, and no tangible proof against the accused to boot.

The Council members didn't seem to care that their voices carried. Rhia was glad for it because in their bickering, none of them noticed her once she eased from behind the pillar and approached the Council. As she moved in closer, her senses were on full alert. She might not see anyone right now, but she knew that those loyal to her and RuArk filled both sides of the screened area by now.

A dark cloaked figure emerged from the rotunda.

As the person approached, Rhia noted that though she couldn't see his face, his height, stature and menacing, but graceful movement, were all strangely familiar. A rapid shiver slivered from the back of her neck down her spine. She couldn't see his face, but she recognized him as surely as she knew her own face— the man who had visited her dreams before the Grandfather had come to watch over her.

CHAPTER TWENTY-TWO

The cloaked man moved a bit closer.

Rhia squared her shoulders, ready in light of this new threat. The Council was still griping at one another, and neither of them could be seen from where they stood. So, she decided to nip her little problem in the bud and get some answers.

"Who are you?"

He threw back his hood and she stilled. He was the Bryan-Who-Was-Not-Bryan that she'd seen in her vision. His features were exactly like those of Bryan Collaidh — which made no sense at all — yet there were differences that made this man quite handsome.

His skin was just as pale as Bryan's, but without the pasty, sickly pallor. Though the shape was similar, this man's eyes weren't frog like or flat black like Bryan's. Instead, they were a bluish-white color, almost like glacial ice. An eerie, yet almost tangible intelligence shone in his gaze. Thick, lustrously white tresses hung well past his shoulders. To Rhia's surprise, he was what Bryan would have looked like had he been honorable and even-tempered. The man was just short of beautiful.

And then he smiled.

The sight of sharp incisors in such a handsome face rocked Rhia back on her heels, but only for a second.

"You look like Bryan Collaidh. Why?"

"Never confuse me with my repulsive idiotic brother."

"Brother?"

"Unfortunately. I am Bryan Collaidh's brother, Behn. His twin, actually."

"But you're a Noman. How could the two of you be twins?"

"It is a long story indeed. After we are wed we can lie about and speak of it all. Or you can ask your new father-in-the-law since it is completely his fault," he said with an unexpectedly sophisticated and condescending sniff.

Yep, he's definitely a Collaidh.

"New father-in-law? Here we go again. We can't be wed, you blasted Noman. I'm. Already. Married. It seems to be something I've had to repeat to you folks far too many times and I have had it." Rhia's katana cleared its scabbard with an echoing *schwing*.

"No, you have not had it, yet, but I will give it to you. And often," he spat, his expression lewd and assessing. He continued his approach undaunted by the sword she'd drawn.

"Rhia, we will make beautiful children together. Simply surrender." He stopped just out of slicing range. She guessed he hadn't survived all these years by being a fool.

"It's amazing," she said, not meaning to speak the words aloud. "You look so much like him. Are you sure you're a Noman? You look like a man."

He smirked, displaying a genuine, though chilling smile. "I look like a man? No need for insults, my dear."

He even has a sense of humor? What in the ever-loving' hells is going on here?

A strange blackness began to creep over Rhia's mind, just behind her eyes, as if someone were pulling a fuzzy soft blanket over her thoughts. She gasped as the hairs on the back of her neck stood on end with a familiar tingle. The bastard was using the Gift against her.

But that wasn't supposed to be possible.

The image of the creature standing before her began to ripple and sway, reminding her of the soft waves created when a small pebble is thrown into a still pond. The white haired man changed before her eyes. His skin stretched and darkened to a glorious golden hue, genuinely masculine and muscular. His hair was no longer white, but glossy black locks that reached to the middle of his back. And those familiar gray eyes that reminded her of stormy seas she longed to be tossed on forever.

RuArk? No, it's not him. It's not.

Her mind fought against the possibility that her husband, her lifemate, stood before her. It just wasn't possible.

The image continued to ripple, and those ripples reached out for her. Steeling her resolve, she began to push against the blackness that surrounded her thoughts and furiously reached for her Source. The moment she touched it, the bond with RuArk sprang to life.

The awareness was back!

Her eyes said that RuArk stood before her, smiling to her in welcome, but her bond told her that he approached this very room from somewhere below.

Her man was wounded and extremely angry. His anger became her anger as clarity snapped through her mind. She reached for her Source more completely now. Surrendering herself to it, Rhia was rewarded with a surge of power like she'd never experienced before.

With that surge came a determination to be rid of the darkness that tried to sway her. She pushed out in her mind against it. The blackness began to subside and the rippling form before her was again the vile creature he had always been.

Rhia moved beyond furious. "Are you mad? How dare you use the Gift against me," she snarled through clenched teeth, barely holding herself in check. She wanted to strike out and cut the bastard to pieces, but she knew that would bring RuArk's men to her aid too soon. If the Noman who undoubtedly escorted him walked into a melee, they would kill RuArk without hesitation.

There would be no skinning Behn Collaidh. Not Yet. She must play this game out with patience or RuArk would never make it to the Council chambers alive. She forced herself to relax.

"So," she said, "you mentioned children. What makes you believe I would want to have your children? Little sharp toothed, blood sucking creatures with no regard for life?"

"Blood sucking? Yes, that might prove interesting. But they would also have the innate Gifts of magick through your warrior genes. And I must admit, even though you're missing the allure as fangs, you are a most beautiful creature, Rhia."

"And being the heir to the High Counsel of Draema wouldn't have anything to do with it, would it?"

"Oh, well, I guess I am caught. But you are still

beautiful and smart...for a human."

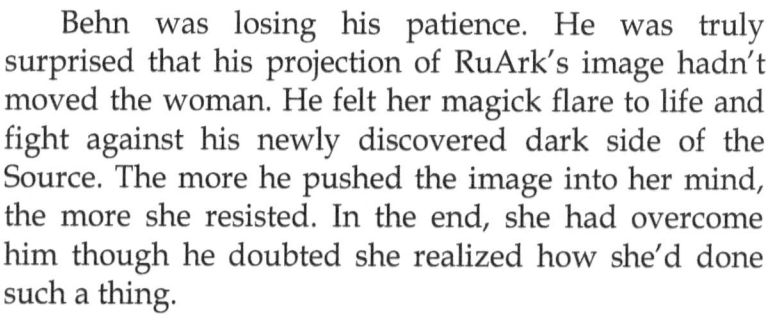

Behn was losing his patience. He was truly surprised that his projection of RuArk's image hadn't moved the woman. He felt her magick flare to life and fight against his newly discovered dark side of the Source. The more he pushed the image into her mind, the more she resisted. In the end, she had overcome him though he doubted she realized how she'd done such a thing.

He didn't see this as a failure. No, this was more of a reason to continue his pursuit of Rhia Greysomne—her magick was very strong indeed. He wondered if he could simply suck it out of her. No, that would kill her. And she was so fabulously made—strong and sleek, like the wild cats that roamed the mountains of the Borderlands. Perhaps he had another card to play to get this wild beauty underneath him. He would plant his seed in her, no doubt about it.

"Come Rhia, this game grows tiresome." She growled in response. *She is magnificent.* "I will make a bargain with you."

"There is no bargain that you can..."

"For the life of your Gaian warlord."

She snapped her mouth shut.

"He is quite a warrior, very skilled, surprisingly swift. Gave us quite a bit of trouble during his capture." Behn spoke calmly, examining his fingernails as if he had all night to take his ease. "Killed several of my pack by himself. We overcame him by sheer numbers. However, he does seem to have abhorrence for chains." His voice trailed off nonchalantly, letting her draw her own conclusions.

Rhia visibly winced as Behn played mercilessly on her feelings for RuArk.

Oh the thought of her beloved in chains, he thought sarcastically.

He almost laughed. Instead he said, "Come to me, Rhia. Sheath your sword and he will go free."

"How do I know he's not already dead?"

"You have my word. He will join us shortly. Make your decision now or let us end this. Shall I bring you his head on a plate?"

She stalled and began to fidget, putting on the most confused look she could muster, all the while calculating. Planning.

"Rhia, I will have your answer," Behn said quietly, painting on the most bored look he could muster. Stubborn wench. The sun was rising. He was running out of time. If she didn't hurry…

"What do you want me to do," she whispered, sheathing her sword at her back.

"Take my hand." If the thought sent a chill of disgust up her spine, the woman hid it expertly. "Admirable. Now, come with me. Denounce your marriage before RuArk and the Council and he will be freed before your very eyes."

She took a tentative step forward, asking, "Why are there no guards?"

"Most of the guards are hunting. The people of Draema are subdued. With no soldiers to protect them they are afraid to come out of their houses."

"But every Draeman is trained at an early age to defend against those like you." She snatched her hand back from Behn and he half-expected her to drop into an offensive stance and draw her weapon again.

"Trained as children, yes. But not trained as men." He held out his hand again and waited for her to take it, knowing she had no choice in the matter. After all, in the end, Blademaster or not, she was a woman with a woman's heart.

"How do I know I can trust you, Behn?"

"You don't," he said coldly, giving away nothing of his thoughts. "Yet, I give you my word that RuArk will go free if you do as I ask. In just a few moments, it will all be over. Some of the hunters in my pack are bringing your soon-to-be-former husband to this very room. Trust me, Rhia. I will make sure you enjoy your decision."

"Well, what does one say to something like that?" she asked coyly, taking the hand he still held out to her. The moment her fingers met his, her eyes widened and she gasped.

She wonders how my hands are so cool, yet my eyes burn with passion.

It wasn't passion at all, but the knowledge of the power he would gain over Draema by subduing her. Seizing his triumph, Behn led the one and only Rhia Greysomne Miwatani into the rotunda where the Council sat and waited.

He was secured with a chain that looped around his neck, then ran down his back to secure his arms, ending at his feet, bound just loose enough that he could walk. He knew he went to his death, even as his Noman guards prodded him to walk faster through the familiar hallways of the High Counsel's Citadel.

They led him down a hall and down the back stairs

to the first floor. As soon as they passed the great hall and rounded a corner he knew they were taking him to the Council Chambers, to the Hall of Judgment.

His thoughts were never far from his wife, safe at home. There was no way she could run into danger all the way from Province Springs to try to save him in so short a time anyway. By the time she arrived, he would have been dead for several days and news would have reached her before she came into the City. If his life ended with her in the safety of their home, then so be it.

At that point he let go of the concentration required to hide the bond from Rhia. RuArk reached for his Source and invoked the bond. He just wanted to feel her essence one more time before he died. It immediately flared to life and filled him with the familiar awareness of the woman he loved. He felt Rhia...right here in Draema Proper. In this very building?

Gods damn it.

What the hells was she doing here! If they made it out of here alive, he was going to challenge her. Her punishment? Forty cycles worth of, as she called them, 'Yes RuArk' days. She would probably be a grandmother by the time they were all done.

The First Commanders serving the Protector of the Realm looked on as Rhia made her way down the gallery toward the Council rotunda. When she was intercepted by a too-handsome Noman who carried himself like nobility, they were amazed.

Marth signaled, "Who do you think he is?"

Sharyn answered, "He is the leader of the Noman. I

saw him in Rhia's Foreknowledge, which is how we came to be here." She looked sternly at both of them as she signed.

They looked on, mouths agape, watching Rhia shuffling her feet and fidgeting about. What in the world was wrong with her?

When she sheathed her sword and tentatively placed her hand into that of the Noman's, every warrior clamped down on their iron wills to keep from attacking the creature who would dare touch their lady, whether it was by her will or not.

"What in the name of the Ancestors is she doing?" signed Linc, mouth agape as he witnessed the spectacle.

"She is buying RuArk time."

"Time for what?" Linc signed back.

"Time for the vile Noman to bring RuArk to this room. Then..." she eased her sword free from the scabbard hidden under her arm, "they are ours."

The Council of Seven was seated at the traditional half-moon shaped table placed upon a raised platform toward the rear of the domed Council Hall. The silvery-gray marble worked into the top of the table reflected the fading moonlight that came in from the skylight above.

Councilman Collaidh, seated in the High Counsel's chair, rose and proceeded to the top of the steps that separated the forum of Councilmen from the conspicuously absent audience. He looked down to where the people of Draema should be and waited with a devious smile. Rhia approached, appearing subdued, hand-in-hand with the creature he loathed most — Behn.

Rhia allowed herself to be ushered up onto the dais to stand directly in front of him. She scowled, having noticed that he'd occupied her father's seat knowing full well he had no right to be there. If she'd been paying attention to the other council members, she would have found their expressions mirrored her own, but her focus was the asshole in front of her.

Then all thought of Collaidh flew from her mind as RuArk was led into the Council Chamber guarded by at least fifty armed Noman. She was proud Behn felt he had to take such precaution where her husband was concerned. Then she began to look RuArk over and bit back the growl that formed in her throat.

His torso was bare. Blood was caked around deep cuts on his chest and neck. His soft leather buckskins were hardened with dried blood about the waist. Angry red welts crisscrossed his back where he'd been beaten. Yet he walked tall, as if he had no wounds at all, his step sure and his expression stern.

Rhia reached through her Source for the bond, hoping to convey to RuArk what she was doing here, and to warn him of the upcoming battle. As soon as the bond was established she felt a flash of cold fury, *his* fury. Then it was gone, snuffed out like a candlewick doused in swift running water.

She looked to Behn, wondering if he was somehow keeping her from communicating with RuArk. She looked back to her husband and those stormy gray eyes were boring right through her. She had never seen him so angry, not even after that dumb stunt where she'd gotten herself kidnapped by Bryan and Ricard.

Didn't he understand that she was here to save him? Self-consciously sliding her hand from Behn's she tried to convey her thoughts through her eyes.

Please, please understand.

RuArk's gaze melted her heart. After what felt like years, he took one deep breath, held his head higher and looked away.

She willed RuArk to look at her.

He didn't.

Councilman Collaidh glared at her lifemate, and then signaled the Noman to remove his chains. Just then Behn grabbed Rhia by a handful of her hair and held her closely from behind. He pulled out a finely tooled, razor sharp golden dagger.

At her gasp of surprise, Collaidh filled in the blanks.

"I have had the chains removed, but if you move I will have her killed," he said to the very large, very powerful man who stood before him with the stature of a king.

"You said all would be well if I surrendered," growled Rhia, not bothering to keep her voice down.

Behn yanked her head back just enough to gain access to her neck. He rubbed his teeth back and forth against the tender skin. "I promised he would go free if you surrendered. I said nothing of you going free." He kissed a surprisingly hot path down her neck and then smiled mockingly at RuArk.

The sensation of his teeth on her skin brought images of her prowling about the province at night seeking weary travelers to feed on.

Ewwww!

She shivered, wishing she could sink into the floor.

But RuArk wasn't looking at them. His gaze remained on Rama Collaidh and Rhia could almost hear the rage seething through him.

"RuArk Miwatani, are you aware of the charges against you?" Collaidh asked.

RuArk said nothing. Rhia hoped the proceedings would drag on another hour or so. By then, the sun would be rising and they would be rid of Behn and his hoard until evening.

"RuArk Miwatani," rang Collaidh's voice, "I hereby accuse you of the death of the High Counsel of Draema, Grey Greysomne. I further accuse you of taking the lady Rhia from Draema against her will and call your marriage to her void and of no account. Have you anything to say in your own defense?" Collaidh sounded more bored than anything else.

To her surprise, RuArk responded.

"I levy charges against you, Councilman Collaidh, and both of your sons, the Noman, Behn Collaidh and Bryan Collaidh."

A collective gasp rippled through the ranks of Councilmembers from one end of the table to the other. Charges against a member of the Council? It was unheard of. But it was also unheard of for Draema to be overtaken by Noman, have the First Heir wed to one of them, and the High Counsel supposedly murdered by an ally such as the Protector of the Realm of Gaia.

Collaidh ignored RuArk and continued with his charges. Rhia closed her eyes, steeling herself to execute the move that would remove her neck from beneath Behn's finely wrought dagger.

"I further say," Collaidh went on, "that any children produced from your false marriage are disavowed and have no claim on the High Counselship of Draema."

What? He was passing sentence on her children? And without any authority? She was done waiting.

Done with the whole business.

Rhia's right hand shot out to squeeze Behn's fingers tighter around the dagger he held to her throat. Her left hand shot up and back to grab a fistful of his hair, and yanked with all her strength while dropping into a crouch. She came away with the knife as Behn sailed over her back to land flat on the dais, stunned.

Just then, one of the closed screened doors opened to the left of RuArk. Out stepped Grey Greysomne, the High Counsel, tattered, bruised and well-armed.

Collaidh screamed and began to back away. The Councilmembers all at once began yelling, and Rhia was still in a crouch making sure Behn held still. Collaidh turned to run. One of the council members stuck his foot out from underneath the table and tripped him. The idiot fell hard, knocked his head against the marble corner of the large table, and landed on the floor out cold.

Behn sat up and it was pandemonium as he yelled, "Kill them!"

The Noman turned on RuArk, but each time he made to face an assailant they were suddenly downed. Warriors had cut through the screening on both sides of the room and now poured into the chamber to take on the Noman.

The High Counsel had quickly shuffled all the Councilmen out through the rear entrances and quickly returned.

To Rhia, he gave a peck on the cheek.

To RuArk, he turned and tossed a weapon. "I recognized your distinct blade in the pile of weapons when Sharyn and company freed us from the dungeons. Shall we?"

And they all joined the fray.

CHAPTER TWENTY-THREE

Once RuArk's Noman guards were cut down, there weren't enough combatants in the observatory to fight, so the remaining warriors streamed out of the building to take out the creatures who patrolled the streets and manned the walls.

Rhia went after Behn. He'd slipped through one of the observatory doors and was making for the nearest exit. He was a competent fighter, but he obviously had no intention of continuing to fight a battle for his now-deposed father.

"Not so fast."

He was cut off on his right by a fuming Rhia, as an even angrier RuArk came up on the left.

"Hold, Rhia!" She didn't miss the edge to RuArk's tone, and she acknowledged him without ever taking her eyes off of Behn.

"Oh come now, Rhia, does this mean you don't wish to have children together now?" Behn smirked, playing for time to figure out how to either get around Rhia or get around RuArk. "I felt you shiver when my teeth were on your neck. Come closer, sweet. Let me taste you again."

She took a step forward with every intention of

running him through, but caught herself. This was exactly what he wanted. He expected her to be ruled by her emotions and do something stupid. And she really, *really* wanted to.

Instead, she shut her feelings away and put on her stoic warrior's face.

"You look so upset, Rhia. Is it because you will not have the pleasure of wrapping those strong thighs around my waist as I take you?"

This time Behn's words rolled off her. And he knew it as she set herself into an offensive stance oblivious to everything except RuArk.

"Rhia, do you wish to challenge him?" RuArk asked, his voice hard, with no inflection, no emotion, as if he were himself made of steel.

She started to say that she absolutely wanted to challenge Behn. But they'd been here before. She knew that this was RuArk's way of asking if she trusted him enough to regain her honor, as well as his own.

She loved this man with all her soul. In this moment, she would give him whatever he wanted.

"No. I give my right of challenge over to you." With that, she stood down, not quite lowering her sword as she edged toward the closest exit, leaving her husband to his business.

Back in the Council Chamber, the High Counsel closed in on a semi-conscious Collaidh as he lay sprawled on the floor with his robes tangled around his ankles. He became fully aware and cringed as Grey Greysomne, renowned leader of the Society of War, picked him up by the scruff of his neck and slammed him into one of the chairs at the council table. Taking the very chains that had held RuArk, the High Counsel twisted them tightly around Collaidh's body.

"It was Behn! It was him! He did everything!"

"Shut. Up. Save it for when my daughter and the rest of the Council gather to judge you," Grey snapped.

The High Counsel kept guard over Rama Collaidh until the fighting was done. He would not let this maggot wriggle away. No, Grey Greysomne would be the rock that crushed this spineless worm once and for all.

CHAPTER TWENTY-FOUR

Behn plunged his sword into the nearest Noman bowman, ignoring his look of bewilderment. RuArk's reach was simply too long and his sword only made that reach longer. He knew there was no way to beat this man hand-to-hand.

Behn snatched up the discarded bow and quivers, and took off at a dead run, trying to put any amount of distance between himself and RuArk. He turned and fired a swift arrow that caught RuArk's left shoulder. But it seemed just a scratch to the warrior and didn't slow the man at all.

They were now in the courtyard outside the Council chambers. A fast-moving summer storm had made the cobblestones and fine tile slick and treacherous. Behn fired again, and again. Each time RuArk deflected the arrow with his blade or wrist guards and sent it skipping along the stones to land harmlessly in the wet grass along the sidewalks.

Each time Behn shot, RuArk gained ground. He was now no more than fifteen feet away. In two strokes, Behn fell, his lungs pierced by a cold piece of steel Gaian death at the end of RuArk's arm.

As the day dawned, the grizzly carnage in the Council Chambers was revealed. The rain continued to fall from fluffy white clouds, illuminated from behind by the shining sun that waited to break through them. Muted light streamed through the skylight and reflected off pools of blood. The early summer morning heat quickly caused a stench to rise in the room. Thankful for the downpour and the tiled floor of the observatory, the now-free Draeman soldiers went up to the roof and opened the skylights to let the rain in to wash away the filth.

The Noman in the Citadel had been slain where they stood. The few who had survived saw their cause was lost and fled the City, even as the sun rose.

Collaidh was taken to the dungeons where he would await trial for treason.

RuArk was amazed at the sheer number of warriors who had come to his aid. He was grateful to many of them...but not grateful to all. With the High Counsel, and all three of his First Commanders looking on, he stood in the rain and waited for Rhia to come to him.

Arms crossed over his chest, he tried and failed to hold onto his temper. In truth, his anger was born of fear for her safety. Period.

"You placed yourself in danger."

"Yes, RuArk, but I..."

"There is no excuse for this recklessness. My only purpose in life is to protect my woman, yet here you are in danger of being killed." He pointed at the blood on her clothing, though in truth most of the blood belonged to others. "If a warrior cannot protect his woman, he does not deserve to keep her. I can see that I can't protect you, even from yourself. I am done."

He turned on his heel and began to walk away.

RuArk had never felt this kind of vulnerability in his life. Not on any battlefield, not in any fight. And not for any other woman. When he saw her standing in the Council Chambers next to those Collaidh bastards, he had truly been afraid for the first time in more years than he could remember. And all because he couldn't bear to lose her. Not now. Not ever.

"RuArk, stop!"

His face may have been stoic, but he was amazingly angry at the danger Rhia had placed herself in. The earnestness in her voice as she called to him was unsettling, as if her very heart was breaking. He stopped walking.

"I know you are angry with me for coming here, but I couldn't leave things the way they were, knowing what I knew. Won't you at least turn around?"

His granite expression firmly in place, he turned slowly, bloodied sword still in hand. He clenched his teeth and said nothing. She would try to explain her way out of this one, but there was no excuse. None.

Rhia took a step back.

He looked around quickly and saw that Joan and Sharyn were having similar conversations with their mates though they were not exchanging words. They were all just... *glaring* at each other, and no one was backing down.

"RuArk, the Ancestors had me come here." He started to turn away again, but something in her words struck home and rang true. Could it be that the Ancestors had taken Rhia's safety out of his hands for a time?

"RuArk, I had a vision of Foreknowledge. I told you about it ages ago, but it hadn't come true so I ignored it last summer. But this time I knew you were in danger. I had to come. There was no way I could ignore what the Gift showed me and let you walk into a trap and be killed along with all our people. Even your mother came and took the children to safety with timing that matched what I was being shown." The rain continued to fall and Rhia stood, soaked to the skin, but determined to make him listen.

She went on to tell him everything — about her first vision in Sharyn's quarters, and the very moment she realized that the vision was about to come true, as well as how they'd carefully made plans to come after him.

"I love you more than my own life," she said.

He was beginning to thaw, but only just...

"I couldn't let you walk into this situation without doing something. I've spent almost my whole life surrounded by people, yet alone. And you promised me you would never leave me alone. You promised! I know I was shown what was happening in order to help you keep your word. I know it sounds simple, but if you are going to stay mad at me then you have to be mad at the Ancestors, too, damn it!"

She yelled at the top of her lungs, one hand on her hip and the other on the hilt of her sword whose tip was point-down in the mud. "And please don't be angry with our warriors. I forced them to come with me. I take full responsibility for my actions."

He turned to fully face her now.

Rhia walked to within a foot of him and knelt at his feet. Her knees sank into the mud, covered with the gore of battle.

"What are you doing?"

She didn't answer. Instead, she wiped her blade on her own clothing, held out her sword to him with both hands and swore fealty to the Protector of the Realm.

"I give you my honor, my loyalty and my sword. I place your life above my very own."

RuArk couldn't remember ever seeing a woman in all the realm of Gaia ever gift her lifemate with her blade. Ever. It didn't matter that most females of his home province chose to forego the sword. Even for a hardened warrior like RuArk, it was a humbling experience.

It was one thing to have a soldier under your service swear, but a lifemate? A wife? It meant more than simple words could convey. It meant that she would serve him in whatever way he needed for as long as he wanted, whenever and wherever she was needed. But it also put her under his protection, which was all he'd ever wanted in the first place.

Rhia continued to give him the words, not seeing her father nodding his approval. She didn't see both Gaian and Draeman warriors with admiration shining in their eyes as they sank to their knees and swore their oath anew. And she didn't see Behn, laying no more than twenty feet from her, reach for the bow that had fallen from his grasp when RuArk had slashed him with his blade.

The bastard sat up just long enough for one more shot.

The arrow slammed into Rhia's back and threw her forward into the mud.

"No!" RuArk leapt over her body, his blade a blur as one swing took the Noman's head clean off his shoulders.

———◆————————◆———

She felt herself being gently lifted. The was sharp pain enough to cause her eyes to snap open for a moment.

"Rhia, if you die now I swear I will take you over my knee."

"RuArk," she lifted her hand to his face, but it didn't make it to his jaw. It fell limply to her side and the jolt caused a groan. She tried to keep quiet, not wanting to alarm him anymore than he already was.

Geez, here she was dying and she was worried about her strong, stoic warrior's disposition? It was actually quite funny.

Her chuckle came out a pain-filled gasp. Rhia closed her eyes and began to slip into the welcoming void, grumbling when her trip was interrupted by a gentle shake.

"Rhia, come back to me!"

She tried, she really did. But the darkness beckoned her. And it was so peaceful. But then she thought of her beautiful children, Taté Icamna and Relaina Grey and suddenly, she didn't want to drift into the peaceful darkness.

She tried to tell RuArk that if he could just get her to the Society of Physicians they could have her on the mend in no time. Better yet, if Sharyn…

Her energy had run out. She was still trying to talk, but had no power left to get the words past her lips. Her head fell back, her body limp, as her lifeblood flowed, warm and sticky, from the wound in her back.

Then came the bellow of a torn man, telling her how much he loved her.

The memory of her warrior's tears falling onto her

cheeks with the light misting of the rain, played over and over in her mind as Rhia slipped into unconsciousness.

CHAPTER TWENTY-FIVE

Rhia awoke on her stomach. She opened her eyes and found familiar surroundings. She was in her old tower apartments in the Citadel.

Sitting up too quickly caused a wave of dizziness so wildly off-center it threatened to carry her back to the shadows of unconsciousness. She fought, but the pain was simply too intense. She lay back down and wondered at the dressing stretched around her torso and splotched with specks of dried, brownish-red blood.

Owwww!

Her back was on fire.

And where was RuArk?

Damn it, now she remembered. The fighting was done and he'd turned to leave her, believing that he couldn't protect her. She'd tried to explain what had brought her to him, even giving him her sword arm, swearing to him.

He wasn't here. Not his scent or his presence. Not daring to sit up, she rolled to her side and looked around. The curtains were open and the room was bright enough for her to see that none of his weapons or his clothes were there. He'd really left her. He must have, otherwise he would be here by her side, especially while she was wounded.

Energy spent, heartsick and sore, she lay quietly, not bothering to try to touch the bond with her husband, nor stem the tears that flowed hotly down her flushed cheeks. She'd known the consequences of her actions before she'd ever left Province Springs. Known that there was always the possibility that things wouldn't work out as planned. She accepted those consequences, knowing that her coming had kept him alive whether he was still hers or not.

But what would she do without her lifemate? Without her RuArk?

A knock came at the door. She didn't call out an answer. What was the point? It wasn't RuArk, so she didn't want to see whoever it was anyway.

Her father poked his head in.

"Rhia? Are you okay?"

"Fine." Her voice quivered on a sigh. She took a deep breath and tried to compose herself. Making her father worry wouldn't help any.

Tousling her hair, he said gently, "You've been asleep for two days now. How are you feeling?"

Two days? RuArk had a two-day head start back to Gaia? She wouldn't go after him, though. If he couldn't forgive her, then there was really no point. She turned her head to look at the High Counsel and noticed that his cuts and bruises were practically healed.

"Your face? How…?"

"The Sensuan are Gaian and some of them have been able to tap into the Gift of Healing. With so many injured during the fighting they have been invaluable. You were in pretty bad shape, Rhia. That son of a bitch, Behn, had too good an aim. You had a punctured lung and a lot of internal bleeding. We thought we were going to lose you, girl." With a watery smile, he cleared his suddenly dry-sounding throat. Ever the soldier, he refused to let his tears fall, but he didn't fail to tell her the words she needed to hear the most.

"So, uh," she stammered, trying to change the subject. "What happened to Rama Collaidh?"

"He'll go to trial in the next few months. But right now, I don't care about that at all. I love you, Rhia. I don't know what I would have done if you'd left us. Sharyn saw to yours and RuArk's wounds personally."

So, that was why she was still alive? Sharyn. If she ever saw the woman again she would kiss her feet upon demand.

"I love you, too, Father," she whispered, closing her eyes against the pain in her heart. Her father loved her, but she'd never felt so alone in all her life... which she honestly didn't think was possible.

"Father, do you think you can send someone to the Queen of Gaia asking if I can see my children? Maybe she would agree to have them brought to me? Even if it's only for a day or so?"

Another voice sounded from the door that she hadn't noticed was still ajar.

"And what of their father? Have you no wish to see him?"

RuArk! Larger than life and right here.

"I thought you had gone. I mean..." She tried to get herself together. Even tried painting on her diplomat's face. Besides, she didn't want to put all her feelings out there in case he'd actually come to say goodbye.

"I could no more leave you than I could leave this world of my own accord."

"I think I'll take my leave," said the High Counsel,

pressing a kiss to Rhia's forehead before rising making his way to the door.

RuArk came all the way into the room then, holding both Taté Icamna and Relaina Grey in his arms. How in the world had he gotten her children here?

"My mother and Sharyn have been watching over you. And yes, I have been here sleeping beside you as well." RuArk laid both babies on bed.

"Really? You didn't leave?"

"I told you, it's not something I can do. To leave you would be to leave a part of myself behind. And our children are precious to me. As precious as their mother."

Rhia stretched and turned her stiff neck to see Taté Icamna's midnight black little head, barely visible among the thick bedding. He was contentedly stuffing the covers into his mouth, chewing on them. Relaina Grey had a handful of her brother's hair in one hand, and her father's finger in the other.

Rhia reached for the nearest baby, then changed her mind and reached for her husband instead. The movement caused her to wince. A dull ache creeped up the right side of her back, but she was so happy and fulfilled that she just didn't care.

RuArk returned her hug, and much more as he leaned over to practically bury her with his body. He gathered her in his arms, careful of the silky gauze dressing covering her wounds.

"I love you, my wonderful warrior," she whispered.

"It is said that warriors do not love, or at least they should not. But this one does, Rhia. With all my heart. I love you."

"So, you're still my Wind Storm?"

"I am. And you are my Fire Storm." It was a statement of fact, without the slightest hint of a question.

Sealed with a kiss, there was no doubt that the Gathering of the Storms was an advent of nature, indeed.

ALSO BY AUTHOR
T.J. MICHAELS

Carinian's Seeker, Vampire Council of Ethics One
Serati's Flame, Vampire Council of Ethics Two
Hatsept Heat, Vampire Council of Ethics Three
Seeker's Solace, Vampire Council of Ethics Four
Juicy, A Twilight Teahouse Story
Luscious, A Twilight Teahouse Story
Succulent, A Twilight Teahouse Story
Silk Road, Seals of Destiny
Spirit of the Pride, a Pryde Ranch Shifter Story
Niah's Pride, a Pryde Ranch Shifter Story
Pursuit of Pride and Pleasure, a Pryde Ranch Shifter
Story
Shiftin' Sassy: Derria Pryde, a Pryde Ranch Shifter
Story
Winter Blues, a Pryde Ranch Shifter Story
Gathering of the Storms ~ Wind and Fire
Gathering of the Storms ~ Reckoning
Just Peachy
Jaguar's Rule
Forever December
Egyptian Voyage
On the Prowl
Entwined Hearts
Elemental Heat
Caramel Kisses
Hide No More

ABOUT THE AUTHOR

USA Today and New York Times bestseller, T.J. Michaels, is also an award-winning author of several romance genres, including paranormal, fantasy, sci-fi and urban fantasy romance. Writing like a madman, T.J. hasn't lost steam. Her mind? Yep, that's gone, but steam there is a-plenty. A true Taurus, T.J. isn't slowing down and she's definitely too stubborn to stop when she sees the fence!

No matter the genre T.J. is penning, her favorite thing to do is build worlds. To take you somewhere extraordinary. To transport you to a place where you can close your eyes and slip into your fantasy…

Visit T.J. Michaels online at her Website
www.TJMichaels.com

T.J. MICHAELS

www.ingramcontent.com/pod-product-compliance
Lightning Source LLC
Chambersburg PA
CBHW031303170626
46807CB00001B/295